The Man Who Loved Jane Austen

Previously Published Work

Cape Breton is the Thought Control Centre of Canada, 1969
Lord Nelson Tavern, 1974
Century, 1986
A Night at the Opera, 1992

The Man Who Loved Jane Austen

❊ ❊ ❊

Ray Smith

The Porcupine's Quill

CANADIAN CATALOGUING IN PUBLICATION DATA

Smith, Ray, 1941–
The man who loved Jane Austen

ISBN 0-88984-202-7

I. Title.

PS8587.M583M36 1999   C813'.54   C99-930262-0
PR9199.3.S64M36 1999

Published by The Porcupine's Quill,
68 Main Street, Erin, Ontario NOB ITO.
Readied for the press by John Metcalf; copy edited by Doris Cowan.
Typeset in Galliard, printed on Zephyr Antique laid,
and bound at The Porcupine's Quill Inc.

Represented in Canada by the Literary Press Group.
Trade orders are available from General Distribution Services.

We acknowledge the support of the Ontario Arts Council,
and the Canada Council for the Arts for our publishing program.
The financial support of the Government of Canada
through the Book Publishing Industry Development Program
is also gratefully acknowledged.

I   2   3   4   •   OI   OO   99

The author gratefully acknowledges the assistance of the Canada Council for the Arts without which the writing of this book would have been much more difficult, if not impossible.

* * *

Over many years,
two writers and two painters
have been exemplary friends.
Each deserves the dedication to an entire book,
but mine come slowly,
so I dedicate this book to them together,
with friendship, admiration, and gratitude:

Ken Tolmie
who inspired me

John Metcalf
who encouraged me

Kent Thompson
who sustained me

Paul Young
who consoled me

Snow

Through the air above Mountain Street, snow flurries drifting, gleaming in the Christmas lights, veiling Mount Royal, the face of the mountain lit from below, dappled in black and white. Frank sidestepped away from a car sliding to a stop, stood back from a knot of shoppers with their bundles. On the sidewalk he paused behind the group of children who stood watching Ogilvy's window display of automata – bears, raccoons, squirrels popping out of windows, climbing stairs, opening doors. The children seemed less impressed than their parents; no doubt the pizzazz of television and computers had educated their tastes to spectacular expectations beyond their parents' memories of childhood. At the main door, Frank slipped a few dollars into the Salvation Army globe and wished the attendant a Merry Christmas.

Heart-quickening scene, a touch Dickensian, *A Christmas Carol* suitably updated.

Inside the department store he paused. He had all the main presents, could use perhaps a few whimsical stocking stuffers for the boys. Where were toys? Basement? Fifth floor? He had not been in Ogilvy's since the makeover a few years ago when much of the familiar and comforting dowdiness had been replaced by the franchised boutiques of international couturiers. Stainless steel, smoked mirrors, and clothes he couldn't afford, didn't want. Who could afford them? Did Montreal still have enough rich people to support this extravagance?

Down the spiral staircase to the bookstore, which had a good children's section. Simon didn't have *Postman Pat's Busy Day*, but Jonathan was more difficult. What the boy really needed was *The Eight-Year-Old's Introduction to Algebra*. At last he picked a glossy hardcover on the heavens – too expensive and too big for a stocking, but the pictures were carefully accurate, and the text sober and reasonably technical. As a balance, he added a Thomas the Tank Engine anthology for Simon.

On the way to the cash, Frank stopped to leaf through *Drawing*

Room and Garden: The Inside and Outside of Jane Austen. It would make some fine slides for his course. He looked at the price sticker. Perhaps after the Christmas bills were paid off.

'You don't remember me, do you?' said the clerk.

Not if she had been more than a term ago, no.

'You were in the Dickens course? Last spring? Carmen?'

'The Brontës, two years ago I think, and it's Mary.'

'Considering the season, I should have remembered Mary. It's the hair, you're wearing it shorter, aren't you?'

'Not really, but I do it differently, with this flip. And a little help from the bottle.'

'I'd never have noticed!' That was true enough. 'Then I'm forgiven, am I?'

Another customer saved him further chat. He wished her a Merry Christmas and escaped to the stairs.

Eight thirty-five – time to call the boys and say good night. Frank had delivered them to their grandparents in the afternoon.

'I'm glad you called *at last*,' cried Mrs Hatcher. 'They should be in bed so they'll be fresh for tomorrow, but they've been waiting for your call since supper and I didn't know when ... Oh, here's Simon, say good night to him, Simon.' She was adding barely heard complaints that 'It's way past ... hours ago ... allowed altogether too much ...' as Simon began his halting, confusing list of grievances about his brother's cruelty, selfishness, violence, malevolence.

'... I'm sure he didn't mean it, Simon ... And you didn't do anything, I suppose? ... yes, well, if you kick him, he ... no, it's not right, but ...'

Simon abruptly broke off to explain in great detail the traps and confusions of level six of a computer game.

Frank wished him love and good night, then talked with Jonathan. '... yes, I realize that, but he is younger and smaller, and you were like that when you were his age ... yes, I love you, too. Now, it's time for bed, and ... I know you don't have school ... yes, you are older, but Grandma wants you to ...'

Mrs Hatcher came back on the line and they arranged Frank's arrival late the next afternoon for Christmas Eve dinner. 'Of course, if the butcher's shop is crowded, which it likely will be, I may not be home just at four, but you won't mind waiting on the steps, I hope …'

'That's not a problem.'

'And if you really *have* to sleep over Christmas Eve, I'm afraid we're having Betsy's old room done over, but I expect I can make up the Hide-A-Bed in the basement …'

Frank would have preferred being within earshot of the boys in case they woke during the night, but he was content to sleep in the basement. It was not the sleeping over he cared about, but the tucking into bed on Christmas Eve, the getting up in the morning.

'But the boys are going wild,' she cried. 'I must go.'

Perhaps fifteen minutes to closing time. Last chance: anything else? Anyone? The main floor counters offered women's jewellery, accessories, hosiery. Among the perfumes he noticed a small display of Shalimar nestled in flourishes of ribbon and tissue. Shalimar was one of the few perfumes he could name. He waved the tester bottle past his nose: yes, that was it, powerful, unmistakable, Middle-Eastern – sandalwood? … frankincense? … myrrh?

The two saleswomen were discussing the tallies before closing their cash; the black-haired one, with just a touch of irritation, gave him the prices of the boxes in the display. All the perfumes were far too expensive. When Frank was reluctant to buy the cheaper eau de toilette, the clerk produced a miniature of perfume from below the counter.

'If the lady likes it,' she said, 'the full-sized one would make a lovely present for Valentine's Day.'

She ran his credit card through and they exchanged a 'Joyeux Noël'.

His bags were light, the evening pleasant, so he set out to walk the two miles home through Christmas-card Montreal.

For once he need not hurry … how rare! Usually, he had to keep an eye on the clock, think of the sitter's schedule, cheat five minutes from the end of a class, decline a friend's happy-hour invitation, smile at the suggestion of lunch, a movie, a vernissage, a stroll downtown. Tonight he could dawdle along, glance over a bookstore window, browse over some magazine racks in a late dépanneur. Why, he could even stop for a beer in L'Arrêt-court, his and Emma's bar before the boys were born.

Although he hadn't been in L'Arrêt-court for a year or so, Denise behind the bar remembered him and wished him season's greetings. Frank was just settling onto his stool when a hand dropped onto his shoulder: 'Sneaking a beer for Christmas cheer, Frank?'

Billy Charles taught political science in another college.

'Merry Christmas, Bubba,' said Frank. 'I was wondering I might run into some of the old gang tonight. Still a regular, are you?'

'Not usually, in fact, but I was doing some last-minute shopping and …'

Billy and Frank and their wives had been companions a decade earlier. Now the two settled in to their beers and catch-ups on school, renovations, friends, bellies, thinning and greying hair, the Habs, the N F L playoffs.

'I think I watched some of the first half of the San Diego-Miami game with Jonathan,' Frank admitted.

'They didn't show the San Diego-Miami game here this year.'

'Last year? Good game, anyway.'

'As you recall, Frank.'

'As I recall, Bubba.'

'Did you hear the one about the tongue trooper and the tattooed hooker?'

They would have to review politics for a while.

'… but to read it in English you have to go to the back of the display and bend down.'

It was better than the punchline Frank had heard: 'But you have to pay double to read it in English.'

'I've got another one,' said Bubba.

'Give it to me.'

'What's the sourest joke in Canada?'

'Sour? Canada? I can't believe …'

'Newspaper headline: "Fresh Constitutional Initiative".'

The closed arguments of Quebec politics. Ruefully, necessarily, the absolute minimum of coded remarks and replies, a quarter century and more of an exhausting, never exhausted subject.

'Bubba, do you ever think about getting out?'

'Yeah, I do, but what's the point? After the P Q won in '76, they were the stick, and jobs in Toronto and Calgary were the carrot.

Now there's a stick, but no carrot.'

'Not for the likes of us, anyway.'

'Colleen got out,' said Billy.

'Did she? I didn't know.'

'After the divorce she was visiting her sister in Markham, near Toronto. She met a lawyer from a small firm specializing in property, estate planning, that sort of thing. He said, "Hey, a Quebec lawyer, we could use someone with Code Civil training. You can parlay fransay and all, can you?" "Are bears catholic?" she said, or words to that effect. "Want a job?" he said.'

'Just like that?'

'Just like that. Well, there had to be interviews, a competition, but the fix was in.'

'And the kids? What do you do about visitation rights?'

'Oh, the break-up was fairly amicable – and Mother Charles didn't raise her boy to get into a custody battle with a lawyer. Anyway, maybe you're forgetting their ages – they were fifteen and thirteen at the time. Mind you, we all logged a lot of klicks on the 401, and I can tell you more about VIA Rail meals than any civilized person could want to know. For a couple of years I had the kids most of the summer, but now they both get summer jobs. Kevin's doing science at Western, and Shirley's in pre-law at U of T'.

'They're grown up!'

'That's about the size of it.'

'And I can still remember the time you had to leave the dinner table to lie in bed with Kevin until he could go to sleep.'

'These days, you couldn't fit a female gymnast in the sack with him, he's that big. At least he has a mother to handle any paternity suits.'

'That was a great meal, as I recall. Wasn't that the year we were all doing Thai?'

'Malagasy, I think. Remember chayote?'

'I see it all the time in the supermarket; somehow I never get around to buying it.'

'Chayote sliced and deep fried, chayote breaded, chayote baked with tomato and garlic…'

'Chayote with those hot little green peppers, blanched chayote

salad with Spanish onions, garlic, and merguez sausages. Not a bad
salad if you add lettuce and tomato.'

'And hold the chayote.'

Denise set two more beers in front of them.

'Hey, Bubba, did Colleen ever wear a perfume called Shalimar?'

'Shalimar? No, she wore Chanel No. 5. I think. She didn't often
wear perfume when we were a feature.'

'Too sensuous?'

'No, that wouldn't bother her – she was all Montreal. Remember
that black cocktail dress, hem about here?'

'Those were the days.'

'You ever wonder why we humans are the only animals whose
females are more decorated than our males?'

Denise paused with a tray of table orders.

'We do it all for you, Bubba,' she murmured.

'When's your shift over, babe?'

'Three a.m.'

'Aw, shucks, I have to be in bed at eleven.'

'I might be able to find you some Viagra.'

'My doctor told me not to mix Viagra with my Geritol.'

Denise chuckled and walked away.

'They do it all for us? I don't think it scans. Damned if I know any
guys who care much about perfume. Do you?'

'Care about it? Not much. I asked about Shalimar because I …
noticed a display in Ogilvy's earlier. And it's the only one I recognize
by smell.'

'I know the name – can't say I know the smell.'

Denise was back behind the counter; Frank asked her if she ever
used it.

'No, I don't wear perfume a lot, and when I do, I prefer lighter
scents. Shalimar is a bit heavy for me.'

'Okay, but tell me, if you were at a party and some Shalimar
woman was talking with your date, what would you do?'

'Nail her feet to the floor, then feed the guy lots of onion and garlic dip.'

So the conversation wandered its silly, comfortable way through
the smoke, the laughter, the chatter, the comings and goings of

regulars barely remembered from the old days. But then Bubba said:

'So that stuff about Shalimar – you got Emma some for Christmas, but I'm thinking it's more like a gift of kinky lingerie – a gift for you, not for her ... Am I right, or am I right?'

A deep breath.

'I guess you didn't hear about it.'

'Uh-oh, cowpat incoming?'

'Emma died six months ago ... June fifteenth.'

Shock, chagrin.

'Sorry Frank – I did hear, but I forgot, I haven't seen you since ... and missed the funeral ... in North Carolina visiting my mom ... I should have ... Emma was ...'

'Never mind, Bubba, it doesn't matter. All that matters is that ... Emma is dead.'

Sympathy, brief questions and answers: Emma was on her way to an academic conference in Lethbridge, in a rental car from Calgary with two others, a sudden thunderstorm with hail, bad visibility, car hydroplaning, off the road, others unhurt, Emma in the front passenger seat, neck broken, all over in a moment, woman, daughter, mother, scholar, teacher, wife – a life gone.

As he told the tale, Frank went through the brief, familiar selection of apt details from the whirl of memories made up of phone calls, arrangements about the children, the flight to Calgary, police reports, arrangements about the body, the funeral, phone calls, notes on slips of paper, credit card offered hourly, the newspaper notice, Emma's department at McGill, the paperwork with the personnel department, at his own College, the Palais de Justice, the notary's office, probate ...

'Because it happened in June, I didn't have daycare problems until I started teaching again, so I got that under control without ... No, she had term insurance through the university, so that paid off most of what we still owed on the house, and ... rare indeed, but with the boys taken care of, this is the first time since it happened that I ...'

Ten minutes sufficed, Billy finding emotions excessive, a welcome discretion.

'How are the boys taking it?'

'It's hard to say. They miss her, talk about her, sometimes the little guy would ask when she's coming back. He doesn't ask any more. But he cries for her. Come to that, so does Jonathan. So do I.'

'How old is he, the little one?'

'Simon, he's four and a half, and Jonathan is eight and a half. Both have birthdays in the spring.'

'And Simon remembers, does he?'

'He remembers some things – when she took him skating, that she often cooked him Chinese food. But whether he remembers her, really remembers her, I don't know. I got some photos of her enlarged and put them in their bedrooms. And I have about four minutes of videotape – we don't have a camcorder, but Irwin Gutman got some of her at his wife's fortieth birthday party. Emma was sort of in charge of handing her the presents. I got a copy and I showed it to the boys on her birthday.'

So they would remember the characteristic lift of her chin as she smiled, the deft movements, the hand to her heavy black hair, her restless eyes.

'So you're getting by?'

'Yeah ... we're getting by, the boys and I.'

'And you don't miss all this?' – waving at the room.

'Miami and San Diego ... politics ... perfume? ... No, not really. And it's no big change. You and Colleen kept up your social life after your kids came along, but Emma and I found we somehow didn't have the time. Didn't have the money either, though I suppose we could have found a bit. But we had ten years of restaurants and dinner parties. Now a brew or two in front of the tube seems decadent.'

Soon enough, with promises to call, get together, season's greetings, they parted, and Frank walked the remaining mile home, through gently falling snow.

Frank was momentarily surprised to find the house in darkness – but no boys were sleeping above, and no babysitter shedding potato chips on the couch in front of the television.

No children.

No Emma.

He stowed his shopping bags and outer clothes. Eleven-fifteen. He made a cheese sandwich, microwaved a cup of coffee, and turned on the television. An enthusiastic woman tried to convince him that upgraded toilet facilities would make a Christmas present the whole family would appreciate for years to come: 'It's called a bidet, Simon.'

He took a bite of the sandwich and flipped through the channels. The only possible show was a black-and-white English movie with Ralph Richardson as a country parson; he seemed to be hosting his family for Christmas. *A Midnight Clear? The Feast of Stephen?* The dowdy stay-at-home daughter, Celia something, who would look dowdy in a ball gown and tiara. John Gregson, familiar and trustworthy as a pair of old slippers. An army private played by ... Denholm Elliot! Celia Johnson, that was it, the dowdy daughter, who, surprisingly, many years later, played the headmistress in *Jean Brodie*. The glamorous alcoholic daughter, wasn't she the wife driven to distraction by Peter Sellers as the lecherous retired general in ... *The Waltz of* ... something or other? He reached for the television supplement: the movie was *The Holly and the Ivy*, with only Richardson and Johnson listed for the cast.

Emma would likely have enjoyed it.

He began to suspect the movie was worked up from a play, all the scenes in several rooms of the parsonage, vicarage, rectory – always forget the differences – and groupings of the cast appearing for their little passages of tension, neatly organized.

Margaret something, the glamorous daughter.

Emma's memory was much better than his, she would have known.

Frank got up and rummaged in his shopping bags. The blue-and-gold Shalimar box ... He sniffed at it: hints of something, but not Shalimar, just the ambient smells of the store's perfume counter, he'd have to open the bottle to release the scent. He rested the box on his lap and sipped his coffee.

Waltz of the Toreadors. Margaret ...

Emma exuded conviction, was decisive about ordering the new furnace, the colour of paint for the rooms, plants for the garden, excursions for the boys, detection of their ailments, couples to invite for dinner ... while he proceeded by doubt, questions, uncertainty. And with Emma gone ...

He let the tears flow for a minute before wiping them.

He put the Shalimar on the coffee table.

Margaret Leighton was the glamorous daughter.

Toward the end of what was clearly the third act, Christmas morning, the tensions were coming to a resolution. Dowdy Celia Johnson agreed to marry Old Slippers Gregson and leave the care of her father to Margaret Leighton who was going to get off the sauce, give up her job with the London fashion magazine, move back to the village, keep house, trade gossip with heavily accented rustics, tend the garden in her wellies, cook for Ralph Richardson, 'Giant toad in the hole, Father,' I'll believe it, thousands wouldn't.

Play the video clip of Emma? No, but take it up to her parents' for the boys to watch tomorrow. No, don't take it, show it only in this house, Emma's house, for the boys, for himself.

He took the cup and plate to the kitchen, turned out the lights, the televison, picked up the Shalimar.

At the top of the stairs he turned toward Jonathan's room, then paused.

The silence. No one drawing breath, no rustle of the sheets as a slim body turned, no thump as Simon rolled against the wall. No sigh from Emma.

As he turned, the floor creaked, sharp through the silence.

He put the Shalimar on his bureau.

In bed, he glanced at the night table for something to read: *Investing for Retirement*, Eric Ambler's *A Passage of Arms*, Dr Spock. The Ambler appealed briefly but would keep him awake. He turned out the light.

Emma exuded conviction; he doubted.

Would Emma have worn Shalimar?

I'll believe it; thousands wouldn't.

Christmas

The Hatchers lived up the hill, above Sherbrooke Street and above Côte St Antoine, but below The Boulevard. In the neat geography of Westmount, this meant they were very comfortably off, rich by the standards of most Canadians, but not wealthy. Frank understood these distinctions in a general sense: the flat part of Westmount where he lived was middle class, halfway up the mountain was upper middle class, the top was upper class. Perhaps that would be, more accurately, middle and upper income. The Hatchers thought in terms of class. They could draw much finer lines based upon ancestors, ancestral finances, length of residency, private schools, universities, location of country house, possession of country house, religion, incidence of French blood, Jewish blood, any other blood.

Frank had heard Mr Hatcher remark of a family further up the mountain, 'More cunning than conscience in those genes.'

Mrs Hatcher once condemned a neighbour for hanging lingerie on her clothesline.

According to the Hatchers, residents of Summit Circle naturally paid for gardening service and snow clearance; halfway down the hill, healthy people were proud to exhibit their taste by doing some of their own gardening and would have a snow blower, preferably a riding model, if they cleared their own driveways; for people below Sherbrooke to hire help beyond a twice-monthly cleaning lady was pretentious and probably Jewish or worse.

Emma ignored all this; her parents were beyond hope, beyond change, Westmount Rhodesians.

Although he usually walked up, Frank took the car because of the presents, and because he would be bringing the boys back when he came. He arrived just after four.

'Well, here at last. Aren't you lucky the butcher's shop wasn't busy, and I was able to get home to let you in.'

The logic of this seemed to be that he was both too late and too early. He just managed to stop himself from apologizing.

'Yes, wasn't I lucky. How are the boys?'

'Doing just famously. They're always so happy to be here. Although I think they do play those games rather too much, they're so violent. I bought some videos for them. They were meant to be Christmas presents, but they were so excited that …'

'Season's greetings, Mr Hatcher.'

'The same to you, Frank. Still snowing?'

In the living room, George Hatcher was seated in his leatherette recliner reading *Newsweek*.

'No, it's stopped. If you'll excuse me, I just have to go see the boys …'

Frank hid the bags of presents in the coat closet and went down to the rec room. The boys glanced about when they heard his steps. On the screen, Jiminy Cricket advised Pinocchio to let his conscience be his guide.

'Grandma got us a new video,' said Simon. 'Do you know what it's called?'

'No, what's it called?'

'Dad knows what it's called, Simon. He wasn't born yesterday, you know.'

'Liar, liar, pants on fire.'

Frank could have sworn he had checked with Mrs Hatcher: he had also bought *Pinocchio* for them. It seemed a waste to have two copies. But then having one here might be just as well if they liked it enough. On a side table lay another new video – *Mickey's Christmas Carol* with the miserly Scrooge McDuck cast as his namesake.

'Have you watched this one yet?' he asked.

Jonathan turned round.

'Not yet.'

Frank examined the box: lots about the magic of Walt Disney, but no mention of Charles Dickens … no, Dickens was there, buried in the blurb paragraph on the back of the box, along with several further mentions of Disney and his magic.

He moved to the couch between the boys. Simon, thumb in his mouth, snuggled against him.

'Daddy,' Jonathan asked, 'when are we going home?'

'Tomorrow evening, I expect. After Christmas dinner.'

Simon pulled the thumb from his mouth.

'Grandma always says "Sit up straight," and "Eat with your mouth shut."'

'And "Don't put your elbows on the table."'

'Well, you should sit up straight and eat with your mouth shut and keep your elbows down. You're a pair of little piggies at the table.'

'I'm not a piggy. Jonathan is a piggy.'

'You're a liar.'

'Am not, am not, am not.'

'Are so, are so, are so.'

'Enough, guys. Remember what I asked you, eh? No screaming or fighting while you're here.'

'Daddy,' said Jonathan, 'do you think Santa might bring us the computer program of *Magic: The Gathering*?'

Did Jonathan still believe in Santa Claus, or was he pretending to believe because Simon was there?

'Could be. Did you put it on the list you sent him?'

'Yes, and I also explained that the version ...'

The game was produced by two different companies, one British, one American, as far as Frank could tell; he was grateful that Jonathan's list had specified the one wanted.

'But Santa's a busy fellow, so try not to be too disappointed if he doesn't bring it.'

'That's all right, Daddy.'

Simon was pondering the broader issue:

'Santa has to take presents to every little boy and girl in the whole world, right, Dada?'

'He tries to, but I'm afraid he misses lots of children every year.'

'Well,' said Simon, 'if he misses me this year, I won't mind because maybe it's not my turn for presents, maybe it's some other boy's turn.'

This generosity of spirit was likely inspired by we-are-the-world explanations from pre-school, but Frank hugged them both.

After a few minutes he went upstairs, moved by the vague sense that he should offer to help, aware that any help would be refused.

'Heavens, no. Too many cooks spoil the broth. You go put your presents under the tree.'

'Ah, Frank, you'll need some Christmas cheer, I'm sure. What'll it be, Scotch?'

'Perhaps a very small one. I've never been much for hard liquor.'

'Nonsense, my boy, spirits of the season. Chivas good enough for you?'

'Fine.'

'I wouldn't vouch for the ... ethical standards of some of Sam Bronfman's empire-building manoeuvres, but he knew quality when he saw it.'

Mr Hatcher poured heavy drinks for both of them.

'Well,' he began, 'what are the chances the Liberals can find a leader who can win the next election?'

Frank focused hard on the Lismer beach scene hanging just above his father-in-law's head. 'Well, I'm not sure ...' he said. It took Frank five minutes to change the subject to house renovations. He managed to pour most of his drink down the sink when he washed his hands.

The main course at supper was tourtière because, as Mrs Hatcher announced, as she always announced, they lived in Quebec and it was the least they could do to share in the traditions of French culture. Some years earlier, Emma had remarked, at the table, that it was a shame René Lévesque hadn't known about this sharing because if he had, the separatist movement would have come to a screeching halt in the early seventies.

'Eat the crust, Simon,' Mrs Hatcher directed, 'and you eat the filling, Jonathan. It's a shame to let food go to waste.'

Jonathan glanced at Frank and lowered his head; Simon made a gesture at the crust with his fork. Frank saw that she had put out the second-best silverware.

'This was Mama's house when she was a little girl, wasn't it Grandma?'

'It was, Simon, dear, and we hope you'll think of it as your house, too. Wouldn't that be nice? Such a big house to play in, so many rooms, and such a big back yard.'

'Let me top you up, Frank,' said Mr Hatcher as he filled the wine glass to the brim.

'George, you should know enough not to fill a wine glass more than halfway – it's vulgar.'

'Frank can handle it.'

'You both handle far too much, if you ask me.'

Mr Hatcher winked at Frank.

'And wasn't it nice to sleep in a proper bed last night? You'd never have to worry about falling out of that bed.'

A month ago Simon had bloodied his nose in the small hours.

'And try to eat with your mouth shut, Jonathan, dear. Santa only comes to good little boys and girls.'

'Well, maybe he's not coming to me anyway, because maybe it's not my turn this year.'

'Oh, I'm sure he'll bring presents to you, Simon, who's been telling you tales like that?'

'Marie-Claire at pre-school said Santa doesn't bring toys to lots of kids who live in other places.'

'Well, I'm sure he'll bring presents to you, but only if you are a good boy.' She turned to Frank: 'It's never too early to teach them, I always say.'

'Babs always does say that,' added Mr Hatcher with a conspiratorial wink from behind his raised glass.

'We've been working at it,' said Frank, hoping to deflect her with the ambiguous 'we', which might evoke Emma-and-I as well as Jonathan-and-I.

'George, not in front of … If you can't say something nice, don't say anything at all. Isn't that right, Jonathan? And, yes, I always say that, too. The truth bears repeating.'

'Very pleasant wine, this,' said Mr Hatcher. 'Best of all, it was a little Christmas consideration from old Charlie Jones, hasn't missed a Christmas in twenty-eight years.'

'I suppose that's a little perk you'll have to do without after you retire,' said Frank.

'I dread the day,' said Mrs Hatcher. 'May Duluth was saying just the other day that when Al retired he was underfoot all the livelong day. I'm hoping George will take up a hobby. Or at least find something to keep him out of my hair.'

'If I'm *underfoot* I'll likely be *out of her hair*, eh, Frank?'

'Perhaps you want to audition as a stand-up comedian,' said Frank with what he hoped was a bright smile. 'As I recall, Bob Newhart was an accountant, wasn't he?'

'Now there's a funny comedian,' said Mrs Hatcher. 'Nothing risqué about his humour, he's always so nice.'

When dinner was over, Mrs Hatcher refused Frank's offer of help, but insisted the boys carry their plates to the kitchen because it was never too early to learn. When the dishwasher was running, the boys were ushered into the living room so they could hang their Christmas stockings and open one of their presents.

Sensing any number of troubles, Frank tried to steer them toward gift boxes containing identical drinking cups with Montreal Canadiens decorations, but Mrs Hatcher had her way, so that Simon got Sesame Street pyjamas, which he loathed as much as Jonathan loathed his Mickey Mouse set. Making it clear that the mix-up was entirely Frank's fault, Mrs Hatcher insisted she give them their baths and put them to bed.

'And you won't splash, will you, or Santa may not come with your prezzies,' she added.

Mollified by the promise of an exchange of the pyjamas, the boys went upstairs with reasonably good grace.

'I'll come up and read to you,' Frank promised. Mrs Hatcher protested, and they compromised: she would read a small book to Simon, while Frank would do a chapter or two of *Around the World in Eighty Days* with Jonathan – they had been doing long books together for several years.

'Something for the digestion?' asked Mr Hatcher when they were alone.

'No, thank you, the coffee's fine.'

'On Christmas eve? I insist. A splash of cognac.'

'Well, since you insist. But I also insist – just a finger this time.'

Nonetheless he got two fingers in a very wide balloon glass.

'Been giving any thought to the future?' asked Mr Hatcher when they were settled.

'As much as I can, considering.'

'You must have very little room for manoeuvre, I expect.'

'Well ...' Frank talked casually about salary freezes and cuts, babysitting expenses, pensions. 'And once I have the last bit of the mortgage paid off ...'

He and Emma had bought the house with a small commercial mortgage, and a large mortgage from her parents at a few points below commercial rates. They paid off the trust company in three years, and by the previous spring owed the Hatchers just over $54,000. Emma had $25,000 in group life insurance from McGill with double indemnity for accidental death. When the insurance claim was settled in the fall, Frank had paid the entire fifty thousand to Mr Hatcher and was now paying off the balance at $200 a month. It was not a great amount to pay out, but it would be a welcome cushion every month when he could keep it.

'And yourselves?' asked Frank. 'Have you made any decisions about this house, your retirement?'

'Well, that's something I've been meaning to discuss with you, Frank.'

Frank put his glass carefully on the coffee table and sat up.

'Well, we have definitely decided we're going to get out. But I don't need to tell you that real estate values in Montreal have been pretty flat for nearly ten years now. I hung on because I hoped things would settle down, but that damn Mulroney wouldn't let well enough alone, then the referendum, and with Bouchard likely to win the next election, and then another referendum ... well, you know all about that. But the upshot is that I don't think values are going to pick up for a while, so I'd rather not sell just now.'

'I expect you've had an agent in to appraise the place?'

'No, but I've been following sales on this street, on Roslyn, Lansdowne, the neighbourhood, and I have a pretty good idea of what I could get. Four hundred, tops, if you're curious – three-fifty, more likely.'

For a house with a central staircase, rooms on both sides, garage in the basement, that seemed reasonable.

'However, there's a complication.'

'Ahh?'

'Well, as you know, Willis is coming back to Montreal, taking that posting with IATA. He and Betsy will be arriving in the spring.'

Willis Jackson, a diplomat with the Canadian consulate in San Francisco, was married to Emma's younger sister Betsy. Because of their continuous foreign postings over the years, Frank had only met them briefly a few times. A few times had been quite enough.

'Surely they don't need anything this big – they have no children.'

'Willis has to entertain a lot, and Betsy really wants to move back to the house she grew up in. You know how sentimental she is.'

'Ahh.'

Betsy? Sentimental?

'However, three-fifty or four is a little beyond them just now, and the house will be hers anyway one day. Of course it would have been hers and Emma's, or at least the proceeds from it would have been if we sold it. As it is, we thought we would leave Betsy her half of the house now and she could pay us something every month, in effect buying out the other half, building up capital which we'll eventually use to equalize the legacy to the boys. They'll get their share, don't worry.'

'Oh, I wasn't worried. In any case, the boys will have whatever I can leave them ... and let's hope nothing will happen to any of us for years.'

The boys came thundering down the stairs.

'Dada, Dada we forgot to ...'

'Daddy, Grandma says we should leave milk and cookies for Santa Claus.'

'Yes, milk and cookies. And can I have a cookie, please, please, please?'

'Perhaps. If there are any left. Let's go to the kitchen and see what we can find.'

Mrs Hatcher arranged the offering, gave the boys each two cookies, then led them back upstairs. Frank followed Jonathan to his room.

'Daddy, when we finish this book, can we do that other one ... about the guy who has the submarine?'

'Captain Nemo – *Twenty Thousand Leagues Under the Sea*. Sure, I expect I can find a copy.' Under the Christmas tree, in fact. 'So, Phileas Fogg and Passepartout are on their way to Bombay, and Fix, the detective, is on the ship with them.'

'Daddy?'

'Yes, love?'

'You know when Passepartout said he left the gas on in his room in the house back in London and it was going to cost him two shillings a day because Phileas Fogg was going to make him pay for it?'

'Yes.'

'Well, if it takes them eighty days to get around the world, Passepartout will owe 160 shillings, right?'

'Yes.'

'So how many pounds is that?'

'Let's see if you can work it out ... There are – or there were until they changed to decimal – twenty shillings to the pound ... So how many pounds would that make?'

After a pause: 'Eight pounds?'

'That's right.'

'Well, but what would that be worth in Canadian money? I mean, if it was now?'

Frank hugged the boy. For his Jane Austen course, Frank had looked into the slippery subject of historical currency values. The evidence suggested multiplying pounds of 1812 by fifty would give an approximation of the value of Jane Austen's pound in current Canadian dollars. Jonathan listened attentively.

'Now, I don't have figures for 1872 when Fogg and Passepartout go on their journey, but let's guess that multiplying by ... thirty would give a fair answer.'

'So that would be £240 times two because the pound is worth two times the dollar today.'

'No, multiplying by thirty already includes changing the value to Canadian. So it would be ...'

'Two hundred and forty dollars.'

'Right.'

'Is that, like, what we pay for gas?'

'I expect it's about right. Passepartout has a gas fireplace in his room and it probably uses about as much gas as our stove and water heater together over nearly three months. It's hard to compare; this sort of calculation is always a bit vague.'

Jonathan liked certainty, but settled for the approximation. Frank began to read.

When he had made sure both had brushed their teeth and had had a last sit on the toilet, Frank tucked them in, kissed them, reassured them that Santa would certainly visit such good boys, turned off their lights. Passing along the hall, he glanced into Betsy's room; he could see no evidence the room was being done over: the furniture was in place, although the bed was stripped and the mattress under a dustcover. A small meanness. He shrugged and walked slowly back downstairs.

Reading the silence, the eyes, Mrs Hatcher's fidgeting with a handkerchief, he guessed the Hatchers had been having a confidential chat. One subject, at least, had been the Christmas cheer: the decanter was safely stowed away and Mr Hatcher's snifter had been replaced by Santa's glass of milk. Frank's cognac remained on the table beside his chair. At least an hour before he could decently escape to the basement.

'Well, they're safely away. Simon is almost asleep and Jonathan will be gone in a few minutes.'

'Good, good,' said Mrs Hatcher. As she didn't add anything about their improper hours she was evidently distracted.

'Perhaps I should explain it to him,' she said to her husband.

'Well...'

'Frank,' began Mrs Hatcher, 'I've always said you were a very good father, I'd never take that away from you.'

'Yes, Emma always said you were excellent with them, more patient that she was, the way you put up with their crying and their fights.'

'And the meals you cook for them – really, it's just remarkable how you manage.'

'I don't think it's remarkable – I make a decent salary and my work isn't nine-to-five. I have advantages most single parents don't have.'

'But that's the point!' cried Mrs Hatcher. 'Single parents. That's no way to bring up children, with only one parent. Children need two parents, Jonathan and Simon need a mother as well as a father.'

'It has only been six months, Mrs Hatcher. Surely you're not suggesting I should have found another wife already?'

'I wish you wouldn't stoop to sarcasm – it's not becoming.'

'Mentioning I'm a single parent after only six months isn't becoming either. What choice do I have?'

'Well, now, Frank,' said Mr Hatcher, 'that's what we'd like to try to explain to you. Now, I realize you love the boys very much, and you're doing a fine job of caring for them – as fine a job as can be expected ... under the circumstances. But the fact is you have your job, you can't be expected to care for them day in and day out, you haven't the time.'

'If only Emma had married Jock Spencer ... and she wouldn't have had to go to that conference ...' Emma's failure to marry Jock Spencer of Upper Bellevue Avenue, a long-time crewman on ocean racing yachts, was the greatest tragedy in Mrs Hatcher's life. Her handkerchief could barely absorb this grief: she went for another.

'Babs isn't objecting to you personally, Frank. It's just that you don't have the means to care for the boys full time.'

'And when I can't be with them, I have a babysitter at five bucks an hour, three or four hundred a month during term.'

'And that's another thing,' said Mrs Hatcher as she returned, 'That Linda, a welfare case from Verdun, for heaven's sake, you can't expect her to be a very good influence on the boys. The clothes she wears, the way she talks, her grammar, I mean, really, and does she ever wash her hair, I wonder? And she has young ones of her own from who knows how many different fathers.'

'It shouldn't be too difficult to calculate the maximum number of fathers involved in two children.'

'That sarcasm again!'

'In any case, Linda is reliable, flexible, sober, and relatively cheap. And the boys like her.'

'Frank,' said Mr Hatcher, 'have you considered that this Linda is collecting welfare, she's getting an allowance from welfare to put her own kids in daycare, and then using the time to look after your boys and taking money under the table for it.'

'Possibly.'

'Well, she's breaking the conditions of her welfare. If the authorities find out, she's in serious trouble.'

'Would you prefer she while away her free time drinking in a brasserie and scratching lottery tickets?'

'How she might spend her time is no concern of mine – the point is she is breaking the law, she's taking advantage of a social service and earning money on which – you know perfectly well – she is not declaring income. In the eyes of Revenue Canada and the Ministère du Revenu du Québec, that's a felony.'

'And you've been declaring the interest you've been earning on the mortgage Emma and I have with you …'

'Now just a goddamn minute here, young man …'

'George! Language!'

'Just as I'm sure you intend to report whatever Betsy and Willis will be paying you.'

'Those arrangements are not the same at all, they're entirely within the family, adjustments because of Betsy's legacy.'

'I wonder if Revenue Canada and the Ministère would look at it in quite that way.'

'It is a private family arrangement whereby Betsy gets the house which would be hers anyway, and we get a small monthly allowance. It's not the same thing as cheating the welfare.'

A small monthly allowance? Surely it could not be less than a thousand a month? But perhaps they would not be charged the 7.5 per cent interest he and Emma had paid the Hatchers.

'No, it certainly isn't – you'll be enjoying a comfortable retirement in Toronto, while Linda is trying to scratch out a living for herself and her two kids in a Verdun tenement.'

'It's entirely her own fault,' cried Mrs Hatcher. 'She has no one to blame but herself.'

… and decrease the surplus population. Perhaps Linda should have had an abortion, as Emma had done after Jock Spencer impregnated her twenty years ago. But the Hatchers did not know that.

'Look, Babs, let's leave this Linda out of the discussion. Let's just say that no matter how good she is, she is not a real mother to the boys, and that's what they need, a real mother.'

'And you're proposing to find one for them, is that it?'

More glances exchanged. Mr Hatcher had the running.

'A mother for the boys, yes, but we aren't trying to suggest you get married again, I mean, heavens, no.'

At last Frank understood.

'Is that what ... You think I should give the children to Betsy and Willis?'

They're family ...

They have no children ...

They're so loving ...

Their need is greater than ...

This big house ...

Their mouths worked over the words, spilling them out. Frank closed his eyes, shook his head, slammed his brandy glass down on the end table; it broke at the stem and the balloon rolled across the table, spilling cognac. He made a grab for it and knocked over the lamp which crashed to the floor. He reached down on the other side of his chair and pulled the plug from the wall.

'The violence!' cried Mrs Hatcher. 'In our house! Didn't I tell you, George, didn't I say he was out of control and prone to violence? Oh, Frank, can't you see that you shouldn't be near children, you shouldn't be near Emma's children, you don't know how I worry about them when ...'

There was no point talking about the lamp, the glass, the accusations of violence and drunkenness – the Hatchers had worked it all out – it was a closed argument. Frank wondered whether to rouse the boys and take them home now. Waking them when they were just asleep, packing all the presents ... The whole business was so grotesque. He was frozen. A closed argument.

He could only try to calm down, make peace. Slow, measured tones:

'Look, let's just say you're concerned about your grandchildren. I'm concerned about them too. But for the time being, I'm getting along, and I'd like to leave it that way. So I thank you for your concerns, but ... no, thanks.'

But Mrs Hatcher was not ready to make peace. She had not had time to air all the arguments which she had obviously been working at, turning over, fitting together for, what, weeks? months?

'I told you George, he is incapable of seeing things in any way except from his own selfish point of view. He simply refuses to see that we're only thinking of the boys' best interests. They need a mother, they need family, they love this house, they'll be so much better off living up the mountain like this, they'll have the best in private schooling, they'll meet friends who can give them a hand up in life ... the better sort of people ... the select ... But if you insist on having your own selfish way, they'll grow up down there, brought up by a welfare cheat and a violent drunk and attending public schools with who knows what sort of riff-raff and hoodlums, blacks and Hindus and Greeks and Italians, what sort of start in life will that ...'

'The boys are likely to be up early. I'm going to bed. Good night. And merry Christmas to both of you.'

'So hard ...' Mrs Hatcher was saying as he left, 'so sarcastic ... such a bad influence ...'

School

The students were getting up, gathering their stuff.

'… so anyone who still has ice storm problems, come see me at your convenience. Otherwise, don't forget – chapters four to twelve of *Northanger Abbey* with a three-hundred-word summary – not a précis – of those chapters.'

'Sir, is that to the beginning of chapter twelve?'

'No, Gino, to the *end* of chapter twelve.'

'Aww, *sir*!'

The others, caught off guard, paused.

'Always read to the *end* of the assigned chapter.'

'Couldn't you give us a break, sir, for the beginning of the term, like?'

'Sure, Gino, what would you like me to break – your left arm or your right?'

Several students stiffened.

'Perhaps your Camaro?'

'I sold the Camaro – it's a Nissan Sentra now, very conservative, sir, respectable, like.'

'Gino, you're engaged!'

'Well … sort of, yeah …'

The others began to relax, to laugh.

'Are you really engaged?' Frank murmured as they left the room.

'It's true, sir, sort of. Me and Mirella haven't made an announcement, but we have plans. We're, like, serious.'

'Well, congratulations to you and to Mirella.'

'Thanks, sir.'

'And this term you're going to be serious, too, aren't you?'

'Eh, sir, always!'

Frank felt the usual flattery that Gino had registered for a second course with him: Gino would be perky during a slow class, but not disruptive when Frank had a good holler going.

'And after you graduate?'

'I'm going to apply for Business at Concordia. My uncle, he's into wholesale fruit and vegetables, see, and he says if I …'

Gino sketched a reasonable future for himself, one in which, reasonably, Jane Austen would play no part.

At the stairs, Gino went down and Frank up toward audio-visual. Outside, under a grey January sky, the smashed trees, branches littering the grey snow, the grey ice; such devastation. Well, think rather of the term stretching ahead toward the green grass and blue skies of May.

After returning the slide projector, Frank looked in at the office of some friends.

'… and this is no joking matter – we're talking about "Real Quebecers" and prospects for the future of the place if all the unreal Quebecers leave.'

'Doesn't Camilli claim the ice storm was organized by Louise Beaudoin?'

'Makes sense to me.'

'It was supposed to take out ethnics and money, but it got out of hand. And stop frowning, Frank. Sit down, you might learn something.'

'I've already learned the only lesson of any importance around here: I'm a middle-aged, middle-class, white male anglo swine who should be put down for the betterment of the collectivité.'

'True, but aside from that, have you heard the one about the tongue trooper and the tattooed stripper …'

Frank slipped out. Others always seemed to have time to sit about with their feet up and their hands behind their heads. But it was doubtless an illusion. Many office doors were closed – teachers trying to get some grading done, others were in class, in the library, at photocopy, in meetings, working at home … Nonsense, all nonsense. He mustn't get angry, mustn't feel sorry for himself.

Get on with it.

He propped open his own door and glanced through his mail. Administrative memos announced meetings, reported the results of meetings, explained the need for further meetings; brochures from publishers announced that *this* introduction to college writing would motivate his students to write better – to write as well, it was implied, as Joan Didion, Lewis Thomas, or Maya Angelou.

'Goody, goody, free books for me, too?' His officemate Sid, trailing clouds of body odour, shambled in.

'No, but you can have this one.'

'Hey, that's good for a buck from the second-hand buyer; you mean it?'

'A token of my love and respect.'

A precarious armload of books and papers slid onto Sid's desk, onto the floor.

'Let's see.'

Frank finished scanning the table of contents.

'Orwell's "Shooting an Elephant" is missing. Do you suppose it's gone out of fashion after all these years?'

'About time. I never could get to them with that one. British India, the Raj, downtrodden brown men – all that imperialist shit.'

Sid had done a masters on Faulkner at CCNY in the sixties and had apparently read nothing since.

'Throw it on the chair. I've got some crucial work to get through.' He winked lasciviously.

'One of these days, Sid ...'

Based on what he saw during the first week of class, when many of the girls were wearing dress-up clothes, Sid imposed what he called his 'Armstrong Seating Plan', a scheme of such apparent complexity that none of the students could understand it. For good reason, because its only purpose, carefully disguised, was to place the girls with the highest hemlines and lowest necklines in the front row. Sid claimed vast erotic success; taped to his filing cabinet was a photo of Neil Armstrong's footprint and the caption 'One small step for a man ...'

'It's a joke,' he had explained when he put it up. 'First to the *moon*... see?'

Frank guessed the girls twigged at once, and were in jeans and bulky turtlenecks within a week.

Futile.

Juvenile.

Sid.

When Sid was gone to his class, Frank opened his briefcase and exchanged the texts and notes from the last class for those of his next. The lecture for *Anna Karenin* was ready, but he scanned his notes from Riazanovsky and Pipes on political and economic changes during the 1860s and 70s, wrestled yet again with the complexities of the emancipation, the implications of the zemstvos, the opening of the universities. He leafed on to review Calder on the position of women in Russian society, Russian fiction, other hints of the vast dramas sweeping that strange, exuberant, sad land ...

'How's it going, old fellow?'

'Can't complain. Yourself?'

'I'm fine.'

Eleanor Rowan shared the next office. They had drifted into friendship over the years because of mutual respect for books, hard work, humour, survival. They traded their brief ice storm tales, and then she asked, 'How was your first Christmas without Emma? You made it through?'

Frank chuckled.

'It's ironic, really. Dealing with the Hatchers is like dealing with Quebec nationalists ... or the Inquisition. Their world view is entirely closed, virtue and truth are clearly defined, there are good guys and bad guys, you're either fer us or agin us, you're either inside the fort shooting out or outside the fort shooting in, praise the Lord and pass the ammunition. Any argument must start from their premises, the logical structure is monolithic and inexorable, all disagreement is anathema, and any accommodation you try to make, any refusal to choose sides, is wrong, illogical, evil, you're a traitor to family, language, race, state, God, ein Volk, ein Reich, ein ... what were the three?'

'Flag? Führer? Anyway, you're hiding something: what are they up to?'

There were no secrets of this sort from Eleanor; she winkled the whole story from him straight away.

'But even if they take you to court, they can't win, surely? You're the father, you're a good father, you're working, the boys are happy and healthy ...'

'Oh yes, I expect you're right. But you never know what can happen in court.'

'But they wouldn't.'

'No, they probably wouldn't. But they might. What about *A Handful of Dust*, *Sword of Honour*?'

Eleanor was a critic of Evelyn Waugh and had published several well-received books on his works.

'Those are novels, this is real life.'

'That's what I keep telling myself.'

They worried it over for a few minutes. Eleanor wore her sanity like a glory.

'Never mind, old fellow. You'll come to dinner soon. I'll be in touch.'

Ten dollars for wine, ten for the cab home, and perhaps thirty for babysitting.

'Just name the date.'

He thought of closing the door after her, but with only twenty minutes before class he had no time for anything useful. After spending the first half of the class on Russia, he would try to point them for their weekend's start on the novel. On the whole, students seemed to like *Anna*, which was half the battle won. Gallumphing Levin was always a problem, with his schemes for improved farming methods, fairer, more efficient financial arrangements with the peasants, grumblings about westernizing modernisms. Interesting historically, interesting as a structural device in the book, interesting to Russians, interesting to Frank, but not gripping material for Montreal teenagers; with Levin, get them focused on his pursuit of Kitty and keep them there. In the meantime, signpost the opening scenes with Stiva, the immediate crisis being adultery, Nabokov's note about the German clockmaker winding the clocks, winding up the novel, Tolstoy's dislike of Germans also in *War and Peace*, Anna's announced arrival by telegram, telegrams inextricably linked with the development of the railways, railways booming under Alexander II, quote Tolstoy's letter to Turgenev saying trains are to travel as brothels are to sex, note the train game being played by Stiva's children, Anna's arrival by train, watch the railway workers muffled and bundled, Anna first seen through Vronsky's eyes, essential Tolstoyan method, seen again most dramatically in Kitty's observations of Anna at the ball, '... she was enchanting, but there was something terrible and cruel in her beauty …' the passage itself is on a right-hand page …

But, as he hefted his briefcase, how best to do it, to do it so the words come off the page, so the work gleams in their minds, sparkling into significance, dancing through their minds? Oh well …

It was showtime.

He could hear the phone ringing as he put the key in the office door; five minutes to clean up and head home to release Linda, and here was some student, no doubt, calling to say he couldn't make it to class tomorrow.

Damn.

'I wonder if I could speak to Professor Frank Wilson, please?'

Professor was polite, but wrong; professeur in French, yes, but lecturer was more accurate in English.

'Speaking.'

'The Frank Wilson who did that lovely paper on *Emma* in *EBN* last year?'

Lovely?

'Yes?'

'I'm so pleased to have tracked you down at last – you seem to have survived the ice storm?'

'We were in the dark for a few days, but it wasn't a problem.'

'Glad to hear it, glad to hear it. But I must a tale unfold …'

'After the ice storm, I trust it'll not freeze my young blood.'

'Ahh, you're quick, you're quick, and you know your *Hamlet*, and I expect you know your Jane Austen better. Now, I'm with the Department of English here at the University of Eastern Ontario. I believe we have a friend in common …'

The caller, Ellery something, mentioned Einar Sorensen, a prof in Winnipeg that Frank had met once at a conference, and remembered vaguely.

Linda, the sitter, had very little elasticity in her late afternoon movements. Frank walked to and from school for the exercise; a few more minutes of this rambling and he would have hurry home, bundle his boys into the car and drive Linda to her daycare, which would make their own supper late …

'... but to get to the nub of the business, as I believe Bertie says to Jeeves ...'

On a rather barren day in the Wodehouse workshop, no doubt.

The nub of the business was that the Department of English at the University of Eastern Ontario was expecting several retirements this term and might just have a tenure track opening next fall or winter for someone in nineteenth-century British novel, especially Jane Austen.

'Look, I have to be honest: my dissertation was not a sparkling performance,' said Frank. Unlike Emma's. She had been passionate about her work, but he had rushed his studies through evening classes and patched his dissertation together from notions he would otherwise have spread across a dozen articles. Respectable churning, but entirely pedestrian. Although he had enjoyed developing the arguments, he had done the degree solely in order to boost his salary after Jonathan was born.

'I expect you have dozens of eager young Ph.D.s clambering up the ivy-covered walls with British novel qualifications, unfathomable deconstructionist depths, and pages of publishing credits....'

People like Emma.

Ellery Whatever was not to be denied: the opening was likely, and Frank, on the strength of his publications, and despite indifferent credentials, must apply. Frank agreed to send a CV, took down the addressing information – the name was Ellery Culp – and grabbed his coat. Too late to walk: he would need a cab home and even if he drove Linda she would be barely on time at the daycare.

Tenure track at a university? An unsolicited invitation: it seemed so unlikely.

And yet, why not? Perhaps in Ontario things were different – perhaps there they were hiring. But hiring Frank Wilson?

Ellery Culp was probably deranged or simple.

After getting the children off the next morning, Frank went to his study to correct papers. The Culp note lying on top of the stack offered a half-hour delay. He started the computer and retrieved his CV and bibliography. He had not updated the file in six months, so he went to the end of the document and entered the two articles which had recently appeared. There was rarely anything to add to the CV, but as soon as he thought of it, he realized there would be one change. He returned to the CV page:

> M. (1979) Emma Hatcher; two children:
> Jonathan (b. 1989), Simon (b. 1993).

He tried:

> M. (1979) late Emma Hatcher ...

But that made him seem a ghoul. Perhaps:

> M. (1979) Emma Hatcher (d. 1997)...

Too cold, statistical. But leaving her name out would suggest he had given birth himself. No, the boys had to be there, so Emma had to be there as well. Surely he could work out a more graceful formula ... Ten minutes later he found he was investigating the WordPerfect Setup menu and was now reading the manual on Delimited Text Options. He hastily returned the manual to the shelf, typed:

> M. (1979) Emma Hatcher, Ph.D. (English, McGill) (d. 1997) ...

printed the document, and composed the covering letter.

Such nonsense.

As an afterthought, Frank jotted a note of thanks to Sorensen for the recommendation. The idea was so outlandish that the thanks were disingenuous, but if Culp was a fool or a prankster, perhaps the note would prompt an exposure. Frank had no address for Sorensen, but in a file from a different conference, he found a list of Canadian university addresses.

University of Manitoba? University of Winnipeg?

Manitoba.

He addressed the envelopes, stamped them, and laid them by his billfold.

The papers waited, brief précis of the opening three chapters of

Northanger Abbey, simple exercises to find out where everyone stood.

He sighed, sat.

In the early years, when he was young and fresh and keen and intolerant, such writing angered him. The kids were lazy, illiterate, stupid; the school system no longer taught anything as boring, as paternalistic, as repressive as grammar; bad grammar flourished in newspapers, on radio.

But the students soon educated him.

They hadn't made the school system, they didn't write the newspapers. Indeed, they didn't even read the newspapers. So how could they be expected to write well?

Even the graduates of private schools, the privileged kids from the Hatchers' neighbourhood, wrote with little grammar and less grace. For the generality of students, English was a compulsory course, an incomprehensible trial on the way to a job. Then the kids with the millstones of poverty, drugged and alcoholic parents, broken homes, homes without books; immigrants kids just off the boat, kids with jobs, kids who were street-fluent in three, four languages … And none of them planning a career in the lit-crit trade. Reasonably enough.

Off the boat? Off the plane, surely.

But you couldn't blame the kids.

So start from here, wherever here happens to be:

In the opening chapter, of Jane Austen's great and famous book 'Northanger Abbey' you can't help of liking Cathrine Morland because the writer describes her, as being very much like a modern girl who even plays baseball …

Groceries

Frank was finishing the Saturday *Gazette* when the squealing from the living room told him the Nagano Olympics had gone to a commercial break. He pulled the shopping list from under its magnet.

'Okay, guys,' he called, 'time for groceries.'

'Awww, not groooceries.'

'We'll miss some of the Olympics.'

'I'm afraid we do have to eat. Anyway, they'll repeat the important events.'

'I guess.'

With fits and starts they made their way to the basement.

'What say we take some bottles and cans back, guys? Can you carry this bag, Simon? I bet it's too heavy for you.'

'Silly Dada, of course it isn't too heavy for me.'

'What are we having for supper, Daddy?' asked Jonathan.

'I'm not sure. What would you fellows like?'

'Tacos,' said Jonathan.

'Burritos!'

'We had burritos last week, Simon, and anywise, I said tacos first.'

'I wanted to say burritos first, but you didn't let me.'

'Well, you didn't say it first, so I win, so shut up.'

'Shut up yourself, you chicken butt.'

'You cow flap.'

'You rhinoceros burp.'

'You wombat dung.'

'It's charming, guys, really charming – from a discussion about what lovely food to have for supper to wombat poop in five easy steps.'

'I didn't say poop, Dada.'

'That's what dung is, Jonathan.'

'It is?'

With races to the corner, scufflings in the snow of gardens, snowballs at stop signs, they made their way around the corner and to the next street. Just as Frank was wondering if he was bringing up two violent, scatological monsters, Simon took his hand to cross; Jonathan took the other hand: did stout Cortez stare at the Pacific with anything like this satisfaction?

Or Elizabeth Bennet at Pemberley?

The squabbles began again with the can recycling; Jonathan was reluctant to let Simon put his share into the machine, and Simon, who was barely tall enough to reach, dropped several.

'Simon, people are waiting,' Jonathan hissed.

'Okay, guys, let's just get the job done. Here, Jonathan, you press the button, and Simon, you take the receipt....' Everybody returned bottles and cans on Saturday. Frank would have brought them on a weekday, but the boys were thrilled that they could get money for garbage. They got in line for their refunds.

Stephen and Melanie are out west ... she's just had her third, a little girl

must miss them

last fall when the baby was born

out to Calgary and

'How much are we getting, supercomputer?'

'It's going to be three dollars and forty-five cents, Dada.'

'I expect you're right.'

He dropped the three forty-five in his pocket and followed Simon who had run off for a cart. When they had agreed it was Jonathan's turn to walk and Simon's to stand on the front of the cart, they moved off toward the meat aisle.

says meat is much cheaper in Atlanta

everything is cheaper in

what they win in heating bills, they lose in air conditioning, so

was only off for four days, and we had power for a few hours on the Monday, I think it was

Drifting through his mind was the melody of ... what? A Glazunov quartet? Something haunting, melancholic? No, poignant, from far away ...

He dropped a packet of ground beef into the cart and found an opening in the crowd.

'Dada, that man hit me with his cart.'

'Does it hurt, Simon?'

'Only a little bit.'

Which likely meant not at all.

'Okay, I guess you'll be all right. It must have happened when I was looking at the meat, did it?'

'I think so. Yes, that's when he hit me. The idiot.'

The man was out of hearing.

'You idiot.'

At least he hadn't yelled it.

'Okay, I'll try to be more careful about driving the cart, and you guys try to keep out of the way of other carts. And let's all be patient – it's not a morning to be in a hurry.'

'People should be more careful, shouldn't they, Daddy?'

'No doubt they should, but ...'

'Or they don't realize they've bumped into a little kid like Simon?'

Frank ruffled the boy's hair.

'Very true, Jonathan.'

'He's a idiot, he's wombat dung.'

'Well, Simon, if you go around calling people idiots every time something annoys you, you're going to get in a lot of fights.'

'So?'

'So you'd better eat lots of vegetables so you grow big and strong. Or learn to control your impatience.'

Jonathan picked the box of taco shells and Frank got the packet of spices and a bottle of sauce.

Not Glazunov – Arensky, the trio!

'Hey, Frank, how you doing?'

'Not bad, Sholem – yourself?'

'Can't complain. Keeping busy?'

'As you see,' Frank chuckled.

The kids had begun to squabble, so Frank made a motion to pass on. Sholem paused then gestured him closer.

'I heard something about you the other day ... I can't remember if it was in the faculty club or at a vernissage.'

'About me? It must have been an excruciatingly boring conversation.'

Or did he perhaps mean he had only just heard about Emma?

'I can't remember who said it – honestly, although it will come to me – but the message was loud and clear – since last spring, you've been hitting the bottle pretty heavily.'

'Oh, always. I've got a flask of whisky in my coat pocket. Want a slug?'

'That's what I said, that I couldn't believe it. But someone does. Now I remember, it was at the faculty club. Marjorie Kovacs, she's married to Tibor Kovacs in history.'

'I don't know them, but I think I'd recognize them. Big sleek guy, she's small, rather sleek herself?'

'Right. But the point of it wasn't the slander, it was that the boozing is so bad you're … questionable in regard to …' and gestured at the boys.

'You're joking?'

'No, I'm not. I can make a guess from a hint Marjorie let slip – do you have a sister-in-law?'

'Do drug dealers have pit bulls?'

'Then I'd tread carefully, if I were you.'

'Enough said. Thanks, Sholem.'

'Take care, fella.'

'I'll try.'

They patted shoulders, passed on.

Coffee, bananas, pears.

say the schools are better in British Columbia, so the kids
spent one night in a shelter, then went
in the old days
people sleeping all over the house, so it was almost like an old family
Christmas
missed Montreal terribly at first

Lettuce. Don't forget the Monterey Jack and the black olives.

The Kovacses were not friends of the Hatchers as far as he knew, but he had a vague recollection of hearing that Marjorie had been a schoolmate of Betsy's.

Monterey Jack a bit expensive this week.

'Jonathan, go get a number at the deli counter over there, could you, please?'

everything so flat, not even a hill for a thousand miles
have to admire the workers up those towers

a dry cold, but it's still darn cold, I say ...

As Frank made his way through the crowd, Jonathan got the number slip, glanced at it, and returned, beaming.

'It's a special number, Daddy, thirty four.'

'What's so special about thirty-four?'

'It's the square of five plus the square of three.'

What luck, what providence has so favoured me?

'Thirty-six would have been even better, do you know why, Dada?'

'Uhh ... it's just slipped my mind for the moment.'

'Thirty-six is the square of three plus the cube of three.'

If only Emma ...

The clerk called his number and he got a container of black olives.

'And thirty-nine is three plus three squared plus three cubed ...'

On the bottle?

After a swing through the fruits and vegetables, they got in line for the twelve-item express cash.

yes, we've talked about it too, Toronto, but
no, I know, but after a whole lifetime here, you don't
those poor people on the south shore who are still
of course, if they get reelected, we're seriously
and they even have restaurants in Toronto, they say

Jonathan slipped away to search the candy machines for unclaimed goodies in the slots.

'Can I help you get the groceries out of the cart, Dada?' asked Simon, leaning into the cart.

'That would be a big help. But perhaps I'd better do the eggs.'

'No, no, I'll be careful, really I will.'

When they had as many items as the belt could take, Simon gestured to Frank to bend down, then hugged his neck and kissed him on both cheeks. 'I just wanted to do that, Dada.'

'Thank you, Simon, it's most appreciated. Here, two kisses back.'

'What a lovely little boy,' said the woman behind. 'And so handsome.'

Simon glanced at her briefly, but evidently decided lifting out the rest of the groceries was more important.

'Is he always so loving?' she asked Frank.

'When he's not threatening mayhem, he is,' Frank murmured.
'Yes, he's generally very affectionate. And although he didn't speak to you, he's often chatty with strangers.'

'Oh, I know, they're like that, though it's usually the girls, I find.' She tried to catch Simon's attention. 'And what's your name?' she asked.

'Come on, Simon, tell the lady your name.'

The boy had obviously decided the woman's tone was somehow wrong, and busied himself with putting more groceries on the belt.

'Children can be like that,' she said. 'I have four grandchildren myself, and they're just the same. They're in Kingston, but I see them every few months. It's not so far.'

'Do you drive or take the train or the bus?'

'I take the train, it's my little treat. It's more expensive than the bus, but much nicer. And I've never liked the 401 … and you can never be certain it's quite safe, not in the winter.…'

'Yes, I agree.…'

She decided to give Simon another try. 'So Daddy's taking you shopping, so your Mummy can have the morning off, eh, Simon?'

Frank wasn't quick enough to see the disaster coming.

'Or perhaps Mummy is home getting a head start on her spring cleaning, is that it?'

'No, my Mama is dead.' He looked her straight in the face. 'You idiot.'

'Simon!'

'You wombat dung.'

The conveyer belt moved forward, making them a space, so that Frank was able to distract Simon with the last of the items. The woman busied herself with her handkerchief and her own groceries while she and Frank tumbled out their scraps of apology and reassurance. These intimacies confused the cashier: she had checked half a dozen of the woman's items onto Frank's bill before they spotted the mistake, and was frosty as she deducted the charges. Explanations were impossible. The cashier flourished the baton for dividing orders and gave the woman a lecture in rapid-fire French. This time the woman burst into tears.

When he at last had them out of the store and along the street,

Frank put his bags on a bench and sat down.

'Twenty-eight would have been good, too,' said Jonathan. 'The square of two plus the square of three plus the square of four. Or fifty, which is …'

But who looked with wild surmise? Surely Cortez's *men* looked at each other with wild surmise while *Cortez himself* stared, silent upon a peak in Darien. Wasn't that it? He must look it up when he got home.

'Let's go watch Bjørn Dæhlie try to win more gold, guys.'

Dinner

Sitting in the bus, the bottle of wine on his lap, Frank found himself musing over *The Manchurian Candidate*, which he had watched the night before, musing over an exchange between Janet Leigh and Frank Sinatra on a train a few minutes after they have met. The Sinatra character, Major Ben Marco, is preoccupied with his problems, and is having trouble concentrating on the conversation. At one point, for no apparent reason, he asks the Janet Leigh character if she is Arabic. A minute later:

J.L. Are *you* Arabic?

F.S. ... No.

J.L. Let me put that another way – are you married?

A neat non sequitur. Gratuitous. Serendipitous.

At the Rowans', after he had gone through the greetings, after he had his coat and boots off, when he had a drink in his hand, he tried the Arabic anecdote on Eleanor's husband Magnus.

'It's a non sequitur, Frank, but pretty?'

'And it is, let me suggest, a model for discourse between the sexes.'

'You think non sequiturs encourage marital concord? "Honey, do you know where my squash racquet is?" "Your what?" "Let me put that another way – are you Arabic?" I don't know, Frank, I'm not sure that would work around here.'

'"Work around here?" You must be talking about me,' said Eleanor, pausing for a sip on her way by to the dining room. 'Here, have some of these sausage things before they're all gone.'

'See, a non sequitur. That's why you two are happily married.'

'This isn't a non sequitur,' said Magnus, taking a bite, 'it's a pig in a blanket. What's the Arabic for *kosher*?'

'Dead,' said Eleanor, and whisked the sausages away.

As the others arrived, Frank was relieved to find he knew most of them at least socially. For years he had had Emma to carry the load with strangers, to start the conversation, make the appreciated enquiries. Now, talking to the Rosenzweigs, he asked about the wrong children – 'Stephanie, *of course*, memory like a sieve' – and congratulated Marnie and Seymour Melcher on their new house, the house they had moved into, he soon learned, two and a half years ago. At least the Rosenzweigs and Melchers knew him.

'And we've even got the mortgage more or less under control,' said Marnie.

'So "more or less" that we actually ate in a restaurant a month or so ago.'

'Try early July, dear. Remember sitting on that patio? We had about the only table with good shade.'

'July? I could have sworn ...'

'You probably did. Trust me, it was July, maybe June.'

'I think hot weather goes with Greek food on the patio,' said Frank. 'When it's really hot, I think of grilled fish or kebabs.'

'I think of air conditioning,' said Marnie, 'and well chilled muscadet sur lie. Or vinho verde.'

'Retsina?'

'Don't talk about retsina.'

'Don't talk about air conditioning in February.'

Silliness, giddiness, alcohol. Perhaps some wit. Frank used to think he had a sense of humour; now he wasn't sure. Little he said seemed amusing to him, though others laughed at times; his students laughed; the boys laughed sometimes. Did he laugh? But would any of tonight's efforts have passed for wit among the people who wrote such scripts as *The Manchurian Candidate*? Would Jane Austen have sent an approving account of this dinner party to her sister Cassandra? No.

'Come along, old fellow,' said Eleanor, after she had rousted the others through the door. 'Soup's on. Don't stand there being glum.'

'Speaking of happy marriages, I am one of a large number of men who took his model of the perfect marriage from William Powell and Myrna Loy in *The Thin Man*.'

'Banter, booze, and a substantial independent income.'

'Emma and I did our best. Why do I suspect that if I went searching for Myrna Loy now, I'd likely get someone out of Evelyn Waugh?'

'Because you're glum, just what those bright young things need as a foil for their own glitter.'

'When they're coming down the steps of the Chelsea Registry Office or the Brompton Oratory or whatever, are they called "Waugh brides?"'

'That's good. Did you just think it up?'

'Mint shiny to me. Is it new to the world?'

'It was in 1931, I expect. Get in to dinner.'

Twelve sat to table. Eleanor steered Frank to the first chair at her end, with Marnie Melcher next along. Toward Magnus's end sat the several people Frank didn't know; all were introduced over the candlelight, but he missed the names.

As Eleanor passed the plates of feta in filo, Marnie leaned toward her: 'How do you do it, Eleanor? You serve up these elegant meals and you never seem to spend any time at all in the kitchen. I'm always up to here in grease and down to here in sweat, but you look as fresh as a cucumber and you never spend more than two minutes in the kitchen.'

'I have my secrets.'

'Marnie, you're just a New Yorker,' said Leon Rosenzweig. 'You wouldn't understand elegance. Eleanor's a Montrealer. Montrealers have elegance born in.'

'You're such a sweetie, Leon.'

'My wife's not a Montrealer,' Magnus called from the other end of the table. He explained to the man on his left, a friend visiting from the west, 'She's from the Town of Mount Royal, nothing but vin nouveau – her elegance is all a fraud.'

'Spoken like a true Calgarian.'

'We Calgarians pride ourselves on our honesty. Down to earth. Blunt. Look the bull straight in the eye.'

'Well, that makes a change, Magnus – I associate Calgarians with the other end of the bull.'

Eleanor finally replied, 'There are two secrets to this elegance. The first is you buy everything ready-made from the caterer.'

'You see,' said Magnus, 'There's your TMR elegance – you've got a problem, throw money at it.'

'Lucre may be filthy but it's cleaner than the stuff Calgarians throw around.'

'So who's the caterer?'

'That's the other secret.'

As the others went after Magnus, Frank turned to Eleanor.

'Did you know that when I left Nova Scotia after I graduated, I came to Montreal first, stepped out of Central Station, walked up to St Catherine, and found I was terrified.'

'On St Catherine Street?'

'I was, really. Everyone seemed so sophisticated ... so fast, so flash, so knowing. They all seemed to be wearing stylish clothes, and moving their hands like movie actors, and smiling because they knew things I didn't know.'

'So you got back on the train to Halifax?'

'No. I wanted to live in a big city, but I wanted to start with a small big city, like a big Halifax – so I did five years of Toronto as practice for Montreal.'

Laughter.

'Today it would be the other way around.'

Less laughter.

Magnus took up the slack. 'When I moved here,' he remarked, 'I came to a cheerfully open and international city – it reminded me of Amsterdam. Now it resembles one of the nastier and more narrow-minded villages in Belgium.'

'At least you have something to talk about,' said the western visitor.

'Yes, but that's all we have to talk about. The Quebec nationalists have hijacked all our serious concerns: I'll never forgive them for the banality of our conversation.'

The westerner missed the point, and pursued his political interests. As the middle of the table went haring off after Chinese signs, Hebrew signs, the next election, Frank turned to Eleanor.

'I often wonder if I haven't diminished myself because I didn't tackle New York or London.'

'You not too old to try it.'

'I am too old to try it. But you're not. And you're a specialist in Waugh; you could find an opening in London.'

'Sure, sweetie. I could slave away in some Hampstead bed-sit for five years and at the end of it, with tremendous luck, I might have more or less steady work reviewing for the *Sunday Telegraph*. Reassuring chitchat on thirties biographies and travel books – suitable Christmas presents for the wife of Air Commodore Bellyham, retired, of The Larches, Much Noodling, Salop. No, thank you.'

'But you'd be in London. And perhaps you'd be writing for the *Observer* or the *Guardian*. Surely they're acceptably leftist?'

'Yes, dear, but I'm a Waugh scholar. Doomed to life on the right.'

'Umm. I've always wondered how you ended up with Waugh.' Eleanor dissected a tarragoned mushroom.

'It seemed like a good idea at the time. I hate his politics, and he was a nasty man, but I've always respected him for the writing – in most of his work, the performance is stunning.'

'So what's the problem?'

'I should have done what you did – I should have picked someone I loved, like Jane Austen.'

'Yeah, look where that got me.'

'You don't like the mushrooms?'

'Or the company?' asked Marnie, turning from the politics.

'On the contrary – they're equally marvellous, the mushrooms and the company.'

'Are you comparing us to mushrooms?'

'I knew I should have kept my mouth shut; better still, I should have stayed home.'

Frank glanced about the room, at the piano topped with brass-framed family pictures, over the walls of paintings, down the long table with its silver, china, and crystal in the candlelight, read the hands curving distinctions in the chat, the rise and fall of the chat: was this elegance, wit? Professors, lawyers, even an Oscar winner. Fine company, the finest company to which he could aspire, the finest of evenings.

He shook his head to clear away the nonsense, the fatuity: how dare he think of elegance and wit, he whose mediocrity was absolute?

As the digestifs were passed about, as people pushed back from the table, Frank realized that the attractive blonde woman sitting along this side and next to Magnus was not connected with the visitor from the Prairies seated across; the Westerner was talking about their hotel to the dark-haired woman next to Leon. For the first time he wondered who the blonde woman was, and why she was there. Surely Eleanor wouldn't have … He wanted to ask her at once, but she was in the kitchen. As he made to rise, the blonde woman happened to turn his way; she threw him a polite smile before turning back to Magnus. But Magnus was arguing with Leon Rosenzweig about the pronunciation of 'Glenmorangie'; the blonde woman would be turning again in a moment. If Frank didn't act quickly, he was going to have to talk with her; his heart was pounding. He rose abruptly, grabbed several plates, and escaped to the kitchen.

Marnie flourished a dish towel and spoke of elegant dining; there would be no intimate, desperate queries here.

Eleanor read the hint of anxiety and quickly dried her hands. 'Secret negotiations,' she said to Marnie. 'Come with me, old darling.'

'A likely story,' said Marnie. 'Secret groping more likely.'

Eleanor closed the door to the small study, and put her arm around his waist.

'You're going to have to get used to it, you know.'

'You mean you did invite her deliberately? You tried to set us up?'

'No, old darling, Beth and her husband were both invited, but Brad had to fly to Edmonton yesterday, so she came by herself. They're happily married – three kids. You're safe here, old dear.'

Frank considered a photo of Waugh, tweedy and Toadish, on the desk.

'Funny thing, Waugh – he always looks drunk and belligerent.'

'He likely was drunk and belligerent. He was also depressed a lot of the time.'

'Jane Austen wasn't, so far as we can tell.'

'You don't have the figure, Frank.'

Ten twenty-five: he should leave about eleven-thirty. He wandered back through the kitchen, told Marnie three of the glasses were still a bit wet, and ducked into the hall to avoid the flick of her towel. In the dining room, Magnus and Leon had passed to the pronunciation of 'Lagavulin'; Magnus was reading from the *Malt Whisky Almanac*. Beth, the blonde woman, was listening with what appeared to be feigned fascination. With an impulse to make amends, Frank poured himself a finger of Macallan and sat down.

Beth turned to him.

'I always find, don't you,' she said, 'that I learn something interesting whenever I have dinner here.'

'I agree. It's remarkable. Even when the information is wrong ... I said, "Even when the information is wrong."'

'Belt up, Frank, I heard you the first time. Just because you lived in Edinburgh for a year doesn't mean you're an authority on Scottish pronunciation.'

'True. But I can tell you that while you have "Lagavulin" right, you must remember that "Glenmorangie" rhymes with "orangey," but you must pronounce "orangey" as a Scot would pronounce it. Which you aren't.'

'Would the Scot be a Glaswegian or ... what's someone from Edinburgh called?'

'An Edimbourgeois. And the Scottish accent you want is probably from Inverness, whose inhabitants claim to speak the purest English, although Aberdonians ...'

The silliness curled itself like cigar smoke, like whisky fumes; nostalgia charmed Frank, nostalgia for similar blithe evenings, back before the boys, when blithe evenings came most every week, when Emma laughed....

As soon as decently possible, he slipped from the chat, letting Magnus and Leon carry it to Beth, the vestige of a juvenile courting ritual. She was enjoying the display, perhaps flattered by their attentions, a recognition of her charm. Leaning back, Frank glanced at her over the rim of his glass. Her face, animated by the engagement, appeared even prettier now, the angularity of her cheek bones, nose, brow elegant, even patrician in profile, her slim neck rising from the blouse in the long curve of, fancifully, an amaryllis stem. As she bent toward Leon, the fold of the blouse gave him a glimpse of a lacy bra cup cradling her tiny breast, a glimpse poignant, achingly lovely, reminiscent ... Frank turned abruptly to reflect on Leon's jowl; Leon needed a shave; Leon always needed a shave; Leon needed a shave even after shaving.

When the Rosenzweigs went to the hall for their coats, Frank followed.

'You're not going already, are you, Frank?' asked Magnus. 'You're foot-loose and fancy-free these days, aren't you?'

'Magnus, you put things so felicitously,' Frank replied, as Eleanor kicked Magnus's ankle.

'You great lout,' she said, 'you boor, you block ...'

'You stone ...'

'Me worse than senseless thing? Well, I suppose you're right, but the conviviality overwhelmed my discretion.'

'Conviviality? That's a good name for it. Tell it to Glenmorangie's ad agency,' said Eleanor.

As Frank stepped to the door, Beth touched him on the shoulder.

'Like a drive home?' she asked. 'I'm going your way, I think.'

'I ... well ...' But no excuse came to mind. 'Sure, yes, great, thanks, if it's no trouble? Sherbrooke and Victoria?'

'Perfect. I'll just get my ...'

Eleanor's private shrug and closed eyes said, It's all right, don't worry, she's only offering you a ride home.

After she had the car started, and the heater and defrosters adjusted, after they were buckled in, Beth turned to him and shook her head.

'This is something new for me,' she remarked.

'Driving home a strange man?'

'No, being mistaken for a ... fox? A predator, a lonely wife on the make.'

'I'm sorry, I ... have I ... I mean ...'

'Frank, you've been terrified of me since about the time the coffee arrived. Don't deny it. Terrified.'

'Well, not perhaps terrified. My wife, you see ... last spring she ...'

'I know. I managed to get it out of Magnus while you were getting the story on me from Eleanor in the study.'

'I'd never have made a diplomat,' said Frank.

'And I'd never have made a fox.'

She pulled into westbound traffic and sped up to beat a light.

'The great thing about a Montreal winter,' she said 'is getting away from it for a while. Brad and I try to get away for a weekend once a year. We leave them with his parents or my sister and just go. Last fall we had a fabulous weekend in New York: restaurants, *Forever Tango*, the Frick Collection, and ... being together.'

'Sounds marvellous. People say the Frick is ...'

Talk of travels occupied them; soon he saw Westmount City Hall out the side window; another two minutes.

'Emma had so much work to do finishing her thesis that we kept putting off New York....'

'And now you see no point going alone?'

'Well ...'

After making the light at Victoria, Beth pulled up to the curb and shifted to Park.

'You shouldn't put it off, you shouldn't put anything off. Surely that's obvious to you now?'

'Well, I ...'

She shifted in her seat, reached for his hand.

'Here,' she said, 'something you shouldn't put off.' Confused, not expecting it, he let her pull his hand toward her coat, then found it, suddenly, miraculously, inside her coat, her blouse, against her bra. 'Inside,' she murmured, 'my breast, don't be frightened. Please.'

Stunned, enchanted, he obeyed.

'Of course, it was the other one you glimpsed at the table, but they're pretty much identical according to Brad. Of course I noticed – a woman can tell when someone's taking a peek even if he's behind her, you should know that by now.'

'It was that obvious?'

'Don't be afraid, I know this blouse – I did it quite deliberately. It was touching, how quickly you turned your eyes. I was quite charmed. It's very small, isn't it? My lemon – half on one side, half on the other. They used to be as hard as lemons, too, until I had Karin. Your wife, did she have big ones?'

'Regular size, I guess,' said Frank. 'Thirty-four B, I think.'

'When I was pregnant the first time, I was a thirty-six C. I hated it, having these great things hanging from me. I much prefer my little lemon halves.'

'It's lovely. Thank you. Thank you very much.'

He released the breast, began to withdraw his hand.

'Pinch the tip a bit,' she said. 'Yes, that's nice. Squeeze it … another moment … Okay, you can take it out.'

He put his palm on her cheek, smiled at her.

'I'm not really a fox,' she whispered. 'I don't know what put the notion into my head. It just seemed right, somehow.'

'It was a magical gift. I'll treasure it in a very private corner of my memory.'

'I'm glad. Good night, now, Frank.'

'Good night, Beth.'

As he crossed the street, Frank wondered if he could somehow give the Shalimar to her.

Fathers

With coats and scarves fluttering, they got out the door and into the pale sun of the warm morning.

'Look, Daddy, flowers in our garden.'

'Hey, you're right. Look, Simon, see the golden crocuses, the first flowers in our garden!'

'Crosques!'

'Are we the first ones on the street?'

'I don't know. I think there's someone with snowdrops down near the end. Snowdrops are even earlier, I believe. But I do believe we just might be the first with crocuses.'

'Dad, can we maybe get some snowdrops for next year?'

'I expect we could.'

'Then we'd be first? Yeaa!'

'Off the rocks, guys, that's someone else's garden.'

As they walked toward the park, Frank tried to count the panels on the soccer ball. But the boys distracted him, running toward cross streets, whacking bushes with sticks.

The April sunlight through the bare park trees gave warmth only when they could find shelter from the wind, but the children's playground had little shelter. Too late, he realized he should have brought the kite. He scrutinized the boys, trying to judge if their clothes were warm enough. Probably. Neither was happy about the extra sweater, and Simon would take off his hat if not watched. Neither had wanted to come in the first place, preferring television and computer games. Frank had papers to correct, but he and Emma had always tried to take the boys out for at least an hour every Saturday and Sunday unless the weather was impossible.

'If Mama was alive, she wouldn't make us go to the park.'

She not only would have made them go, she would have taken the soccer balls along with sand toys, Frisbees, baseball equipment … and the kite. The boys in their mild resentment, refused his suggestion of a kick-about. Now they swarmed over the jungle gym.

'No, Simon, I don't think that's a very good idea – that bar is too high even for Dada.'

Even at two or three, Jonathan had been cautious about heights; Simon seemed unaware of danger.

Frank found a free bench and sat with the ball in his lap. Emma preferred to play with the boys, engaging them with her enthusiasm and affection; unless they seemed bored or at war, Frank let them play by themselves, hoping to encourage their independence.

'Simon, don't push – the little girl was there first.'

On the next bench, two fathers chatted about skiing. One seemed to have a place in the Eastern Townships, the other in Vermont. They soon shifted to aspects of renting out their chalets, to the relative tax advantages of Canadian and American ownership.

'Like I was saying to the wife, sure you can write off the repairs, but you still have to pay for them.'

'Ha-ha.'

'And with a marginal rate of 42 per cent ...'

Frank turned away. He and Emma had bought a bit over their heads, bought into a neighbourhood of young lawyers and doctors on, as the real estate people put it, their starter houses; and older teachers on their only houses. Neither was bothered that they had a second-hand car while others had a BMW or Mercedes and a van for chauffeuring the kids, for trips to the cottage. They had a short walk to downtown Montreal, good schools, convenient shopping, the nearby city rink, swimming, library, and parks. The real estate agent had been cheerful about the future: 'It may be a bit tight for the first few years or so, but after that ...' After that, inflation and constantly rising salaries would make the mortgage trivial. And Emma would soon enough have her doctorate and a tenure-track job. Emma did her part, but they also got recessions, pay cuts, pay freezes, and the constant nibbling of new taxes and tax increases.

'Well, Emma,' Frank murmured, 'you just about paid off the mortgage all by yourself.'

He lowered his face quickly and concentrated hard on the pattern of the coloured panels on the soccer ball, tried again to count the panels. Twenty-nine, it seemed. He counted a different way. Thirty-two.

'Dada, Jonathan won't push me on the swings and I want him to push me, but he wants to swing himself.'

'That's all right, Simon, I'll push you.'

He reached to take the boy's hand for the walk to the swing, but Simon pulled free and raced ahead, crying taunts at his brother.

When they first moved to the neighbourhood, Frank used to run in the park and gradually got some sense of its times and people. On Saturday mornings in spring and fall, the city ran a children's soccer league on the athletic fields. On summer evenings and weekend afternoons grown-ups played pickup and league softball, while others – recent immigrants from the West Indies, Greece, Iran, it seemed – played pickup soccer, rugby, or even cricket, depending on their origin. Older folks, lovers, people with babies sat on benches near flower beds, and several sheltered, south-facing slopes attracted the sunbathers. After dark, bored teenagers smoked various substances in the gazebo, flirted, and indulged in petty vandalism.

Over the past eight years, with no time for running, he had got to know the park at a slower pace. Jonathan suffered from colic during his first six months and was only comforted by constant rocking or walks in the stroller. It could have been worse: they heard of children who had to be taken for rides on the autoroute during the small hours. It had been hardest on Emma, for she was breastfeeding him. So when he was not at work, Frank took the child for walks while Emma read for her thesis, read for five minutes before slumping into stupefied sleep. At first he would bring a book, but after a few minutes motionless, Jonathan would shudder awake in howls of pain. The next year, when the boy could court the dangers of the sand pit or the baby swings, Frank left the books at home altogether.

Weekdays in the children's playground found mothers or nannies with children, Saturday morning families, Sunday morning fathers, and Saturday and Sunday afternoons families, mostly speaking Greek, Spanish or Farsi, perhaps local or perhaps from neighbourhoods without parks.

The responsibility was a relief, really. Unable to correct papers, unable to read, forced to keep a constant guard against scrapes, broken limbs, maiming, and drowning, against suicidal rushes toward Sherbrooke Street, against sadistic older children, and drooling carriers of impetigo and conjunctivitis, against the lurking armies of child kidnappers and molesters, Frank was relieved of the guilt of shirking.

'Push me high, Dada, push me high.'

'Dad, is this a good day for the kite?'

'Yes, it is, Jonathan, but unfortunately I left it home. Sorry about that.'

'Well, could we go home and get it?'

'Yeah, yeah,' cried Simon. 'Let's go get the kite.'

'Please, Dada?'

If they got the kite now, they would not have lunch until after two; the boys were both visiting friends for the afternoon, Frank still needed groceries for supper, and a stack of essays sat on his desk.

'Let's look at the timing, guys …'

At last they agreed to bring the kite tomorrow afternoon. They again refused to play soccer, and slouched toward the seesaws. Frank found a bench.

'… half my time flying back and forth now that head office is in Toronto,' a father was saying.

'Fun, isn't it,' said his friend.

'So a few months ago, Elly says to me, "If flying's such a drag, why don't we move to Toronto?" "Fine," I say, "I'll check it out." So next time I bring home a *Toronto Star* and give her the real estate section. "Here's one for three-twenty," she says, "We could get three-twenty for this place." "Where is it?" I say. "Richmond Hill. Where's that? Like if it was here in Montreal?" "Try Rosemere." "Rosemere?" she says, "Rosemere! In Rosemere they get moose eating the gardens! In Rosemere wolves attack children on the way to school!" "I hear Richmond Hill has a great wolf control program," I say. "So okay, what's the Toronto equivalent of Westmount?" she says. "Try Rosedale." So she looks again. "Here's one, detached, five bedrooms, two and a half baths, and …" Would you ever think of the word "speechless" in regard to the ball and chain?'

'Speechless? Elly? No, not speechless. What was the hit, about seven-five?'

'Try nine.'

'Makes you see the advantages of the distinct society.'

'And I hear values in Westmount lost fifteen-twenty percent the day Muldoon bought on Forden Crescent.'

The boys had found some friends from school. The girl Simon's age was the daughter of Chris Morgan, who taught in the communications department of Frank's college. Frank spotted him by the jungle gym and strolled over.

'They don't allow weirdos with pigtails in the park, Chris.'

Chris, who was otherwise ordinarily groomed, wore a small pigtail because he was free-spirited and came from Vancouver.

'Pigtail, nothing, look what I got this morning.'

He picked up a vast sombrero from the bench and put it on his head.

'Got it in a yard sale on Arlington – five bucks.'

'Five to take it off their hands? You should have asked for ten.'

'You're just jealous.'

Frank sat, turned so as to watch the boys: a single parent now, the sense of tension never left him.

They chatted about the children, the weather. Presently Chris asked, 'You heard anything about the program evaluations?'

'A bit. I haven't paid much attention.'

'We got the full report at council the other evening. You guys in the English department seem to have held your own.'

'No layoffs?'

'Not this year or next. They say. Of course, you'll be offering a lot of courses in business writing, scientific writing, social sciences writing. Service courses.'

'No literature?'

'It's being cut back, but there'll be some. But it's a back-to-basics agenda.'

'Charming. English as grunt. How to write a report convincing head office to accelerate the pace of new pizza outlets. Non-actionable advice to the new CEO on how to bust a union or pay a bribe.'

'As the man says, "Be glad you have a job."'

'I am glad I have a job, I just wish I could like it more, not less. But ... Oh well, I'm glad I have a job.'

After a bit, Chris took off the sombrero.

'Getting along all right? ... By yourself, I mean?'

'Yeah, getting along.' Frank paused while Simon walked a wobbly balance beam. Nearby, two fathers smiled as a third said: 'You have to pay double to read the English!'

'It's odd. Apart from Emma, I have as good a life as anyone could ask for, better than all but a slice of one percent of the human race in all of history. Good health, good job, super kids, solid house in perhaps the best neighbourhood in Canada, no real money problems, lots of food shipped in from everywhere, a civilized country more or less at peace ... All the basic needs in abundance. I've never wanted luxuries. So I have it all ... so do you, right?'

'Well, Frank, I could use a better fade feature on my camcorder.'

'The gods aren't fair, I agree. But defective fade features aside, life is ambrosial.'

'The very word I was going to use.'

'So why do I feel like hell all the time?'

Chris stroked his chin, asked pensively, 'Have you considered that maybe you're a jerk?'

'You think that could be it, eh?'

'A definite possibility.'

'I wonder why I never thought of that?'

'That's just the point, Frank – a jerk wouldn't think of it.'

Chris picked up a stick and began scratching the dirt. A passing father was saying to another, '... have to spend next weekend at the squash club for the provincials, so ...' Chris said, 'That guy has the right idea – perhaps you should take up squash, get your mind off things.'

'Beating sweaty balls around white rooms, no, thank you.'

They talked about the pressures of time, of two parents working, of a single parent working. With his stick Chris was filling in the ears of a large head of Mickey Mouse: Frank realized he was being gloomy, boring.

'Never mind, Chris – as I said, I couldn't ask for a better life. Look at them.'

His boys were playing tag with Chris's Rhiannon and Jonathan's friend. They shrieked with laughter, eyes bright, bodies stretching to avoid the tag.

'And summer's on the way,' said Chris.

'Yes, it is, isn't it.'

The children's laughter turned abruptly to screams: cheating, betrayal, *I was safe, no you weren't, was too, was not...*

'I think I'd better get going,' said Chris. 'Too much of a good thing for four-year-olds.'

As they strolled toward the kids, Chris patted Frank on the shoulder. 'Take care of yourself, guy. The boys need you, but they need a you who has some life of his own, you know.'

'I know.'

'And,' Chris added as he put on the sombrero, 'don't take everything too seriously.'

Chris took his daughter's hand as they walked toward Sherbrooke Street.

The game broken up, the boys wanted to play soccer. Jonathan's friend wanted to come too, so Frank was led to his father and explained where they would be playing. 'James Buller,' said the man, and glanced at his watch. 'Look, perhaps I can leave Sean with you while I run an errand. Fifteen minutes.'

'Sure, no problem.'

Beyond the playground, Frank kicked the ball forward to the running boys. They improvised a goal and Frank played goalie.

After a time his back began to ache, so he begged off and leaned on a tree to relieve it. His watch had ten to twelve – surely they had been playing since about eleven. He looked over the people in the playground, tried to see to the parking lot by the library. No James Buller.

High cloud was moving in and the wind had a sharper bite now. Even running, the boys would probably not be sweating much, nonetheless the moment they stopped playing they would feel the chill. He worried about colds, or worse. Linda might well not be able to come every morning when both boys were normally out of the house, and he could ill afford the extra expense. He could certainly not be sick himself. Where was the wretched man?

After another twenty minutes, the boys were clearly tiring of the game, and Simon was hugging himself. They should be home by now having lunch. When Frank suggested the library, they abandoned the ball.

'But what about the groceries, Dada?' asked Jonathan. 'Aren't we going to get the groceries?'

'Well, we have a problem …'

Frank had the sense of an unspoken rule that parents were not to betray one another to children. But surely James Buller had forfeited that protection. Frank explained that they could not abandon Sean, and had in fact promised to stay where they were.

'Couldn't we take him home to his place?'

'Good idea.'

But it wasn't. Sean actually lived with his mother over a mile west in NDG, while his father had an apartment half a mile toward downtown.

'Dad lives there with Chantal,' the boy explained. 'She's his girlfriend. She's not home today. Mum isn't home either.'

What could have happened? Car broken down? Or an accident, and Buller in the hospital? Dead? Or sitting with some cronies in a bar? If they left the playground, where would Buller think to look? And was Frank legally responsible for Sean? It was, as Frank understood, against the law to leave a child under twelve or so alone in a house; was there a law covering this? Could he leave him in the children's library? In the front hall of his father's apartment? Should he take him home with them then keep trying the father's telephone number? But with his own boys going out …

The library was the only possible answer.

'You guys go read some books, and no screaming or squealing, and stay out of the elevator, Simon. I have to stay here where I can see the playground in case Sean's dad comes back.'

Standing by the window, Frank felt his frustration building toward rage, but he could not afford the luxury of rage, the luxury of losing control. Yet he was pinned down by unknown circumstances, by obscure obligations.

After a time, Frank decided they would have to take Sean home with them and keep telephoning his parents. They would go at one, two hours after Sean had been left with them. As they were coming down the front steps, Buller came from the parking lot, grinning, a hearty greeting. Frank froze, unable to trust himself to move, to speak.

'Dropped into the office for some papers and got lost in some work.'

'You said fifteen minutes,' Frank managed at last.

'Well, hell, you didn't have to stay here – the kid is nine, he can take care of himself.'

Frank turned away. It was clearly pointless trying to explain his story, the legal burdens, the moral trust. James Buller had built his own version of events.

'So, what's got up your nose?'

The boys stood mute, aware of the tension, not knowing what to do. When Frank reached out to them, they each took a hand. They started off along the path across the park.

'Hey, don't turn your back on me, fella, you don't know anything about it, I've got problems you can't even imagine.'

As Frank was clearing away the lunch dishes, the phone rang. Frank assumed it was a parent calling to confirm timing or pickups of one of the boys – it was not.

'Frank, old pal, Willis Jackson ...'

'Willis, I thought you weren't due back for a week or so....'

They sorted out the details, did the courtesies.

'Look, Frank, you free this afternoon? I thought we might look in on a good ol' pub, une vieille taverne, suck up a few draft, watch some sports on the tube, relive university days.'

Relive? They hadn't known one another in university. And Frank had that stack of papers.

'Now, Betsy and Mrs Hatcher will be happy to take the boys for the afternoon. Don't say no.'

Frank explained about the boys. Willis had a whispered exchange off the phone.

'Are you sure that's settled ... Okay, so be it. But all the more reason for you to take a break. I'll pick you up, and I'm paying.... No, really, I insist.'

He would have to do the papers tomorrow when he had planned to do his income tax returns.

'Okay.'

Willis was distressed to discover that he was behind the times – the grubby, comfortable men-only tavernes he remembered from the sixties and early seventies had in the late seventies been the victims of changing times and tastes.

'The Sportsman?' he asked as Frank pulled the car door shut.

'A parking lot.'

'The Mansfield?'

'A parking lot, I think.'

'The Peel?'

'I don't know what's inside, but there are always teenagers lined up to get in. And it advertises on TV.'

'The Central?'

'I'm not sure. I do know it's no longer in operation.'

'The Rymark? Toe's? I'd love a knuckle.'

'Toe's is an office tower, and the last time I went in, the Rymark was giant screen sports and heavy metal.'

'The Royal?'

'A hole in the ground.'

'Jesus, it's like Dresden. Or Singapore.'

'The Stanley was still there the last time I looked.'

Willis was dressed in rumpled cottons with California labels on the outside; his floppy cotton hat had brass fittings. A tall, slim man with a pot belly threatening, he didn't look as if he was going on safari, but as if he was pretending he was going on safari. The three customers who glanced from the TV screens didn't seem bothered, interested, or impressed.

'By God, Frank, this brings it back. Eh? Doesn't this bring it back?'

'Yes, it sure does.'

Willis was vastly nostalgic when Frank ordered a twenty-two-ounce bottle, unavailable elsewhere in North America. He peeled a ten from his money clip and told the waiter to keep two.

'Memories are cheap at the price,' Willis remarked with a wink.

'So, tell me about the delights of Frisco ... Fisherman's Wharf ... Following the trail of Sam Spade ...'

Having handed him the ball, Frank sat back to nurse his beer and wait for Willis to work around to the point. It was certainly something to do with the boys, or with the Hatcher estate; it certainly wasn't bonhomie. It took an hour – baseball, football, basketball, the Olympics, beaches, beach houses, recreation generally, Frisco and Montreal being the two most dedicated recreational cities in North America – skiing, bicycling, perhaps include Vancouver, Denver, and Miami, recreation the culminating condition of the American Declaration of Independence.

'Life, we have, liberty we have – so the pursuit of happiness is open to us, as it is to damn few people in this world. And I've seen more of it than most, as you know. Manila, Nairobi, Lima. My God. And recreation is the thing for kids, they should have it, it helps them grow. And for old folks, it's the reward for all those years of hard work. Now ...'

Frank finished his beer and ordered another to help Bwana Willis follow the spoor into his diplomatic jungle.

'Now, believe me, Frank, I'm on your side in this ...' The Hatchers, it seemed, were deeply distressed about the boys' welfare, their happiness. They felt it their duty to stay in Montreal as long as things were 'unsettled'. Naturally Betsy and Willis were delighted to share the house with her parents, but the arrangement wasn't doing the Hatchers – or the Jacksons – any good. Mrs Hatcher refused to give up the kitchen to her daughter, but whined endlessly about the extra work. Mr Hatcher wanted to get on with his golfing, but didn't know whether to renew his membership at his club here; equally, he'd be 'precipitate' to join a club in Ontario before they bought a house.

Frank considered stopping it abruptly, but couldn't resist letting it run: how would Willis put it?

'Now, I understand the Hatchers made an entirely unwarranted proposal to you last winter – having you simply give the kids to us. Ridiculous. Well, no parent with the least love for his children could accept that. You were angry, I hear, absolutely furious. I understand, Frank, I really understand. And I'm on your side. But you know as well as I do that Mum and Dad Hatcher are not the most ... subtle or ... thoughtful people in the world. Agreed?'

'If you say so.'

'And I thought I was the diplomat. Now it would benefit all of us

– the Hatchers, Betsy and me, you and the boys, all of us – if we could develop some reasonable solution to this … untenable situation. I mean, surely you see that? I mean, as long as the situation is unstable, it's bound to be full of unresolved tensions, some at least of which – the ones we're labouring under up the hill – I have described, and I know perfectly well you have your own unresolved tensions – financial, babysitting, scheduling, getting on with your work, what you will. And your own recreation, don't slight that.

'I mean, what's the point of your life and your liberty if you haven't any time left for the pursuit of happiness? Eh? You mentioned a while ago that you should have been grading papers this afternoon, and doing your taxes tomorrow. So where's the free time? Admit it, Frank – you don't have any free time, nil, niente, nada. No free time, no pursuit of happiness.'

'I'm doing all right.'

'Don't give me that shit, pal, excuse the language. But you know it's shit. You are hanging on by your fingernails. 'Now, those are your boys, and you are a fine parent, obviously. No one would try to take that away from you.'

If not, you're doing a good imitation.

'But since last year, since the tragedy of … well, you must admit, it's a bit too much for one person to handle, especially when the money is a bit tight. It's dragging you down, Frank. And what if you have some sort of crisis? A new roof, a car accident, new furnace – you can't just go on from day to day hoping and trusting that things are going to work themselves out. That's why we – I mean all of us up the hill – want to help out. Now, don't you go all proud, and I'm handling things, I'll work it out. For now you're getting by, sure, but what's it doing to you inside? It's killing you, Frank.'

That's my cue:

'So what are you proposing, Willis? A nice basket of blue chip shares? Full subsidization of daycare? A Danish au pair? A new wife?'

Willis shook his head.

'Mrs Hatcher warned me about the hostility.'

He drained his glass.

'Do you remember Hitler's conference with Franco in '40 or '41?'

'Not offhand.'

'Forty, I expect, not long after the fall of France. Hitler took his train down to the Spanish border and met Franco. Trying to get Franco to enter the war, or capture Gibraltar, or at least sweat the Brits a bit. He stayed a day or so but got sweet nothing. Then he travelled to Italy for a conference with Mussolini, and Mussolini – or maybe it was Ciano – asked about the conference with Franco. And Hitler replied, "Rather than negotiate with that man again, I'd prefer to have all my teeth pulled."'

'I didn't think Hitler had a sense of humour.'

'I believe that's the only example. Now don't you turn all Franco on me. Stay Frank.'

'Of course, Franco did make it through the war, which is more than you can say for Hitler and Mussolini.'

Willis paused.

'Touché, old pal, touché.'

And I'm not your old pal.

'Anyway, all I ask is that you hear me out. I am on your side in this, even though I know you don't believe it. I want to put a proposition to you. A human proposition. And I think it may help us all out of this morass.'

Your morass. My life.

'Of course, suggesting you give up the kids entirely is absurd. That's the mistake the Hatchers made. And I'm not sure that Betsy ... well, that's irrelevant. But what about we give you a bit of a break on the full-time caring? Look, you teach, what, six months of the year? Seven? At any rate you have four months or so off in the summer, and a fair chunk of time off in December, January as I understand it. Right? So how about letting the boys live with us during term, and with you during the holidays? And we can see about weekends. Doesn't that make sense? The Hatchers are relieved and they get on with their move to Ontario, Betsy – who adores kids, who adores your boys – Betsy gets to do something besides flash the plastic along Greene Avenue – and you get all the time you need for grading, along with a bit of time for the pursuit of happiness. The boys get a full-time family, no harassed dad, no surrogate mom on welfare, all the benefits of upper Westmount – and that means, and

I'm pretty sure we can swing it, private school – St George's, L.C.C., St Crispin's, you name it. Those boys are bright, they deserve the best education money can buy. What do you say? A win-win situation. Win-win-win situation. How can you refuse?'

After a pause:

'As any parent would.'

Willis sighed, pondered, decided.

'There's another possibility: have you thought about getting a job somewhere in the Toronto area? I mean, it wouldn't be as dramatic a change as the other suggestions. If the Hatchers could at least retire nearby knowing they'd be close to the boys, I think they'd be ... well, not happy, but at least pacified.'

'There are no jobs.'

'Hey, look, I know about downsizing, believe me, but there must be ...'

'There are no jobs.'

'Have you at least looked? Universities must have to hire sometimes, the first wave of the people they hired in the sixties must be getting on to retirement by now.... There must be ads in journals, word-of-mouth, and you have a Ph.D. ...'

Frank gave him the tired story: what few jobs were going were not on offer to middle-aged, middle-class white males with mediocre degrees in unfashionable areas of criticism and the wrong kind of experience.

'Emma found a job. I suppose you'll say it was because of her tits.'

'The fact that she was a woman would have been a factor had all other things been equal. But Emma got that job because she was special, a vedette, the best applicant they had. I'm not a vedette. Anyway, the way they look at it is I already have a job.'

'But have you tried? Have you at least ...'

'When Emma was looking, I looked too, but no one wanted to take both of us.' Emma, certainly, but not with a dreary husband in tow. 'And I keep on looking,' Frank lied. Thinking about Ellery Culp and Eastern Ontario, he added, 'But they'd be crazy to hire me when they could get a hotshot just out of grad school for far less than I'd have to ask. It's just not on.'

'I find that hard to believe. I think you're just being pessimistic.'

'I'm a Canadian, not an American. A Quebec anglo.'

The continued pessimism clearly irritated Willis, but he mastered himself.

'At least think about the possibilities, consider them, keep looking for a position in Ontario – you never know when something might turn up. Failing that, consider the offer we're making – to help with kids during the term – don't slam the door on it without going over it, giving it your mature consideration. From our side, it looks unassailable. I mean, every party to any negotiation has to be willing to move a bit. Without negotiation ... well, without negotiation life is intolerable.'

And diplomats are out of a job.

'Willis, I have to be honest with you. Not blunt, but honest. It's not easy being a single parent, but I have managed for nearly a year. The longer I stay with it, the more I learn the routines, the easier it gets. I want to keep on trying. I may not be actively pursing happiness in the hot spots of Montreal, but even in the last few years when Emma was alive we didn't go out much. As I said, I'm not an American. That's not as fatuous as it sounds. I don't expect to pursue happiness; endurance is more my virtue. As long as I think I can manage it, I want to keep on enduring. As for the future, we'll see.'

'So I can report that there is a window of opportunity, albeit not a very big one, but a window nonetheless?'

'Willis, you can report anything you please. But for the foreseeable, I plan to keep the boys. Not just on weekends and holidays, but all year round.'

'And if circumstances change, you would consider the proposition?'

'If I could read the future, I'd have made a killing on the stock market.'

'You can't be fairer than that, old pal. I accept that.'

Willis threw back his last inch of beer.

'Right. So ... well, I expect you'll be wanting to get on with your chores ... whatever.'

No idle chit-chat now from the great white hunter; he reached for his safari hat. Frank left half a glass.

Mothers

Because of end-of-term fusses, Frank usually found himself scurrying about on the Saturday for a Mother's Day card and a present. This year the day loomed early, clutching at his mind in the pensive times: on the way to and from school, as he cooked, after the boys were asleep. Something different, special, a memorial. But something cheerful: an outing, a bicycle ride with picnic, weather permitting. The video of Emma, then her favourite dinner, a favourite of the boys as well, carré d'agneau, rösti, hot asparagus vinaigrette, endive and orange salad with raspberry vinaigrette ...

On Thursday Mr Hatcher called to remind him they were expected for Sunday dinner.

'Well, actually, I was planning ...'

'Don't be silly, of course you're coming. Babs will not take no for an answer. Now, we'll pick the boys up about eleven, and if you have marking or whatever, you can come later, give you some peace and quiet, eh? You need a break from this single parent nonsense, wearing you to a frazzle, I know ...'

Wearing you to a frazzle equals *driving you to drink*?

'Right, Frank, that's settled, then ...'

Frank breathed slowly in, out.

Why fight this battle he was likely to lose? But at what point in the war did he begin to fight? And what was he fighting for? And why must there be a war?

There were indeed late essays. He began every term threatening failure for missed deadlines, but as the term was winding down, when he had come to know the students a bit, to appreciate their fear, their panic, he always relented. The students in bus admin, science, and the careers programs had their massive term projects to complete; future dental technicians reasonably calculated that compulsory Englit essays had to be put off until the end, tacking them together in desperate all-nighters, producing sloppy, misguided efforts on the over-confidence of Emma Woodhouse, or the spiritual travails of

Constantine Levin. Who could blame them? And what did it matter, really, if some papers were past deadline? If he hadn't been able to bring them to the texts in fifteen weeks, last-minute punishments were pointless.

So on Sunday morning, Frank in his sweats had the boys dressed and at the front door just before eleven, waiting for George Hatcher.

But Betsy arrived. He had seen her at the Hatchers' Easter dinner, but he had been seated with Willis at Mr Hatcher's end of the table, so had hardly spoken to her, hardly noticed her. Today, she was wearing a gold silk blouse under an expensively rumpled black jacket with white jeans and black laced boots. More California elegance, Frank supposed. So unlike Emma's plain things.

'You like?' she chirped, clattering bangles from wrists and ears.

Frank realized with horror and humiliation that Betsy thought he found her attractive, sexy. Before he could adjust, she was in the door with clouds of perfume and enthusiasm.

'I'll have to go over …' gesturing mysteriously upward with her eyes 'you know …' but as he obviously didn't know, 'les habilements de ma soeur … to see if …'

'If you're trying to be secretive, the boys both understand French. And I doubt any of her things would suit you.'

'Of course, of course, how silly of … but we can talk about it later … But here are the little darlings – oh, my, aren't you all dolled up, Simon-eye-mon-eye-mon, such a handsome little …'

'My name is just Simon.'

'Of course it is, darling, Auntie Betsy was just …'

'And my brother's name is Jonathan.'

'Well, we'll just have to get your names right, won't we? And now that she's living in Montreal again, your Auntie Betsy's going to be seeing a lot more of you, Simon and dearest Jonathan, a lot more …'

Her hands were all over the boys, who recoiled in silence and suspicion. Jonathan was frozen in doubt, hanging his head and glancing at Frank for cues; Simon glared at her with open hostility.

'… just the cutest little boy I've ever seen,' in falsetto, 'how about a big kiss for Auntie Betsy, you'll have to think of me as your Mummy now, because on Mother's Day every little boy …'

'My Mama is dead. She died.'

Betsy pulled Simon into a tight embrace, and glared at Frank over the little shoulder.

'She died and she isn't coming back ever.'

'Frank, how could you, telling them brutal things, a sensitive child, really, Mother tried to warn me, but I never in my wildest dreams expected …'

Her eyes were busily scanning the hall and the stairs … where the morning light would be highlighting every dustball.

'… really have to wonder if you're fit to …'

Emma, save me.

Jonathan was hiding around the corner in the living room, his eyes darting about, his long awkward fingers fidgeting. Frank could not remember ever seeing the boy so frightened, so distressed. Frank beckoned, but the boy flourished his hands, his eyes in the direction of the woman on the other side of the wall. Simon broke away and grabbed Frank's legs: 'Dada, Dada, Mama's dead.' Frank bent to hug him.

'… I've never been so …'

Now.

'Go out to the car, Betsy.'

'… that my own nephews should …'

'Go!'

'Why did she slam the door, Dada?'

Lack of imagination, Jonathan.

'Well, Auntie Betsy has been away, so she doesn't understand about some things, guys.'

'Nobody should slam the door, should they, Dada?'

'That's true, but she's a bit upset. Now then, as I explained, I have to mark essays, so you fellows are going to Grandma and Grandpa's place for the day. I'll be along before supper. Okay?'

'But what'll we do there, Dada?'

'Oh, I'm sure they'll have lots of things for you to do. Grampa mentioned a movie …'

'*Mulan?* I hope it's *Mulan.*'

'We already saw *Mulan,* Simon.'

'Now, boys, that's for you and your grandparents to decide. Whatever it is, I'm sure you'll enjoy yourselves.'

'If we go to *Mulan*, Dada, will Auntie Betsy be coming? I hope not.'

After a few more minutes of soothing, he got them out the door and across to the car where Betsy glowered in hauteur. Emma had once described her sister as Joan Crawford with PMS. There was no customary fight for the front seat: both boys scrambled into the back. Frank stood in the middle of the sunlit street and waved to the two little faces which peering back at him as the car pulled away.

After wandering through the silence of the house for a time, putting off the job, hating the stack of papers as much as the students no doubt did, Frank sat down at his desk and began. Freed from the necessity of correcting – most of the essays would sit unclaimed in his office for three years – he made good speed, and the pile on his right shrank as the pile on his left grew. After two dozen or so, he made a sandwich and ate as he worked. By three-thirty he was able to enter the grades in the spreadsheet. He looked through to see if all the best students had indeed gained firsts, if the deserving had their sixties and seventies, and if the failures were those who had not done even the minimum work or who had dropped out. He noted that three students were missing a final essay. They would perhaps have slipped their papers under the office door on Friday, past the absolute, final, unalterable, most dreadful deadline; he would delay entering their grades until he had checked the office tomorrow; he put his calculator in his briefcase. Then he printed the results. The final grades had to be recorded on the official sheets, but this he would leave until the morning when he was fresh and could be careful enough the avoid mistakes.

Anything else? He dealt with the phone and hydro bills, cleared the junk mail from his desk, found the note to Sorensen in Winnipeg, returned two weeks ago 'addressee unknown'. Frank put the note in a new envelope and addressed it this time to the University of Winnipeg.

Silly.

Four o'clock.

He showered and changed, neatened the kitchen, then rang the Hatchers' number.

'We are unable to come to the phone right now, but ...'

Reasonable enough: they were still out, at the movie or perhaps in the park.

But Mrs Hatcher would want to be home soon to start making the dinner.

Frank sat down in the living room with Ford Madox Ford's *Parade's End*.

He called twice before five, both times getting the recording.

His first reading of the situation had everyone at the hospital while the emergency room staff laboured over two small broken bodies; a worse reading saw the flaming wreck of the car crumpled against a bridge abutment beside an expressway ...

But the truth was obvious enough: the Hatchers were not eating at home, but in a restaurant. It would be too far away for Frank to join them, and the phone would be mysteriously out of order ... earlier they would have been unable to reach a phone because ... but the details of the story wouldn't matter. The point was to freeze Frank out of the day, to capture the boys and keep them as long as possible, bribing them with hugs and sweets equally cloying.

That was certainly the scheme.

The sweetness would end abruptly when they returned to find their street blocked by the Westmount fire department, their house a smoking ruin, neighbours eager to pass on the bad news:

spread before we knew what
window frames melting
upstairs and *down*
not a thing anyone could
and when the roof fell in, well

Yes, well, let's be sensible: get the Lismer out first – though from a late period, it was an original. The computer they'd recently bought the boys, perhaps some of the silverware.

No, he was wrong, they would telephone, but would leave it until too late, seven, perhaps, calling from out of town, the Laurentians, Hudson, the Townships. He rather hoped they might try Vermont and run into official suspicion, perhaps arrest, incarceration for trying to take the children across the border; Bwana Willis fatuously flashing his diplomatic passport ...

With nothing to do about it, he tried to concentrate on the long-suffering of Christopher Tietjens.

Who had developed this scheme? Babs and Betsy, almost certainly, no less loathsome than George or Willis, but considerably more petty, more spiteful.

Was long-suffering a noun?

Like loving-kindness?

In ten minutes the book fell forward and he dozed off.

Although he slipped fitfully in and out of wakefulness, the call caught him sound asleep.

'Sounds as if I woke you, Frank. Having a rest from the ardours, of course. I'm glad to find you're happier at home.'

'Willis?'

'Listen, you just go back to sleep. Don't worry about us, everything is fine.'

'But where are you, why didn't you call earlier, how are the boys?'

'We decided to check out the cottage and then we came over here to North Hatley for dinner. Of course, the phone in the cottage hasn't been reconnected for the summer yet. Don't worry, the boys are fine, having a marvellous time, and it has all been a splendid opportunity for us to develop our relationship and to relieve you of your burden. There wasn't room for you in the car anyway.'

'But when are you bringing the boys back? They have school tomorrow. Can I talk to them?'

'You worry too much, Frank, everything's under control. We'll get in touch later. Must go now.'

The line went dead.

Ardours was wrong: Willis wanted *arduousness* or *labours*.

The feeling of impotence, Frank reflected, was more than familiar, it was definitive: the situation was intolerable, but he could do nothing. He could not call the Sûreté, could not call a lawyer, could not sit waiting on their front steps, could not go for a walk, could not call a friend, could not get drunk, could not read a book – certainly could not read *Parade's End*, that thousand-page catalogue of misunderstandings and betrayals.

He could pace the house in the gathering twilight, could turn on the front porch light, could pick at a sandwich, could turn on the television and flip though the channels from two to fifty and back again half a dozen times before turning it off; he could pace the house again, could turn on the lights, could water the plants, could start a load in the washing machine, could sort the rest of the laundry, could select clothes for the boys and lay them out for the morning, could consider cleaning the oven, could close the oven door with a snort of derision, could put the first load in the dryer, could start another load in the washer, could try not to hyperventilate, could try not to quiver, could tell himself that although he was powerless to do anything which would not be misunderstood, misconstrued, actionable, and although he must remain entirely passive, nonetheless things would work themselves out, and he could briefly wonder if this being guilty, being wrong, being impotent was somehow the natural state of the anglo in Quebec: no, no, isolate that thought, wrap it in insulating plastic, return it to its freezer, mustn't think that sort of thought, for that way lies despair, lies madness.

He could wait.

He could, as he had so often been tempted to do, get out the Westmount Directory and find the names of the people living in the Hatchers' block – McGuire, Tam, Corriveau, Patel, Yousipian, Furlotte, Bathurst, Kisner, Couture, Hatcher, Morrison, Théberge, Hampshire, Chin, Marzitelli, Czerniewicz, Sherman, Matika, Colasurdo, Paquin, Sharma, Tzavaras, Horvat, Christmas, Weisz, Dass – could try to list them as oriental (was Matika Japanese or perhaps Czech?), Middle Eastern, Eastern European, Italian, French, and, finally, in Imperial Triumph, British, four names, though the McGuires at the corner were doubtless Irish Catholic, Christmas looked suspiciously made up, while Dr and Mrs Hampshire across the street and up one were, as Mrs Hatcher always mentioned, 'from the Antiguan branch of the Hampshires, though they're very well behaved for …' and never finished her sentence.

Could reflect that the list would mortify not just Mrs Hatcher, but the Société Saint-Jean-Baptiste.

Could wonder if Professor Sharma was old enough to have been born in British India and thus perhaps be classified as British, in which case perhaps Patel and Dass ...

Could reflect that the very making of the list was to fall into the racist ancestor worship, the blood-purity obsessions of the Hatchers, of the SSJB.

Could ball up the list, unfinished, in distaste, in revulsion, could throw it in the wastebasket.

Despair, madness indeed.

Could wait.

Simon's bedtime passed, and half an hour later Jonathan's.

The Hatchers' telephone answering machine remained on.

At a quarter to ten the telephone rang.

'Well, Frank,' said Babs breezily, 'you've had the entire day to yourself – sort of a Father's Day present on Mother's Day – but we were so glad to be able to help you. The boys had ...'

'Where are my children?'

'I beg your pardon?'

'Where are my children? It's nearly two hours past Simon's bedtime, they both have their school tomorrow, Jonathan's books and homework are here, their clean clothes, their pyjamas ...'

'The boys are asleep, of course, they are staying here as planned. What can you possibly be ...'

'Planned? What plan?'

'I have planned this sleepover for weeks, and don't say you ...'

'You might have mentioned it to me.'

'I know perfectly well I mentioned it to you at Easter, but you were probably so drunk that ...'

'I was not drunk at Easter, despite your husband's attempts to make me so.'

'Please don't interrupt. Betsy would have made everything clear to you if you hadn't been so rude to her – virtually throwing her out of the house – yelling like a savage ...'

'Rude? After what Betsy said to me ...'

'I regard your tone as offensive. And on Mother's Day. Really, Frank, you are incapable of showing any understanding, any generosity, and after all we've done for you, why, when I think of ...'

The hours of frustration and worry clamoured at his mind, shouting grievances, insults, threats. But that way lay chaos. As Mrs

Hatcher babbled her justifications, Frank laboured to master himself.

'… and then taking the boys on an outing which was very special to them and to us, so that I am amazed and shocked when …'

During a pause, he asked about arrangements for their school bags and clothes. Twenty minutes later Willis loped up the steps, grinning from under his safari hat.

'Got your marking all done, pal?'

'Willis, the last time we talked, you were all for a diplomatic solution to what you termed an untenable situation. This isn't diplomacy, it's a preemptive attack.'

'Frank, we were doing you a favour, for chrissake!'

'A favour? That's a strange name for this little plan.'

'It wasn't my plan, pal, it was Babs's. And, hey, it wasn't really a plan, it just happened, you know how these things go, you get in the car and you start driving, and you decide to stop for some frits, hang loose, do some window shopping, drop into a craft shop, take a look at the cottage, and then everyone is hungry again, and time flies, and there's no phone …'

'And I sit at home imagining bridge abutments and flaming wrecks.'

'Babs assured us it was all okay with you. Look, Frank, there has to be some give and take …'

'All give from me, all take from you people.'

Willis hefted the boys' bags, went down a step.

'When we had our beers that day, I tried to be nice about it, tried to explain the options. You weren't willing to negotiate. No negotiation, we try other means.'

'Or as Clausewitz put it, "War is diplomacy carried on by other means."'

'Who?'

'And I'm not your old pal.'

'You name the game, we'll play it.'

'And it's not a game.'

'You're finally beginning to get the point.'

He winked and loped to his car.

Interview

As Frank stepped down from the train, he scanned the dozen people arriving, waiting. The man who was obviously Ellery Culp – 'I'll be wearing a narrow-brimmed white tennis hat' – was looking around as well. Culp made his decision, and advanced toward Frank with big smile beneath the hat, and extended his hand. Frank hefted his shoulder bag, managed a smile in return, and took the hand.

'Welcome to Port Simcoe, Professor Wilson.'

'"Professor" is a bit grand for a Cegep teacher. "Mr" is more accurate. "Heysir" is more common. "Frank" will do.'

'Frank it is, then. Well, the car is just there. The university is on the other side of town, which offers you the opportunity to inspect the delights of downtown Port Simcoe. In the last century it was quite a thriving little metropolis, and much of the graciousness has survived, or has been restored under the aegis of our enthusiastic heritage society of which, I modestly admit, I am a founding member. Now, on the left ...'

Indeed, the streets, shops, and houses looked particularly idyllic in the June sun. Ellery Culp pointed out a charming tea shop, a sandwich bar, a few elms – 'all that remain, alas, of the thousand stately elms which earned the town its epithet "the City of the Stately Elms", and we had the name before Fredericton, New Brunswick' – three banks with automatic teller machines, a park suitable for children, a favourite student bar, a more upmarket bar favoured by faculty, a pizza outlet, a gourmet restaurant – 'nothing like Montreal, of course, but the chef worked there for a few years, and he does a mean veal cordon bleu; of course, the wine selection is ... although you'll be surprised at the quality of Ontario wines these days ...' – another park suitable for children, a street of nineteenth-century houses – 'wonderful for renovation if you're handy at that sort of thing, young Stones, our keen young deconstructionist (if you'll excuse an obvious but apt pun), lives in that one on the corner, and he and his wife have done a smashing job on ... you can see how he's restored the gingerbread on the gable ... won an award from the heritage society ...'

Mr Blandings Builds His Dream House.

'As for deconstruction, I'm not sure I'm a convert, but some of their insights are fascinating; some recent critical work is intriguingly provocative ... concept of "the other" ...'

I am an anglo. I am 'the other'.

Cary Grant and ... Myrna Loy? New York advertising executive buys derelict Connecticut farmhouse with a view to remodelling. Comic disasters. No, thank you. A newish ranch-style with minimal upkeep.

Across the road from the university gate, the new mall – 'You'd have to go as far east as Belleville to find a bigger one, though as a Jane Austen devotee perhaps you're a bit standoffish about malls, still, they are a convenience ...'

Frank turned his eyes to the university buildings, and Culp gave a capsule history.

Eastern Ontario University had its beginnings in the mid-nineteenth century as St Augustine's, a small Anglican college. St Augustine of Canterbury, as Culp hastened to add. It had survived more than a century on the tuition fees, frequently remitted, of Anglican divinity students, and of regular students who lacked the grades to enter more prestigious institutions. In the early 1960s, with church support evaporating, the provincial government designated St Augustine's as the logical candidate for massive expansion to service the regional baby boomers. This involved an awkward marriage to a neighbouring agricultural college – 'A marriage of inconvenience, we used to call it, although none of the faculty resentment persists today ...' The expansion had obviously been carried out with neither fidelity to the existing Victorian Gothic pile, nor enthusiasm for the more original architectural impulses of the sixties, but rather with attention to construction efficiency and cost.

'Straight ahead is the Arts and Humanities Centre, where the Department of English holds court ...'

It looked like a Ministry of Administrative Affairs, Ministry of Certain Things, six storeys or so.

Perhaps ten other buildings, of three or four storeys, one about ten, engineering and science probably, all in concrete, steel stripping, glass, cinderblock. Still, no doubt: *commitment on the part of the government of this great province to the future leaders of ... etc.*

'... we do have a faculty club, and a fine one, if I may say so, although it's unfortunately closed out of term, but the student union cafeteria is ...'

Capital G Government? Capital P Province?

'... which on the other hand does offer distinct economic advantages, and in these days of cutbacks – well, I gather you fellows in Quebec have had a few, too ...

Capital M Ministry? Capital E Education?

Silly ...

'And after a bite of lunch, I'll show you around. Living here after Montreal, the town perhaps will seem a bit small, but you'd be surprised how quickly you'll ...'

Ellery Culp was using a surprisingly definite future tense, not a conditional: didn't hirings here need committees, competitions, equal opportunity? And wasn't that a dangling modifier?

No   nearly-dead-able-bodied-middle-class-white-males   need apply? Still, he was a single parent.

'... and, of course, Toronto is just a couple of hours down the 401, so if ever you feel the urge to taste the delights of ...'

Blandings, as he recalled, soon gave up on the old farmhouse and began building a new house. More comic disasters.

'... and we do have a vigorous little theatre group in town ... of the past season were *Plaza Suite* and *Murder at the Vicarage* – bridging the Big Pond, as it were – and the sets and costumes were quite ...'

Student union buildings seemed much the same from British Columbia to Sweden: concrete and cinder block, ads for rock bands and political imperatives, photocopied notices of club meetings, flats to let, theses typed in WordPerfect and printed on laser printers, second-hand computers for sale, new computers, class cancellations, classes rescheduled, summer jobs, summer travel, the campus store with T-shirts, shorts, windbreakers, backpacks, agendas, all with the school logo, custom designed and manufactured in Taiwan, People's Republic of China, the Philippines, and rainbow hangings showing their faded and tattered-hem age ...

'... no, really, a sandwich and salad will be just fine; the food on the train was ...'

Aggressive No Smoking notices. *Commitment to the future leaders of* ... wherever ... défense de fumer, rauchen verboten, roken verboden, rökning förbjuden, vietato fumare ...

They sat by a shady window. After nearly thirty years, the campus trees were well established.

'... of course, it would be more pleasant to have the lake breeze in here, but the buildings are all climate-controlled. It makes perfect sense when you consider that the facilities are most heavily utilized during the winter ... not, I hasten to add, that Port Simcoe gets the sort of winter you've just had, but ...'

Frank gave him a minute or two of the ice storm and then asked about Einar Sorensen.

'I'm sorry?'

'Einar Sorensen in Winnipeg. You mentioned he recommended me for the job. I sent him a thank-you note care of the University of Manitoba. It was returned "addressee unknown" so I tried him at the University of Winnipeg, but I haven't heard back from him.'

Culp gazed vaguely out the window, squinting from the light.

'Sorensen ... yes ... now what did I hear? Sabbatical? Exchange teaching? That's it, Australia, he's on exchange in the Antipodes. Not Sydney, not Melbourne, smaller place ... Flinders University ... University of New England? I expect his department will forward it. I remember when I was in Minnesota for a term ...'

No longer used to chat, to the languid whiling away of time, Frank was about to try pulling him back to the job offer, when Culp asked about 'the political situation in la belle province'.

As he offered the telegraphic notes, Frank watched Culp, trying to guess when his interest would begin to drift, hoping, trusting it would drift within a few minutes, hoping Culp didn't care, didn't have *views*, didn't believe he could convert this anglo-Quebecer to his own theory of ...

But he did.

'... because it seems to me that, living in the middle of it, so to speak, your views may be a bit ...'

This was going to take at least fifteen minutes.

'... see, it seems to me it comes down to constitutional ... *viability*. Viability is the thing. It's not just a paper a bunch of politicos put together in a back room, but a living – viable – arrangement whereby ...'

Twenty minutes.

'... in all modesty ...'

A good half hour, certain.

'... but if you consider, for instance, the differences in constitutional theory between the American and the British models, versus the constitutional *practice*, well, it's surely obvious that ...'

The banality of our anglo-Quebec conversation, Magnus Rowan had remarked.

'Yes, very cogent.' My dear Socrates.

The women behind the cafeteria counter were clearing away the trays, wiping the stainless steel, the glass display windows, laughing, their day nearly done, no evening meals – as the chalkboard warned – during the summer months.

'... and after all, Frank, I was at McGill during my undergraduate years, so I have *some* experience of ...'

Would cafeteria work here be considered a good job?

'... though of course I have no friends there any longer, lost all contact, sadly ...'

Would the cafeteria pay better than something similar in town, in the mall, or in the freeway restaurants? So much unemployment these days, all across the country: how are people to live? Are these women grateful for their white smocks, their hairnets?

'... the art of the possible, as – was it Churchill? – said, but the separatists simply don't ...'

Can't remember, but fairly sure it wasn't Churchill.

And I am considering changing jobs, getting out, building my dream house. Buying a not-so-dream house on a new crescent where everyone has a basketball hoop over the garage door and an RV in front of it. Bring the boys to this small town, take them from their friends, me from mine, such as they are, bring the memories with me? Would the memories fade faster here? Do I want the memories to fade? What am I doing here? What am I doing at all? Going on. Going on going on.

Emma?

'... simply must understand that a *viable* arrangement must also be an *equitable* arrangement, otherwise ...'

'Yes, a valuable distinction.'

'... I mean, it must be accepted that there's just so much elasticity in any constitutional ...'

Ellery Culp, Frank reflected, should have been short, fat, sweaty. Incongruously, he was rather above medium height, slim, and in the climate control looked as if he was just out of the shower. He looked more like an economics professor. Nonsense: none of the economics teachers at home looked like Ellery Culp. All nonsense.

'... not confrontation – which helps no one – not backroom negotiation – which always leads to betrayal or supine concessions, but a third way, a move toward an organic, *inclusive* arrangement which ...'

It sounded like something from Yeats and the Golden Dawn ... The Middle Way? Madame Blavatsky?... Ouspensky?... Aleister Crowley? Or wasn't there something similar in *The Quiet American*? The American was pushing a theory propounded by a professor, probably, State Department adviser, some sort of intellectual with a book, about another way, the Second Way, the Third Road? And the young American ... Pyle, that was the name. As obvious a name as any in early Dickens. But also evoking Ernie Pyle, perhaps, the war correspondent.

'... not perhaps the *complete* solution, but a *workable* solution with a sound *theoretical* basis ...'

Culp glanced at his watch.

'It makes a lot of sense.'

Write it out and mail it to Bouchard, to Bernard Landry.

'But, tempus fugit, so ...'

To the Société Saint-Jean-Baptiste.

'... thought we might ...'

To Australia.

'... wend our way over to the AHC now and I'll just show you around the department. Of course, we're not likely to meet many faculty today, but ...'

The sun hot now, with touches of relief from the lake breeze. Some summer students reading under the trees, four in shorts and bare feet tossing a Frisbee, laughing, and pitch-and-catch over toward the science building.

On the fifth floor, narrow hall, Ellery Culp ducked into a small room and took his mail from a pigeonhole, found a package, then a second, from a wire basket.

W.W. Norton & Co.

Prentice Hall.

Book Rate.

Just like home.

Culp stuck his head in at the departmental office, exchanged greetings and cryptic information with the pleasant-looking, forty-ish secretary. She handed him a file, did the courtesies with Frank, asked what Frank took in his coffee. They got their cups, Frank's with a sunburst, Culp's with Shakespeare, then Culp, juggling impedimenta and keys, led the way along the hall.

The sanctum sanctorum.

'The sanctum sanctorum,' announced Culp, waving Frank before him. Book-lined, blond oak furniture showing the years somewhat, computer and printer, glass vase with three wooden tulips, beige curtains, lake view.

'No lake views for new faculty, I'm afraid,' said Culp. 'Although the offices on this side get devilishly hot on sunny winter days. The climate control for this building wasn't well designed, although it's better than it was. The first eight or ten years here were … well … ahh, take a pew.'

The shelves, the desk were neater than Frank's own. Culp, seated facing the window, opened a file, not the one the secretary had given him, but another from a stack. Inside the file was Frank's letter of application, the CV with it.

'Well, to business. The good news is that old Purdey has indeed been translated to emeritus status: his position is now definitely vacant. The other news, not bad news, but, shall we say, tentative news, is still hanging fire. It's the question of whether or not the dean will approve the hiring of a replacement. As I remarked earlier, I don't need to tell you about budget cuts. However, pre-registration numbers are up slightly, and the ministry is allowing some leeway in budget. In particular, the college has the right, within limits – about 12 per cent – to transfer funds from capital cost allocations to staffing. Plant and facilities has been grumbling about a new furnace and more modifications to the climate control system, and there is some question about upgrading the music rehearsal facility. Phys ed, of course, wants a pool, squash courts, weight room, you name it – a steeplechase course for horses, Olympic soccer stadium – their appetite for capital expenditure is always boundless. We can forget about them. There are other minor requests for some office remodelling, some new furniture – well, see for yourself, these chairs have seen better days – but such minor matters can be fitted into running costs. Which leaves the rehearsal room. Now, there the problem is that the music department, all two of them, to justify the expenditure, would have to hire, and that eventuality is a non-starter. The budget committee sat last Thursday, and pretty clearly untuned their strings, as Iago puts it. Now, there are three other requests for replacements – in chemistry, political science, and classics – but they are just that, replacements, not new positions, as music would be. Now ministry policy, which is nearly complete, will benefit us here – back-to-basics. I expect you have the same sort of thing in Quebec. The point is that back-to-basics means the classics department is dead in the water – who needs Latin to program computers? Personally, I'll be sorry to see the department go, but one must be realistic. Ten years ago they amalgamated with religion – the modern world catching up with the shibboleths of the old. And back-to-basics means the ministry is going to go for an English exit exam, a *compulsory* English exit exam. It's not graven in stone yet, I hasten to add, but I gather the policy is in the final drafting stage, and should be announced this summer. Well, you can see what an exit exam means – more English faculty. Ergo, a position for Professor Frank Wilson. So although it is not iron-clad, it is as near certain as these things ever can be.'

'Yes, I see.'

'So, what do you think? You'll go for it, I hope?'

Frank glanced along a row of Shakespeare criticism … turned toward the lake. A distant sailboat.

'It's tempting, I must admit.'

Throw in Myrna Loy and it's a done deal.

'More than just tempting, surely. Consider the disadvantages of your current situation, and the advantages you'll enjoy here …'

Myrna Loy in *The Thin Man*.

'In the first place, the political ...'

The wooden tulips seemed an odd decoration for such a boorish, bouncy ... Tigger-ish man. And surely such a motif should be picked up in a print, a brightly painted pot. Not in the curtains – they were institutional beige. But wooden flowers seemed ... unlikely. Like ... harlequin underwear.

'... a maximum of nine hours a week in the classroom, a – what did we calculate? – 30 per cent increase in salary ...'

A reverence for the novels of Jane Austen?

'... superior pension plan ...'

All nonsense, this tulip business, these snide perceptions, this knowing analysis, Montrealish superiority. And what was he doing here? There was no departmental meeting, no committee, no interview – there was nothing that could not have been done by phone or mail.

'... and don't forget reduced tuition for your children when they are of age – current government trends are toward user-pay initiatives, so that tuitions are certainly going ...'

'If I'm to catch my return train, I really should be getting to the station.'

'Of course, of course. Now, Frank, I hope this visit and our little interview have clarified your mind on a number of ...'

As Frank stood and turned, he noticed the framed degrees on the wall: BA McGill, 1955; MA McMaster, 1957; Ph.D. Toronto, 1961.

'I must admit I was hoping to get an Oxon. or Cantab. in there somewhere,' said Culp, 'but there's a divinity that shapes our ends.'

'As Nell Gwyn said to Barbara Villiers.'

Culp was, it seemed, stunned by this thunderclap of wit: slap on the shoulder, guffaws, rock the faculty club when it reopens in ...

'If I have the dating right. Which I probably don't.'

Scholarly humour. But it kept Culp occupied until they were well on their way back to town. The platitudes of departure got Frank to the platform. Culp apologetically mentioned a tennis match and departed after comradely smiles, handshakes, and a go-for-it clenched fist.

Settled into his seat on the train, Frank tried to make sense of this absurd trip. The Blandings dream was of escape to a home free of the annoyances of the city. Finally, at a cost far greater than he expected, nearly at the cost of his marriage, Blandings got his house. But this proposed move to Port Simcoe seemed suspiciously dream-like. But then, perhaps a university as undistinguished as the University of Eastern Ontario actually could want to offer him tenure. Emma would have made sense, of course, Emma who could certainly have been a short-listed candidate for a job at U of T, UBC, Alberta, not to mention Eastern.

Build a dream house here? Who could imagine he might want such a dream?

Could he imagine it?

Just possibly.

Family

They joined the Westmount Family Day parade just as it was beginning, Simon in his Batman cape and hood, Jonathan with his pirate's eyepatch, tricorn, and sword. Most of the other children were also as modestly done up in last year's Halloween garb, half a dozen wore spangled gowns or suits rented or bought, while a few were in costumes laboured over by their mothers: banana and pineapple siblings, a golden sun-boy with the planets of the solar system on hoops round his waist, a girl who was perhaps a bird with the shimmering extensions of tail, wings, head, the sort of costume usually found in the Caribbean parade. Frank studied his boys to see if they were aware of the meagreness of their own costumes, but they seemed not to have noticed. Both were looking about and grinning, clearly enjoying themselves, but also impressed by the sense of occasion, by the solemn honour of being in the parade.

'Are we going to walk right in the middle of the Sherbrooke Street, Dada?'

'Well, in the middle of this side of the street. I think they leave the north side free for traffic.'

'That's a good idea, Dada. And you can walk beside me.'

As they turned onto Sherbrooke Street, Simon took his hand and stepped along proudly. Jonathan, chatting with a school friend, took Frank's other hand.

They could see ahead to the fire engine, the air cadets, the Cubs and Brownies, the ponies, goats, and llamas of the hired petting zoo. A teenagers' band, from the high school perhaps, could just be heard from near the front; Frank thought he recognized 'Seventy-Six Trombones' though a moment later it seemed to be 'Liberty Bell'. But it didn't matter: Westmount's Family Day in the Park was meant to be relaxed, casual, simple.

Jonathan said, 'I think that's Aunty Betsy and Uncle Willis at the corner of Prince Albert, Dad.'

Frank and the boys were halfway to Victoria; he looked back and waved. Betsy waved; Willis was tracking them with his video camera.

'Wave for the camera, guys.'

'Maybe you can get a copy of it, Dad.'

'We can always ask.'

'Are we going to get a video camera someday, Dada?' asked Simon.

'I'm not sure. We'll see.'

'Let's all ask Santa Claus to give you one for Christmas. That way it won't cost anything.'

'Now that's an excellent idea!'

Saturday morning shoppers paused to watch the parade, while at the sidewalk cafés people in shorts and sunglasses clapped, pointed, and raised their cappuccinos in salute. Clerks in the shops, the banks, the liquor store stood in their doorways, and even a few cashiers from the supermarket found time to wave through the plate glass.

Jonathan ran briefly to the sidewalk to talk to a schoolmate. Simon slipped his hand free to go and befriend a little girl with fairy wings and wand. Frank did a mental inventory of his shoulder bag: suntan lotion, extra sweat shirts, caps, umbrella, fruit drinks, crackers, camera and extra film. Perhaps a photo or two now.

'You guys hold hands while I take your picture.'

He rummaged for the camera, ran ahead, turned and look through the viewfinder.

'How about holding hands ... yes ... keep walking ... there!'

Presently the parade passed by the top of the Park, then down its long side to St Catherine Street, then back to the playing field for dispersal.

'Wait a minute, guys, wait a minute. Now look, there are lots of things to do, and lots of friends to see, but there are two of you and only one of me. So we are going to have to have a chat about staying together and what happens if you lose me or if you need a pee. First of all, do you see that shed down by the tennis courts? Look where I'm pointing, Simon. Now that's the Public Security office, and if you can't find me, or if I can't find you ...'

They listened impatiently as he went through the instructions, made them each repeat them, mentioned some of the likely parents they knew and could ask for help.

'Okay, costume judging over in front of the Public Security hut. Let's go!'

Poles with tapes marked the boundary of the race area. Halfway along the field, rows of chairs sat before a stage for exhibitions of magic and dancing. Through the trees, along the main path, various organizations, charities, and shops had booths for handouts, craft demonstrations, bake sales, face painting, and advertising.

Frank helped the boys remove their costumes and stowed them in his bag, then warned them not to leave the race area, told them to listen to the age group announcements. The activities moved genially and apace. Everyone entering an event got a purple and gold participant's ribbon, so that by the end of the costume judging, the foot races, the tug of war, the novelty races, the water balloon toss, and the egg toss, all the children and some of the parents had two or three ribbons. Simon came to Frank with all his trophies before running off to his friends. Jonathan was always in sight, but came less often: growing older, more independent, growing away. At nine, halfway to college. Almost a year since … She had had so little of it to enjoy.

'Simon, do you want to see the fire engines? But first we'll have to get Jonathan …'

They made their way to the far end of the playing field, where the firemen had parked their trucks.

'Fire trucks are pretty sturdy, guys, but try not to break anything. And don't push any buttons or switches or whatever …'

Firemen pointed out hose engines, gauges, axes, and helped the children into the cab.

'They're patient with the kids, aren't they.'

Jane something, mother of … Ashley, schoolmate of Jonathan.

'Yes, more patient than I could be, I expect. Do you suppose it comes with the job?'

They chatted about patience, the good weather for the day, the ice storm nearly forgotten now, stratagems for keeping the kids from irritations.

'… always a lineup for the pony ride, but the army rope ride is best during lunch hour, and …'

From the roof of the big school on the south side of the park, firemen were preparing a demonstration of rappelling. Jonathan and Ashley, veterans of numerous school visits to the fire station, were watching a fireman suspended thirty or forty feet up.

'I'm not sure if I'm happy that my son is interested in scaling buildings. Are you a mite …'

'Nervous about my daughter? Yes, it's terrible, isn't it? You worry about everything even remotely dangerous, but you know they have to try things …'

Simon had finished with the driver's seat of the truck and had crossed to the other side. Frank walked around the front of the truck and arrived just in time to see Simon squirm away from the fireman who was helping the children down. The boy slipped, bounced off the running board, and fell forward on the ground. Frank and the fireman bent to lift him up. Simon was crying, though clearly more in surprise than in panic or pain.

After a quick check for broken bones, after hugs, soothings, reassurances, they examined a slight scrape on his knee, and a bruise high on the thigh where he had bumped on the running board.

Simon's crying was, as usual, quickly over.

'The knee is just grass-stained,' said the fireman, 'and the bruise looks worse than it is. I think you'll be all right, young fellow.'

In one of the pockets of the bag, Frank found a wipe in an individual pack, a leftover from Simon's diaper years. The wipe still had enough moisture to clean the scrape.

'It stings, Dada!'

'I know, I'm sorry, little guy, but it will go away in a minute.'

To distract him, Frank gently palpated the bruise.

'That still hurts a bit, I think.'

'A bit, Dada. But not too much.'

'Not enough for us to take you home to bed, eh?'

'Maybe after the pony ride I might want to go home to bed.'

'How's the knee? Does it still sting?'

'A little bit.'

'Well, you didn't much want to play at the game booths this afternoon, did you?'

'Or maybe I won't have to go home at all.'

'That's the stuff, young fellow,' said the fireman. 'Maybe when you grow up, you'll be a fireman.'

The crisis over, they watched the rappelling for a while, then strolled over to get in line for the pony ride. After fifteen minutes, they were among the six waiting to go next, when Mrs Hatcher and Betsy appeared.

Tempted to ask where they had parked their brooms and why they were out during the daylight hours, Frank smiled as cordially as he could, and when the current ride ended busied himself with getting Simon safely mounted. A helper came to steady the boy, so as the ponies began their round Frank got out the camera. But at last he had to turn to the women.

'What's that terrible bruise on Simon's leg?'

'He slipped getting out of a fire truck.'

'When did it happen?' cried Mrs Hatcher. 'Have you taken him to the hospital?'

'It looks uglier than it is. He says it doesn't hurt.'

'You should at least have had him looked at. Don't they have a first aid station here? They should have a first aid station, all the dangers for the little ones, I can't imagine why you haven't ...'

Frank let her rattle on, trusting that Simon, when questioned, would disarm criticism. Indeed, the boy struggled from his grandmother's embraces, claimed he could not feel the bruise, and insisted on explaining how brave he had been in the saddle.

Jonathan pulled Frank aside.

'Dad, can we go to the rope thing over the lagoon now? You said we might go about lunchtime.'

The women wanted to take both the children, but with the Mother's Day business hanging in the air, they didn't insist. Finally it was agreed that they would take Simon for lunch, while Frank waited with Jonathan at the rope ride – for which Simon was, in any case, too young. Frank handed over the boy's fruit drink, and Simon went with them cheerfully enough, giving precise instructions about the garnishes he wanted on his hot dogs. Jonathan was obviously relieved when Betsy at least was out of sight. Frank wondered if he should run after Simon for a reinforcing application of sunblock, but reflected some would get on the boy's hot dog. High summer hadn't arrived; after lunch would do.

However, he was not soon enough. Jonathan had his turn on the rope after only fifteen minutes, but when they found the others, Betsy was busily applying lotion.

'He could have burned to a crisp, Frank,' cried Mrs Hatcher. 'I don't know how you can ...'

Frank showed the sunblock in his hand, explained his reason for delaying.

'Nothing since nine-thirty? And Simon so fair-skinned? I think you could have put some on while you were waiting for the pony ride, it would have been well soaked in by the time ...'

Ellery Culp and the University of Eastern Ontario were beginning to look more appealing.

'And we took Simon to the first aid hut, didn't we, Simon, to treat your boo-boo. They sprayed it with solarcaine, and he didn't cry at all, he's such a brave little fellow. And they cleaned and bandaged the gash on his knee ...'

'Mrs Hatcher, it was not a gash, it was a scrape, the skin wasn't broken, there was no blood, and even the fireman, who is no doubt trained in first aid, didn't think it needed a bandage.'

'Well, I'm sure that if you have better things to do than care for the cuts and bruises of your children, it's a good thing they have family who do care.'

'But ...'

'And I'm not at all sure I like your tone of voice. How can you carp and complain when we are only doing our very best for ...'

What would Emma have said to such an attack? But Mrs Hatcher would never have attacked Emma, had indeed been terrified of Emma.

Betsy smirked.

When he felt the tears, Frank bent down to embrace Simon, his other arm reaching for Jonathan. With head bowed, he held the boys to him, trusting his sunglasses to hide his eyes.

Mrs Hatcher missed it, but Betsy guessed at once. She knelt before him and took his head in her hands.

'Frank,' she murmured, 'What's wrong? Is Mom hurting you? She doesn't mean it, you know that, it's just her way, she cares for the kids so much, don't take it to heart, we love the boys, we love you,

you're family, we just want what's best for them and for you and for everyone, please let us help you, you need help, because we understand, we really do, but we can't help you if you keep us at a distance, if you won't open up to us, I know Emma's loss has been devastating for you, it's hurt, it's wounded all of us, but if we stick together we can get through this, but we have to stick together, you have to let us help you, just say the word, just tell us what you want, tell us what you need …'

She stopped when Frank put a finger to her lips.

'Just go,' he whispered. 'Thank you for offering to help, thank you. I'm a bit … tired. But I'm okay, the boys are okay. Just let me and the boys finish the day alone, together. Okay? Please.'

'If that's what you truly want, we'll go. But don't keep us from you, Frank. Don't push us away, we only want to help. But for now, we'll go.'

She stood up.

'What's wrong?' asked Mrs Hatcher. 'Is it something I've said? I didn't mean to cause trouble, I only want what's best for …'

'Never mind, Mom, everything's fine, I'll explain later.'

'But this anger, this hostility, when I'm only trying …'

'Not now, Mother, come on, let's leave them for now, everything's fine, Frank just needs to be alone.'

Mrs Hatcher, her voice querulous, her hands fluttering, was led away. Betsy turned to blow them a kiss.

Frank lifted a hand in acknowledgement.

'Well, guys, anyone hungry?'

Relieved that the incomprehensible drama was over, the boys began to chatter about the food. But each took a hand.

Schedule

As the boys put on their shoes and Frank checked the bag of swimming gear, the mailman came up the steps and pushed the delivery through the slot. An alumni magazine, offer of investment services, phone bill, letter from school, discount coupons for garden supplies. He pushed them into the equipment bag.

'Ready guys? Oops, sunblock.'

'Oh no, not sunblock!'

'It stinks, Dad!'

'The life guards and the swimming instructors wear it, so you wear it.'

'You don't wear it.'

'I'll be sitting under a shady canopy on the observation deck. Anyway, my skin is old and leathery, while you guys ...'

The boys stood impatiently as he applied the lotion, then ran down the steps. By the time he had washed his hands and locked the door, the boys were at the corner of the street. He loped after them – no hint of sweat, a deliciously cool July morning, not so cool that the boys would shiver coming wet from the pool, but not hot, the close Montreal heat that makes so many summer days languorous, heavy.

'A perfect day, eh, guys? Just right for swimming lessons. A day to dream of all winter long.'

'Dad, can we maybe go for a bike ride later?'

'Sure, Jonathan. We won't have much time between swimming and your sports camp, but how about I make up a picnic lunch and we'll take it along?'

'A picnic, yea!'

'Perhaps we'll take the bike lane out de Maisonneuve, try one of the parks in NDG. What do you think? Simon, do you think you can go that far?'

'I'll try not to be too tired, Dada,' he said solemnly.

Simon had discarded his training wheels the previous summer, a month after Emma, declaring with the same solemn tone he had just used that he thought he was ready to ride a real bicycle. And he had indeed wavered down the Sunday-morning street, gaining confidence quickly, so that in five minutes he was riding his little two-wheeler. Last summer as well he had declared one evening in the baby pool that Frank should take his hands away because he thought he could swim by himself. And with his little face tilted up, his eyes squinched, Simon dog-paddled the six feet to the side. In an hour he had managed to swim the length of the baby pool, perhaps twenty feet, without touching bottom. Within a week he could do twice the length of the adult pool. Such a miracle! Jonathan had been a year older when he learned to swim and to ride a two-wheeler. Still, a miracle too. How old had Frank been? Surely eight or nine, ages older than his sons. They were a miracle.

When the boys were in their bathing suits, with caps adjusted, towels over their shoulders, Frank saw them to their classes, then went out through the locker room and up to the observation deck to while away the lesson time. He exchanged nods with several of the half-dozen mothers on the deck, but they were already settled into their conversations, so he slipped onto an isolated chair. On the pool deck below, mothers chatted in the shade, while others were stretched on deck chairs, tanning. The instructors with their clip-boards and whitened noses strolled toward the seated groups of children. Simon looked up and waved.

After ten minutes of watching the boys smiling, grinning, chatting with the other kids, Frank remembered the mail. He put the magazine on his knee, held the school letter, dropped the rest back in the bag. Administrative bumf? No, above the letterhead was scrawled the name of Arty Hodge, the head of the department. His fall schedule!

He tore open the envelope and glanced at the grid of the week. Early morning classes every day but Thursday, no midday classes at all, Monday and Thursday ending at four, Tuesday and Friday ending at six. It was the worst schedule he had ever had. Linda couldn't possibly come at seven in the morning; she couldn't stay until quarter or twenty after six, the earliest he could conceivably get home.

How am I to manage this?

Somehow.

Keep going on.

The last time he had calculated his work load, he had come up with sixty-five hours a week. Without Emma he had had to cut back on work at home. Now ... what? ... at least twenty-six hours a week in the office, another ten to twenty at home ... And Eastern Ontario promised nine class hours in the fall term and six in the spring, with a like amount for office, eighteen one term and twelve the other, with hometime added. And thirteen weeks a term instead of fifteen.

And Ellery Culp.

And Port Simcoe.

And the Port Simcoe Heritage Society.

And the Port Simcoe Little Theatre Group.

And the Hatchers retired nearby.

Here, forty-plus hours a week of school work.

And Betsy and Bwana.

And politics.

And the boys.

At least I have a job, hard times, thousands would love to have my position, easy job it looks, mustn't complain.

Keep going on.

After the bicycle picnic, Frank telephoned Arty's home, then the office.

'He was in a few days ago, but he's likely at his shop,' said Carmen. 'He spends most of his time there in the summer.' She gave him the phone number and address.

Frank tapped the first few digits, but decided to try seeing Arty. He drove Jonathan to the park for his sports camp, then with Simon headed for the West Island.

'Why can't I sit in the front seat, Dada?'

Because it's called the death seat, my precious one.

'The back is safer, Simon, especially when we're going fast on the highway.'

'I wish we didn't have to be on the highway.'

'I don't much like it either.'

Vin Maison was in a strip mall in Pointe Claire or Kirkland – Frank could never keep the West Island town borders straight in his head. As he walked across the hot parking lot, he made Simon promise not to touch things.

'There'll be lots of glass, so you must be careful not to break anything.'

'I'll try, Dada.'

'And you have both your video games?'

'Can I play with the sound on?'

'Better not.'

'Aww … okay, Dada.'

The air conditioner in the transom was racing and dribbling condensation that Frank saw just in time to keep Simon out of the stream. Despite this noise and effort, the shop was slightly too warm for comfort. A pretty teenaged girl turned from the shelf display she was rearranging and greeted him in both languages.

'Is Arty about?'

The girl's T-shirt said 'Megadeath.'

Before she could reply, Arty appeared from the back carrying a carton with four boxes of concentrate. He was bathed in sweat.

'What's that game?' he demanded of Simon. 'Is that Sonic 11? I bet I can beat you in Sonic 11. My name is Arty the Terminator, what's yours?'

He set the box on top of others and mopped his brow.

'My name is Simon. I can beat my Dad.'

'Everyone can beat your Dad. At least in Sonic 11. Tell you what, you play it for a while until you get your highest score, then I'll see if I can beat you. Is that a deal?'

'All right.'

'Great.' To Frank he said, 'Don't even bother asking, it's carved in stone.'

Frank had never seen Arty in shorts: his white legs were unexpectedly hairless – Arty's chest was a jungle – and the knees puckered and faintly obscene.

'Somehow I thought you might say that.'

'You got problems, Sid's got problems, Eleanor's got problems, Mike's got problems, I've got problems.'

'Yeah.'

'The administration's got problems.'

'From what I hear, the administration's problems are a signal lack of intelligence, ability, morals, and backbone.'

'True, but aside from that they've got the bozos in Quebec City on their backs.' Arty sat down on a case. 'This latest régime from the ministry is a real pain in the ass for the administration.'

'For them!'

'Awright, for you too, yeah, I know, and for me and for everyone. "Object-Oriented Learning" for chrissake. You any idea what it means?'

'I've looked at the memos. Grids? Student names down the column and oriented objects across the top. Check off the objects achieved. Something like that?'

'Something like that. So what are you going to do about it?'

'I'll do the paperwork.'

'And keep on teaching the way you always have been?'

'I expect so. The memos haven't been very clear on the procedures.'

'They never are, are they? Actually, it's not a bad idea, except for it to have any meaning, they have to start teaching grammar in about grade three. Which they're not going to do because that would be repressive fascist elitism. So we deal with it. In my Modern American Lit course, for example, I'm ...'

Frank realized Arty was keeping away from the schedule, but accepted that Arty was better having his say sooner rather than later. Arty had early noticed that departmental chairmen got releases from teaching in recognition of the dreary work they had to do running their departments. Arty took the job when no one else was interested. He had quickly learned how to keep the paperwork down, which administrators to flatter, how to arrange scheduling goodies for friends and potential enemies. He didn't snow the teachers with pointless memos. On the whole he was fair, and, so far as Frank could tell, did not bear grudges. He seemed to spend at most four or five hours a week on departmental duties. His major concern was Vin Maison, and the money it could pump into his retirement savings – the word was Arty had salted away half a million; it could be true, but Frank expected it was considerably exaggerated.

'It's dog-eat-dog, Frank. You can be a winner or you can be a victim. The choice is yours.'

'I'm too busy taking care of this little fellow and his brother.'

'In other words, you're a victim.'

'I expect so.'

A customer had questions the girl couldn't answer, so Arty spent five minutes advising him with serene confidence. The customer, Frank could see, spent more than he had planned.

'Want a good start-up kit?' Arty asked when he was free.

'No, thanks.'

'I'll give you a deal: cost plus 10 per cent. Spread over four batches, your unit cost will be down to a dollar, dollar-and-a-quarter a bottle depending on the concentrate.'

'I don't drink enough to make it worthwhile. Look, about the schedule ...'

'Frank, you're missing the point. Let me give you my reading. An election this fall, next spring, Charest is just a pretty boy and no friend of yours in any case, and when Bouchard is done with him, he's road-kill, because ...'

Arty gave his reading of the political future: election, neverendum, federal blundering, Reform Party yahoos, navel-gazing nationalism, bond rating agencies, xenophobic paranoia, the provincial debt, doses of reality quickly ignored, downsizing, buyout packages.

'But it's still Montreal,' Arty concluded, 'it's still my home, so I'm staying. But staying with the gas tank full. Things get to be too much of a nuisance, I unload this joint, unload the house, and I'm outta here. I got my eye on a couple of locations in Ontario, BC, maybe the States.'

'And a time-share in the Bahamas.'

'Myrtle Beach, actually, and it's not a time-share, time-shares are for suckers. Even if they're aboveboard, which they often aren't, you gotta know what you're doing, you really gotta know contracts and the tax set-up.'

'I don't know contracts and tax set-ups. I don't know how to run a business.'

Arty played with Simon and monitored the girl as she sold two cartons of merlot concentrate. When he was again seated, Arty said,

'You know your problem, Frank? You're an idealist.'

'I hadn't thought about it.'

'For "idealist" read "jerk". You take it all so seriously, you and Eleanor and Bernie and that bunch. Coterie papers on Jane Austen, for chrissake! International scholarly conferences. You get the travel fund to pay your fare, you read your papers that no one understands or cares about, you write the odd review for journals, unpaid. You stick in your thumb, and pull out a plum, and say "What a good boy am I!" As for school, you know those kids aren't even listening, they aren't even reading the stuff, they're reading cribs. They haven't the remotest idea what you're talking about. You pretend to teach, and they pretend to learn. It's a scam, Frank.'

'I admit, there are times …'

'Hell, there's nothing wrong with a scam as long as no one blows the whistle – which is what Bozo the ministry thinks it's doing, ha-ha – and especially as long as you don't scam yourself. Which is what you're doing.'

'Enough, Arty.'

'Overstatement? Yeah, well. Look, Frank, I know you're a sincere and talented teacher and you're doing the best you can in difficult circumstances. But getting through to one student in ten is not a satisfactory payoff for a sane man. And trying to do it as an anglo in this place …'

'So I should invest in a home wine franchise?'

'You could do worse. Because come two or three years from now, you'll still be bullshitting the Tonys and the Stephanies about the glories of Jane Austen and wondering if you can learn to like dog food when they pension you off, and I'm going to be living in some low crime town outside of Quebec, near an international airport, reinvesting my pension cheques, clipping my coupons, banking my dividends, paying minimum wage to kids who want weekend jobs, and raking off enough to cover the day-to-day.'

A new customer greeted Arty by name. Bemused out his earlier anger and frustration, Frank waited. When the customer left, Arty played a round of Simon's video game. He was devastated when he lost, and admitted Simon was a killer player. Simon vowed to do even better next time. Arty turned to Frank and took up another

SCHEDULE

thread, murmuring so the girl couldn't hear.

'You heard me with that guy earlier: I'm fluent in joual, right?'

'Like a native.'

'Now tell me, am I pure laine or am I a tête carrée?'

'I expect you'll tell me.'

'I have French friends, Guylaine here is French, and I deal with half my suppliers and maybe a third of my customers in French, so I am tolerated, but I am still a tête carrée. My kids, they can pass, though, they're in French school, they'll work in French. But you, with your academic French and lousy attitude, you haven't got a chance. So why are you staying?'

'No jobs on offer.'

'Balls – inertia, that's what's keeping you. No teaching jobs, granted, but what about other jobs? The real trouble with dinosaurs like you, is you're pining for the privileged past, dreaming it's going to come back. It's not coming back, Frank, it's gone with the wind and tomorrow is another day. Get real or get out.'

Is Ellery Culp real?

'You're wrong, Arty, I hardly think about this stuff. And, to be honest, I don't think what you say I think. Other than that, you make an interesting case.'

'Yeah, don't I just. And what does this have to do with your schedule? I'm trying to make it clear that times are tough, they're going to stay tough, and no one is going to help you but yourself. So you want six-nine hours a week of low-enrolment lit classes at mid-day Tuesday and Thursday? Don't we all. Show me your schedule.'

Frank handed over the sheet. They talked over some possibilities. After five minutes Arty shrugged.

'Word gets out I fixed your schedule and next term you get the schedule from hell.'

'I don't talk to anyone anyway.'

'Okay. So we have some part-timers tentatively slotted into some time blocks for allocation if the registration numbers are good and admin approves a few sections. I was saving a couple of twelve-to-two and two-to-fours as little prezzies to hand out. What's worse for you – the eight o'clocks or the four o'clocks?'

When the deal was done, Frank still had the eight o'clocks, but had Friday free, and taught no later than four.

'I think I've seen my last late show for a while,' he said.

Arty played three rounds of the video game, losing each time in loud humiliation. Simon left triumphant and asked how soon they could return.

'Not for a while.'

Too expensive.

Drive

With their fine sense of occasion, the boys were entirely cooperative – they dressed themselves, ate their breakfast quickly, and helped pack the car. Simon even took the back seat without complaint, accepting that he mustn't sit in the front on the highway, that Jonathan had to sit in the front or he'd get carsick after a few hours. With a last check of the house doors and windows, automatic light timers, mental check that the paper and mail would be cared for by the neighbours, Frank got into the driver's seat, took a sip of coffee from the cup on the dash, and put his sunglasses in the bin in front of the gear shift.

'Okay, navigator, what's the time?'

'Five after four, Dad.'

'Okay, let's zero the trip meter … start the car … and we're away.'

As they headed downtown on the Ville Marie expressway, the promise of dawn glowed behind mist at the horizon; but even after they were across the Jacques Cartier Bridge and eastbound on Autoroute 20, the light was still not bright enough for Frank to put on his sunglasses.

'We'll make it all the way today, won't we, Dad? Because we left almost exactly on time.'

'I think so, Jonathan. Just hope the poor old car can manage it. If it does, we should make it.'

'Do you want me to pour you some more coffee, Dad?'

'Not yet. Let's see if Dad can make it to St Hyacinthe before he needs another cup.'

He glanced back to see how Simon was doing; in semi-sleep with his thumb and his blanket.

'Do you want something to drink, Jonathan? A carton of juice?'

'Not yet, Daddy.'

'Okay. Now the top map should be Quebec. How about you find where we are and see if you can estimate how long it's going to take us to get to Quebec City …'

The kilometres rolled by. If he kept the pace they should pass

Quebec City by six-thirty, and make it to Edmundston, New Brunswick, well before noon. If he pushed it, and if he was lucky with traffic and construction, and if the boys didn't have to pee every half hour, they'd be in Cape Breton early in the evening.

The question had been whether to fly and rent a car, or to trust the car to do the more than two thousand kilometres there and back. The bank balance and a telephone call to a travel agent answered that question. Actually, Frank rather looked forward to the drive. As much as he feared Montreal's streets and autoroutes, he enjoyed the long rhythms of highway driving. Here he had no responsibility to grade essays, book the babysitting sessions for the week, organize birthday presents for friends, schedule shopping, meals, doctor's and dentist's appointments, soccer, ringette, laundry … Here there was the slow calculation of the tripping kilometres, the gas gauge, the temper of the children, the cars and trucks drifting past, the coffee …

'St Hyacinthe, Dad. Four forty-five. I think we're going to make it.'

'Not bad. Now just as long as there's not too much construction in New Brunswick …'

Where the stretch between Fredericton and Sussex was the worst piece of Trans-Canada Frank had ever encountered. Slow, narrow, twisting, dangerous. Lose an hour there. Lose … Think of coffee. Pray. Make up the hour here, on the fast Montreal-Quebec City autoroute, edge the speed up to 130 km/h. At that speed, the Sûreté patrols ignored you, left you standing as they headed for the next doughnut outlet. So said folklore – the reality might be different.

Drummondville, then an hour or so later Quebec City across the river, magnificent in the early light. Past Montmagny, La Pocatière, St-Jean-Port-Joli, and Jonathan fascinated by the long thin fields stretching away from the river, an essential part of Quebec history. At Rivière du Loup they stopped for gas, coffee, and the toilet. The boys had been so good, Frank couldn't resist a chocolate bar for each. Then inland, over the hills toward the New Brunswick border.

'Watch the signs, Jonathan. There's a great name coming up. See if you can guess the one I mean. A really funny name.'

'Is it funny in French or in English?'

'In both, I guess.'

A Quebec dilemma.

On a whim, he stopped the car and photographed the boys in front of the sign for St-Louis-du-Ha! Ha!

'St-Louis-du-Ha! Ha!?' cried Simon. 'That's crazy. What a crazy name, St-Louis-du-Ha! Ha! That's the most ridiculous ...'

'Why did they call it that, Dad? Why don't they change it?'

'I'm not sure, but the story I heard is that the "Ha! Ha!" is the sound of a loon calling.'

'What's a loon?'

'Well ...'

They chatted away the miles to New Brunswick and into the Saint John River valley. After a burger near Grand Falls, Simon fell asleep again. As they neared Fredericton, increasing cloud cooled the car. Simon woke up needing a pee, a drink, and obviously some more activity.

'Can you wait five minutes, Simon?'

'I think so, Dada.'

Frank crossed the bridge over the Saint John River; following the east bank, they found a safe layby next to a willow-bordered meadow. Here the boys went behind a bush, sipped their juices, and they all played catch with a tennis ball. Although Frank was anxious to get on the road, he thought the boys deserved half an hour. But after barely fifteen minutes, Jonathan glanced at his watch and said they should be going. When Simon agreed, Frank shrugged, and they got back in the car.

As he expected, Frank found construction and slow traffic on the 120 kilometres to Sussex; the stretch took nearly two hours.

Under dramatic clouds – in sunshine and in shadow – they came to the Nova Scotia border with its elaborate gardens and large welcome centre. Frank was surprised to find himself elated as he parked the car.

'They'll likely have clean toilets here, guys, and I can put some coffee in my cup,' he said, but he knew he wanted them to share his excitement: we're in Nova Scotia, we're home. My home, genetically half your home. In the floral garden, the piper was playing a set, and he took the boys across to listen, to be photographed with the piper, with the Nova Scotia and Canada flags bright behind them.

Jonathan was mildly curious; Simon quickly bored, asking for the ball or the Frisbee.

Why not, they're Quebecers.

Rather: they live in Quebec.

Where no Canadian flags fly at the welcome centres.

But let them learn about all that on their own.

For an hour after Amherst the Trans-Canada offers little but occasional hilltop views of rolling spruce forest. Jonathan drifted into sleep. With a full coffee cup, CBC classical music, and good road, Frank edged the speedometer up a tad and made good time to Truro. Neither boy saw the big sign announcing Cape Breton straight ahead, exit for Halifax. No matter. In the humming peace of the car, Frank drove east toward New Glasgow.

Frank had been born and brought up in New Glasgow. His parents had both been schoolteachers and their home life had been pleasant, with two salaries, a large house with glistening, wax-redolent hardwood floors, a wide staircase, and bay windows. They lived in a friendly neighbourhood where during the summer the sun always shone and during the winter snow-covered streets offered sledding every day. John Wilson, a math and science teacher, had served in the air force during the war, teaching navigation at various bases on the Prairies. Although there had apparently been plans of bringing baby Frank and his mother west, nothing came of it, and the father missed the first few years with his only child. When the war was over, both parents were in their thirties. No more children came.

Kate, Frank's mother, was from the vestigially Gaelic village of Tobermory on the west coast of Cape Breton. With her Highland and Island insouciance, she made the home gay with laughter, music, friends. Her quirky sense of humour and musical inclination seemed to have bypassed Frank and Jonathan and had come down to Simon; the Hatcher family had certainly not provided the humour genes for either, and even Emma's humour often had an edge to it.

Unlike their neighbours who built summer cottages at nearby Chance Harbour or Merigomish, Frank's parents built on a piece of waterfront property on Tobermory harbour, Kate's legacy from her parents. For nearly two months every summer they moved to Cape

Breton, where Kate feasted on lobster and salmon, dragged John to square dances and ceilidhs. She made sure everyone knew her son, often taking him along when she visited. Frank, shy but athletic enough, made some friends, and, while his mother gossiped over tea, explored barns and meadows, played for the village baseball team, bicycled to beaches where the local boys swam. John worked methodically, steadily on the cottage, plumbing it, wiring it, adding another bedroom, winterizing it, building a fireplace, a veranda, planting and tending the garden. By the time they took slightly early retirement in the seventies, their home was ready for them. Their pensions, savings, and the sale of the house in New Glasgow were to guarantee what the sellers of annuities call their 'golden age'.

Within three years, John suffered the first of the strokes, and Kate developed uterine cancer. What wealth they had gathered financed their years in serviced retirement homes, in chronic-care clinics, in intensive care. When they died, too soon to see their grandchildren, almost everything was gone but the house and the few acres of waterfront.

Distance, lack of money, work, and the insistent invitations to the Hatchers' place on Lake Massawippi kept Frank and Emma away from Cape Breton two summers out of three. But Frank kept up the taxes and the insurance and sporadically spent a few weeks painting, puttying, repointing, carpenting, mowing, mending fences. The herbaceous border was soon overwhelmed by bush, the garden perennials by weeds. Twice they rented the place out to tourists, and once over the winter to a teacher, but the complications of arrangements and taxes along with the repairs meant they barely broke even. Although Emma enjoyed Tobermory and the beach, enjoyed being free of her parents, she had spent most of each visit on the deck with her typewriter and stacks of books and photocopies.

Jonathan awoke as they approached New Glasgow. Frank considered showing the boys his childhood home, but they would not likely be interested. As the cool of the late afternoon, the cool of ocean air made the car really comfortable, Simon came awake. He seemed inclined to sing, so they had a contest, each singing in turn.

'Do we have to stop again, Dad?' asked Jonathan, lifting his head from the map.

'Just for some groceries and gas.'

'Will it take long?'

'Ten or twenty minutes perhaps. There's a mall just by the highway in Antigonish.'

'In what?'

Frank helped them learn to pronounce it. Simon thought it a hilarious name.

'But it isn't as funny as St-Louis-de-Ha! Ha!' said Jonathan.

'I didn't say it was, you camel patty.'

'I didn't say you did, you rhinoceros dung.'

They pulled into the mall at ten to seven, and although Frank would have preferred getting on quickly, he admitted to himself that he couldn't realistically get food on the table at home before eight-thirty. And if there was some problem with the water or power ... The boys were happy enough to eat pizza, and they were done in half an hour. Then groceries, a case of beer and two bottles of white, a tank of gas. They were away, Jonathan assured him, in forty-eight minutes.

Frank had kept up his acquaintance with some of the boyhood baseball and swimming friends. One of them, Angus MacDonald, kept an eye on the house for him, made sure the repair and utility bills were paid, and forwarded mail. Twice the house was burgled, but the damage was not worth claiming from the insurance. A portable radio, a toaster oven, a shaving kit, half a bottle of rum stolen; dishes broken; the carpet soiled with excrement; the door to fix; black-and-white TV tossed into the bushes. Better than cottagers had a right to expect. Then a young couple built a house across the road and Frank chopped down a few trees so they had a good view of his place. He made a sign for the kitchen window: 'No booze here – I drank it all.' There had been no burglaries since.

Every few months Angus forwarded offers to buy the place – locals, locals coming home from away to retire, couples from Halifax, Americans. When the earlier car had died, when the children were born, Frank had been tempted to sell, but Emma invoked the real estate adage that God wasn't making any more beachfront. Now

Frank was grateful for her stubbornness, though he wasn't quite sure why. Extended summers were impossible, given the boys' activities and friends. And his sense of Tobermory was surely artificial, a memory gilded by childhood, an idealization, an amusing Gaelic vestige straight out of *Whisky Galore*. Wouldn't the Quebec nationalists smirk, sneer, rage at this contemptible folkloric quaintness. But the reality of life in Cape Breton was tough, he knew, yet redolent in twinings, flowerings of life he sensed but couldn't measure. Even if he wanted to retire here, he could not stop working until the boys were at least in university and preferably graduated. Until then – fifteen and more years away – he would try to keep it up. Yet he found himself thinking more and more of Tobermory as a refuge, a bolt-hole. As home.

Some kilometres past Antigonish Frank found some fiddle music on the radio and told the boys, 'That's the sound of home, guys. And I'm not just sure when we'll get to it, but out the left side of the car we'll soon see our first view of Cape Breton.'

'How will we know it's Cape Breton, Dad?'

'It's a view over five miles or so of forest, then twenty-thirty miles of water. What's that, thirty-forty kilometres? Anyway, we see the hills behind Creignish and away in the distance the islands off Port Hood. And even if it's cloudy here, the sun will be shining away off there.' This had been a family tradition from the time the new road was built and this long view opened to travellers. It was surprising how often it was true. And today was no exception, with cloud above, but golden haze off to the northwest toward PEI, and sunlight dappling the hills and islands of Cape Breton. The view disappeared for ten or fifteen minutes, then Cape Breton came into view again, as they topped each hill, as they drew closer and closer to the Canso Causeway that would take them across.

When a long beige four-door overtook him, Frank recognized it with a shock of nostalgia. Not the car itself, of course, but the type, the occupants, the situation. His father and mother had defined it for him in their casual comments over the years. These were Cape Bretoners who had left Sydney, Glace Bay, Inverness, or Arichat, their own movie *Goin' Down the Road*, Jayne Eastwood and Doug ...?

Doug something and the other guy, like these people in the car ahead, setting off to Toronto to find work, a future, a family, a house; but those people years ago and these people, unlike the characters in the movie, returning home, birds of passage that summer and this summer, with two or three kids and, oddly, at least three adults squeezing out the maximum home time by driving in shifts nonstop from Oshawa, Windsor, Sudbury, Thunder Bay, Lloydminster, Grande Prairie, Edmonton. In his youth some had had Michigan or Massachusetts plates – tighter green cards had stopped that.

And this beige four-door was one of them, Ontario plates, low to the ground with six people, a full trunk, luggage rack on the roof, pulling away at 140 to 150 km/h....

'Two and a half days from Timmins, bye,' his mother would imitate, 'and only one ticket, the effin' OPPs just east of North Bay, buggers nailed us comin' off of dis long straight ...' and Frank felt a lump in his throat, remembering his mother's bright comedy, her deadly mimicry, thinking at the same time of the Cape Bretoners away from home for the jobs, coming home for family, for the air, the dances, the rum that only tasted right in the salt air off the North Atlantic ... coming home.

Might it ever be home for him?

Never for the boys, certainly – they might choose Arty's Quebec, learning to pass, learning to dodge and weave through the nuisances of a language and culture determined not to become vestigial; or might choose anything anywhere if they did well enough at university, exploiting one of their obvious talents, math, computers for Jonathan, music, athletics, who knows, for Simon.

They would choose their own homes.

But for him?

Home?

Perhaps.

In fifteen years.

The boys caught some of the excitement as they came down the long hill to Auld's Cove with the Causeway before them, curving under the great naked rock cliff on the mainland side, then across, with the gulls bickering above the rhythmic pht-pht-pht of the guardrail posts, the briny air filling the car.

'See the bridge ahead, guys? It's over a canal and it swings aside so ships can go through.'

'Will one go through now?'

'Let's hope not – we could lose twenty minutes.'

Up the hill to the roundabout. Some traffic took the first exit toward Port Hawkesbury, the rest took the Trans-Canada toward Sydney and the Newfoundland ferries, while only Frank curled round to Highway 19, the road up the west coast. Forty minutes now, and he was wondering if Angus had thought to put any water in the ice cube trays – a beer chilled twenty minutes in an ice bucket would go down well after he had unpacked the car and got the boys to bed.

'There's a boat, Dad. What kind of boat is it?'

'It's called a Cape Islander, I believe. It's a Nova Scotia fishing boat, and you'll see lots of Cape Islanders around Tobermory.'

'Can we perhaps go for a ride on one sometime?'

'Perhaps we can arrange it. I'll have to ask around. Oh, look, see that embankment running along there? That's where the train track used to be.'

'Did they have passenger trains?'

'Yes, a long time ago.'

'Did you ever go on that train, Dad?'

'My mother told me I did once or twice during the War, but I don't remember it. It's supposed to have been one of the most scenic train trips in Canada outside of the Rockies and perhaps the north shore of Lake Superior....'

Meanwhile, they still had the road and Frank was surprised again how much he was moved by the view, by the memories.... Home? Surely not, surely this was the most blatant sentimentality – the hills on the right, the sun westering across the water to the left, everything in the golden glow of a summer's evening. The scenery was all very well, and the *Whisky Galore* comedy was not imaginary, but the larger reality of life here was, for most, those long cars, low to the road, coming home from away where there was work....

Still, it is beautiful, enjoy it for itself...

Through the final twenty miles, Simon sucked his thumb patiently.

Jonathan was curious about the scenery, the ubiquitous satellite dishes outside the houses, the distance signs.

'Will it get to 1500 kilometres, Dad?'

Frank did a quick estimate.

'No, thank heavens. Look up ahead – at that crossroad there's probably a sign for Tobermory and it might have the distance.'

The village looked idyllic in the falling twilight. Home of a sort, at least, and forget reality for a few weeks.

'Fourteen hundred and sixty-nine kilometres, Dad!'

'And how long?'

'Sixteen hours and forty-two minutes. That's with adding the extra hour because of Atlantic Time.'

'Tell you what, you come on in and if the lights are working you can fix up your trip log. I've got to get the car unpacked and see about Simon.'

An hour later, the boys were happily, amazingly in bed, and Frank was seated on the front deck with a cold beer gazing at the stars above the harbour. They had made it.

If only Emma ...

Vacation

After breakfast they had a swim, then drove off to buy some of the last strawberries at the U-pick up the valley. Swimming again in the afternoon, as the boys learned that it was even more fun when the water didn't lap on tiled edges, tasted of salt rather than chlorine, was home to jellyfish and minnows. Paddling along with mask and snorkel, Jonathan stopped suddenly.

'Dad, Dad, I saw some sort of fish maybe, but it was like a snake. Is it a snake? Is it dangerous?'

'It's an eel, Jonathan, and it's not dangerous. It's more afraid of you than you are of it.'

Simon collected shells and pretty stones. Frank pointed out an eagle soaring by, and a kingfisher cackling and diving. When Jonathan asked about the charred remains of driftwood on the beach, Frank said, 'Some of the kids from the village probably came down one evening to roast wieners over a bonfire.'

'Can we please have a bonfire, Dad? And make hot dogs?'

'Sure we can.'

'Tonight?'

'Tonight if you like.'

So they fell into the easy routine of beach life, swimming in front of the house, and at the big ocean beaches beyond the harbour mouth. They did a bit of sightseeing, though only for an hour or so because the boys were not long interested. Jonathan was intrigued to be shown, from the top of a hill by the ocean, the low dark line of Prince Edward Island beneath the setting sun. At home, he got out a map and determined that PEI was more than fifty kilometres away.

'That's really far, Dad. Is that the farthest I've ever seen anything? I mean on the earth. Not like stars and the moon.'

'Must be nearly. Though do you remember seeing the mountains from the lookout at the top of Westmount? Those mountains were in Vermont or New York. They might be farther.'

Jonathan got the Quebec map and decided the mountains were farther.

When rain came one afternoon, Frank tempted them from the television Cup with the boxes of games, still in the same closet they'd been in when he was young. Sometimes they played together and sometimes Frank played alone with Simon while Jonathan went through the bird book to identify which birds he would like to spot.

'Well, how about the American bittern, Dad? The map says it should live here.'

'Read what it says about the bittern's habits.'

'"Common but very shy, the bittern in ... habits swamps and ..."'

'Look, Dada, I just rolled five and I'm way up this ladder. So there's only one more snake to get past and I'll win, yea!'

Although he had no immediate family, Frank knew he had in the neighbourhood numerous relatives whose relationship to himself he but slightly understood; and which the relatives themselves would understand quite well. From his mother's example, Frank realized protocol suggested he visit and present the boys. He remembered some of the names, sometimes a wife's name but not the husband's, remembered some of the houses. Properly done, with all possible visits, it would mean no swimming, no shell collecting, no bird watching. Could he visit a few of them without offending the others? Whatever he did, however, he would have to visit Sarah Ann, called Aunt Sal, but actually his mother's cousin, thus his own second cousin. She would advise him.

In the meantime, he called Angus to thank him for preparing the house and assured him all was well. Angus promised he'd drop in one day.

'Late mornings are best if you can manage it.'

As he was hanging up, Frank said, 'Well, we'll see you when we see you, Angus Rory Mor.'

'You may have been born away, Frank, but you're still from Tobermory.'

Frank was immensely pleased.

Angus arrived the next morning as they were coming up the hill from the beach.

'Kimera-how, Angus.'

'Ha-goh-ma, Frank. M vail gahlic acah?'

'I know what the question means, but I don't have enough Gaelic even to answer "No." You still have the tongue?'

'Och, I'm after forgetting the most of it.'

Angus's parents had been Gaelic speakers ... and the nationalists crying, *You see? You see?*

'And who are these big fellows?'

After the introductions, Frank got Jonathan settled on the deck with the bird book and binoculars, while Simon sat hunched over his video game.

'How's she going, boy? Everything working? I wasn't sure about the fridge, the compressor sounded cranky when I started her up.'

'No, no trouble, the fridge is fine, everything's fine. Come on in. Can I get you a coffee?'

He and Angus settled at the shady table with their mugs, and fell into an easy chat about the view, the house, the water, the boys, Angus's children and wife, the new houses in the village, the new fire hall, and the taxes and other bills, and arranged for one of Angus's children to do some painting. After a bit Angus said he had to see someone about a calf – he worked for the agriculture department – and they walked round to his half-ton.

'So how are things in Quebec?' Angus asked.

'Ohh ... all right, I guess. Ordinary people – French and English – are pretty much the same anywhere, I expect. In Quebec, ordinary people get along pretty well.'

'You speak French, don't you?'

'Not as well as you speak Gaelic, I suspect. I get by. I rarely notice the signs or what language I'm speaking in the supermarket, the bank, stores ... As everyone says, it's not Sarajevo.'

Despite the best efforts of the nationalists – politicians, intellectuals, bureaucrats, journalists – to poison the lives of ordinary folk, poison the buzz and clank of the workplace, the discourse of neighbours, the raising of children, poison the very air ...

'I must admit,' said Angus, 'I don't understand it at all, at all.'

'I sometimes wonder if anyone does....'

So much of it illusion, all the readings of history, of the present, of the future ... so full of lies, wishful thinking, distortions, perversions of truth ... an ordinary fellow hasn't the time or the inclination or the ability to sort it out.

'As for me, Angus, I've got a job, a mortgage, and two boys to raise, so I'm just trying to get on with my life. And to forget ... all that while I'm here.'

'I'll remember next time.'

'Don't worry about it. It's important to the whole country, but you asked a guy who knows nothing.'

'Well, enjoy your vacation. I'll drop in again before you go.'

'Ahh, I just remembered something – the boys asked me if I could arrange a little boat trip. You wouldn't know anyone who could take us out for an hour or so? Are they fishing just now?'

'They're crabbing this month, but, och, someone will take you out, I'm sure. Let me talk to my cousin Dan Archie ... I don't know if you know him, but ...'

Frank waved Angus out the lane, and rejoined the boys.

'Dad, Dad, what's that bird, quick, it's looking for fish, I think, see, there ...'

The bird flapped at a deliberate speed across the inlet. Not as big as an eagle, dark above, very light below, leading edge of the wings crooked, wings arched. Suddenly the bird hovered on flapping wings, then dived feet first, hit the water and soon was aloft again.

'The bird has a fish, Dad, see, isn't that a fish in its claws?'

'The bird caught a fish!' cried Simon.

'Yes, it has a fish, and I think you've spotted a fairly special bird. I think, let's see ...'

He leafed quickly to the section.

'Here, it's on this page, see if you can tell which one it is.'

'Is it ... is it an osprey?'

'Yes, it's an osprey! Congratulations, Jonathan!'

The excitement carried them through lunch. Of course, Jonathan wanted to spend the afternoon waiting for more special birds to fly by the deck, but Frank suggested he might like to try for some birds of fields, gardens and woody edges.

'Where?' suspiciously.

'Well, I wanted to visit a cousin of my mother – I always called her Aunt Sal. She always has a great garden so there are lots of birds around her house.'

The boys were doubtful.

'Tell you what, we'll go this evening, after dinner, and we don't have to stay long.'

'Can we stay here and swim this afternoon?'

'Yes. And Aunt Sal has always been famous for her cakes and cookies.'

'Okay, Dada.'

'Jonathan?'

'Okay, Dad.'

Aunt Sal's husband, Albert, had been a fairly prosperous farmer up the valley. When he became too frail to carry on, and because their children had all moved away, they sold the farm and moved into a small house in a charming dell. Here, Aunt Sal devoted herself to her garden, to baking, and to genial gossip. If anyone could prove Tobermory was *Whisky Galore*, Aunt Sal could. But she would know the Tobermory of *Goin' Down the Road* as well.

When, that evening, they pulled into her driveway, Aunt Sal was gardening. From the bits he had done in his own small front and back yards, Frank could see at once that Aunt Sal was diligent, talented, and patient: it was a fine Victorian border.

'Well, hello, stranger. And who are these quiet little boys? Vexed at your father for dragging you out to see a silly old woman you couldn't care less about, right? You'd rather be swimming, I bet, or playing with one of those Nintendo games, wouldn't you? I don't blame you. Fathers have no business dragging kids away from the fun to eat cake and cookies in a stupid garden. Now this must be Jonathan the math whiz, so this is Simon the singer. If I play the piano for you, will you sing me a song? Of course you don't want to, why should you? And I see Jonathan has a bird book and binoculars. Well, if you come around the side here, I think we might just see the hummingbirds coming to the feeder. And after that ...'

The boys were shown the nectar feeder and the hiding place. The hummingbirds would keep them for fifteen minutes.

'Sit down, Frank, and let me catch up on you while we have time. I'll make tea later, but I suppose you're a coffee drinker ...'

'Whatever's going is fine.'

'Well, you've kept your waistline, if nothing else. You could have rinsed the grey out of your hair, though, you make me feel my age.'

'I'll remember next time.'

'Don't be solemn, Frank, you're too much like your father, a dear, good man, but awful serious. And your mother – well, they were like apples and oranges. But they were happy, don't you think?'

'I believe they were.'

'Yes, of course you'd never have known if they weren't – your father would never show it, and your mother would hide it behind her joking. But I think they really were happy. I'm not surprised he died so soon after her, like the light going out in his life it must have been. But your wife, Frank – well, what can a person say? No words make up for that. You must miss her terribly.'

'Yes.'

'I only met your Emma the once, that time you brought her up to the farm, but she was really something. A real lady, and smart as a whip. And a natural charm, eh? You could sense so much going on beneath the surface, but she didn't make you feel stupid for not knowing what it was – just easy and graceful. Now, how are you getting along on your own, with the boys, I mean? Just fine from the look of them ...'

Aunt Sal kept up a steady line of chat, questions, jokes, qualifications, reassurances. When the boys tired of the humming-bird, Aunt Sal pointed them to the brook that ran along the back of the garden.

'Can you tiptoe, Simon? Show me. And can you be quiet as a mouse? Well then, let's us tiptoe to the little bridge there and we'll look very carefully down toward the pool and maybe we'll see some frogs. And sometimes there's a muskrat comes up from the river below....'

She was gone five minutes. Frank walked along the garden edge. He didn't know the name of one flower in ten. The border girdled the lawn, easily a hundred yards in all, and all carefully weeded. Every section had flowers in bloom, so that it seemed especially a summer display. But on closer inspection, he saw that others, the finished spring flowers were equally spread throughout; and that late summer and autumn blooms were on the way. She had varied the height, the sizes of the blooms, carefully chosen the colours. It was a masterpiece.

'They'll be happy for a while,' she said, linking his arm. 'We'll take a turn the rest of the way round, then we'll go into the kitchen and you can sit in the window and keep an eye on the boys. I suppose they keep you busy here?'

'Yes, but other parents tell me they're easy compared with some. We manage. Angus Rory Mor is trying to arrange a trip on a fishing boat for them.'

'That'll be with his cousin, Dan Archie. They're crabbing these days. Don't be too disappointed if nothing comes of it.'

'How are things for the fishermen with the codfishing stopped?'

'The ones with crab licences are doing all right, I hear. Lobster still does well, and there's been big money for tuna the last few years – the Japanese are paying fortunes for tuna. Of course, they all say things are terrible, but that's just their way. They're afraid you might have friends in the tax department.'

'Well, if it happens, the boys ought to enjoy it. If it doesn't, well, we have our beach.'

'They tell me they both swim – isn't it something, a little fellow like Simon swimming? – but you can't be too careful when they're around water, can you? Every few years a little one around here falls in and drowns. Fishing in the spring, or through the ice in the winter.' She mentioned several names. 'Of course, the roads are much worse. Kids on bikes hit by pulp trucks or drunks. Then they get to be teenagers, and get drinking and the next thing they're over a cliff or into the trees or ... But you don't want to hear about car accidents do you? I hear it was all over in a moment, Frank, that she never knew what happened to her?'

'That's what they told me.' He related what he knew.

'My, oh, my,' she said. 'The things that happen to people. If He had to take a woman, why didn't He take me instead of her? Eh? You can't help wondering, but it doesn't do to dwell on it, does it? You have to grieve, but you mustn't let it weigh you down. Those hollyhocks, I planted them in memory of your mother, she loved hollyhocks, about the only thing she ever grew besides pansies. She was a great gal, Kate, the life of the party, but a gardener she wasn't, your father planted most of that garden, and he didn't have enough time to make much of it, and your mother was … well, let's say she was an original gardener. Do you remember the time I gave her the bulbs and she planted half of them right-side-up and the rest upside-down? Said she wanted to give them a chance to grow up whatever way they wanted! Can you imagine? But the truth was she didn't know which way was up, so she figured she'd get half of them right no matter what. Oh, she was some character, she was. A bit ditzy, as they say. The times we had … And when she and John retired here, I thought it would be just like our school days together again. But then … well, aren't I gloomy tonight. Well, when you're my age you'll find most of your old pals are looking at the flowers from the root end. Now, enough of that. If you'll just help me up the steps there, we'll go in and make tea.…'

The house was small and Dickensian in its layout, its odd doors and windows, its clutter.

'Don't mind the mess. I wasn't expecting company, and the truth is I wouldn't have tidied up even for the minister.'

Frank sat on the bench in the window nook. The boys were still tiptoeing about near the brook, pointing and craning their necks.

'I've been wondering, Aunt Sal – do you think I could live in Tobermory?'

'With two boys to bring up? Not without a private income to support you. You'd never find work. Any job going anywhere on the island of Cape Breton goes to a relative, or to someone who has been in continuous residence for five generations at the least. Unless it's government work, and there you have to be a supporter of the party that's in. That's both federal and provincial. A supporter for ten years at least, and even then the lineups are as long as your arm.'

'That's about what I expected to hear. What about if the boys were in university and I had a pension?'

'Ohh, well, of course. Just you remember, though, that you were only here in the summertime. The winters aren't cold like what you get in Montreal, though we get ice storms, too, now and then, but it takes forever for spring to arrive, and sometimes it doesn't arrive till the third week of September. It's a lovely place in many ways, but paradise it isn't. And not while you've got the boys to bring up. Even if you could get work, it wouldn't really be fair to them. They'd likely be fine, but the city has so much more to offer them. See, for all the fun they have, it's hard on the kids. It's fine when they're growing up and like the out-of-doors, but when they get to be teenagers and the hormone storms sweep through them, all they want are the bright lights and the discos. Mind you, most of them are really decent kids – Tobermory people are mostly good family people. If they can stick to the books and get away to university, they've got it made – as much as any young people have these days, even with university. But you know all that better than I do. Others, if they're keen on a good trade – carpentry or plumbing or fishing – they make it through, and they can usually make a decent life for themselves. We could use a good electronics repair man around here, for example. Your TV or VCR breaks down around here, you have to take it Hawkesbury or Antigonish or maybe Halifax. Fellow who could repair TVs could make a decent living. And a bit extra if he could make illegal decoders for the people with the satellite dishes. I hear that's a growth market.'

'I'm afraid my only skill is telling people about Jane Austen.'

'Elizabeth Bennet! Oh my, there's a girl for you. But what's brought all this on, Frank? You aren't really crazy enough to want to leave a job in Montreal and come here?'

'When I retire, perhaps. There's the house, the beach, and I know some people.'

'In fifteen years' time? I hope you're not expecting me to wait around until you retire? I'll be long gone by then.'

Aunt Sal placed the last tray of the immense feast upon the table and set the tea to steep. While she waited, she sat with her head cocked and studied him.

'I expect that separatism business is getting you down.'

'I'm just tired of having to think about it. Tired trying not to think about it.'

'Yes, I can imagine. Well, I can't imagine, but I can guess. Yes, well, you call the boys and I'll pour the tea.'

After the boys had stuffed themselves on the four kinds of cookies,

two kinds of cake, three kinds of squares, and two kinds of sandwiches, and had washed it all down with a pitcher of lime juice – a
specialty of Aunt's Sal's these many years – and had gone to the toilet, they were obviously ready for bed. Aunt Sal turned on the porch
light and Frank helped Simon with his seat belt. As he stood by the
open driver's door, he tried to find words to express his happiness.

'It's been … a real pleasure.'

'Never mind, Frank. I'm glad you came and brought the boys to
see me.'

'It looks so idyllic,' waving at the garden, the cosy house.

'Come back in December. The sun doesn't get over the hill there
for two months. But it'll see me out.'

'I'll come again before we leave.'

She mentioned three other relatives he might visit, but said she'd
make excuses if he didn't.

'Well …'

They hugged, he started the car, and they headed home in the
deep twilight. Simon was asleep before they crossed the embankment where the railway used to be.

Boat

At nine-thirty in the morning, the fishing done for the day, a dozen boats were tied up at the sheltering U-shaped dock of Tobermory Harbour Mouth. Angus stood talking to a beefy red-headed man in overalls and rubber boots. A girl and a boy sat on a cleat and watched as Frank parked the car in the shadow of the lighthouse. He took the picnic cooler and the beach bag from the trunk.

'Okay, guys, and don't forget your hats.'

Frank was relaxed with Aunt Sal, Angus, and half a dozen more; with other people in Tobermory he usually felt uneasy. His bookish ways were no preparation for their intensely physical lives, their relaxed and efficient movements, their languid, curling banter. But Angus's cousin Dan Archie Gillis greeted him warmly then tousled the hair of the boys.

'Are yez wanting to catch some crabs, now?' he asked them.

'All right,' Jonathan replied.

'I love crab!' cried Simon, and Dan Archie hefted him high in the air.

'But what if the crabs love you? You're not afraid they might eat you? Eat you all up? Eh?'

'I'm not afraid!'

'Good boy yourself.'

Angus called his own children over and introduced them – ten-year-old Brittany and six-year-old Sean. Clearly, the old Scottish names were as out of fashion as they were in Westmount or the West Island.

'Are you coming along too, Angus?' Frank asked.

'No, no summer holidays for country folk.'

After the courtesies, Angus drove off and Dan Archie said he had to see about something in the shed, a large recent building with government brag signs by the door.

'I have a friend in Montreal and his name is Sean,' said Simon, 'and he has Nintendo64 and he lets me play sometimes. I don't have Nintendo64. Do you have Nintendo64?'

'Yeah, we got it for Christmas last year.'

'Cool! Do you have GoldenEye?'

'Yeah, it's some great! But my favourite is Ten-eighty Snow-boarding.'

'Wow, I heard about …'

Simon, as usual, would be fine. In five minutes he would be begging to visit Sean.

Jonathan eyed the girl shyly, but she took up the slack, asking if he had ever been out on a boat before. Jonathan mentioned the Hatchers' speedboat.

'Papa was teasing your brother. But we are going to try to catch crabs. But there mightn't be any in the pots.'

Jonathan looked disappointed, even though he had been told it was just a pleasure cruise.

'They're kind of messy to clean,' she said. 'Papa gets up at three-thirty. I'm sure not going to be a fisherman.'

So they were all right.

'Dad, Dad, some day can I go over to Sean's place? Please, Dad, please?'

'We'll see.'

Dan Archie returned, carrying a small black box with coloured wires dangling from it. Two men arose from their crates by the shed and followed slowly.

'It's getting so's a fellow can't take a few fish without enough navigation equipment for the space shuttle,' he said. 'What's going on here? I tought youse'd all be in the boat with your life jackets on. Are we going out today or are we waiting for Christmas?'

Nonetheless, he made them stay on the wharf until he was in the boat and could help them down the ladder. He gave them life vests and made sure each was properly secured. 'Now do yez have your suntan lotion on? Sean, if you get a sunburn today, I'll be sleeping in the barn tonight.'

When the low throb of the engine settled into a regular beat, Dan Archie looked to the two onlookers; the man on the bow-line cast away. With one hand playing between the gearshift and the throttle and the other spinning the wheel, Dan Archie warped the bow away from the wharf and in a few moments had it neatly turned about; the man on the stern cast away and they were heading out the opening into the channel. A small dinghy skipped along behind.

'Frank,' Dan Archie called from the wheel, 'can yez let out some line on the dinghy, about twenty feet or so?'

The children watched in jealous awe as Frank performed this test of high seas skill; indeed, he had the sense to examine the knot first and tied the same one when he was done.

'Before we go any further, I'm the captain and that means I'm the boss, so yez have to do whatever I say. Do yez understand that?'

The children all nodded solemnly.

'Good. Now there's only one big rule here – keep both feet on the deck. If you keep both feet on the deck, yez can't get drownded. Do yez understand that, now?'

The children nodded.

'Then who wants to see where we're going?'

All the kids did.

'Then come on up here and look.'

The two oldest clambered onto the side benches, while Dan Archie lifted Sean and Simon in the crook of his arms and still managed to handle the wheel.

'Can't a fellow get no help around here? What am I holding you two for but to steer? Grab aholt of the wheel and keep her steady. Mind you don't run her aground....'

They entered the surprisingly deep swell of the harbour mouth.

'See how fast the current is flowing past, then look at the shore and see how fast we're going. Tide's coming in, you see, and the natural harbour flow is out. Who knows what the tide is? How many high tides a day are there?'

Frank knew Dan Archie came from a large family – perhaps that explained some of his naturalness with children. Some. The rest was just Dan Archie.

'Papa, who lives in that house?' Brittany asked.

The house was the last one on the road, isolated near the end of the headland. Three children stood in the field below the house, shading their eyes against the sun and waving.

'That's where Mary Catherine McIvor lives, she's some relative of your mother's. You go out where they can see yez and give them a wave back.' He turned to Frank with a twinkle. 'Around town they call her Saturday Night Live. She's building what you call your mixed paternity family.'

'Likes kids, does she?'

'That's one way of putting it.'

Beyond the last channel marker the swell abated. Dan Archie changed course to starboard, heading north along the cliffs of Cape Tobermory.

'Frank, you'd best go out there with them. There's no sea at all, but kids can get into trouble some fast in a boat.'

Frank went back and sat on the stern deck. The children watched the water, the waves, the sky, the cliffs. Jonathan pointed out a pair of long-necked black birds flying fast and low.

'Brittany says they're called "shag" but there's no shag in the book.'

'People around here call them shag. In the book they're called cormorants.'

'Can you eat them?'

'Brittany, have you ever heard of anyone eating them?'

'No, Papa says you can't eat shag.'

'Yes, I think they only eat fish, so their flesh probably has a fishy taste.'

'They're going home to their nests,' said Brittany. 'They have hundreds of nests on a cliff and Papa says we're going to see it after. It's called the shag roost. I saw it last summer, but you'll see it in a while.'

Presently Dan Archie hailed them.

'See what's coming up ahead, there.'

The children followed his gesture, rushed to the port side and craned forward. Frank joined them. Dan Archie changed course slightly to port. Presently Frank saw what was meant – three low, arching black shapes rising above the surface, and falling again.

Brittany saw them first: 'Black fish!'

Suddenly a plume of water spurted from one of the humps.

'A whale, Dada,' cried Jonathan, 'is it a whale?'

'It's a whale, right enough,' Dan Archie confirmed. 'We call them black fish, but whales is what they are, pilot whales, so you're both right.'

'Whales, Dada!' cried Simon, 'whales!' Life had for once triumphed over television.

Dan Archie cut back to near idling speed, and all watched as the humps rose and fell in their long rhythms, listened to the whoosh as they spouted. Frank remembered just in time to reach for the camera.

Not long after the whales passed into the distance, they came to the shag roost, a colony of several hundred nests tucked onto ledges of the cliff. Birds were coming and going, diving, preening, squawking. Dan Archie brought the boat within forty feet of the rocks, circled a few times, then slowly pulled away. After five minutes, he throttled the engine back.

'Frank, can you take the wheel a bit?'

He gave Frank a brief description of the controls, and pointed to a white-and-red float bobbing ahead.

'Bring her alongside and throttle right back to here. When I've hooked her put her in neutral like this and I'll pull the pot. Whatever you do, don't let her arse swing round to the rope or we'll have the line around the propeller shaft. But if that does happen when she's in gear, throw her in neutral right quick.'

They managed, not with any elegance, but without mishap. Dan Archie attached the line to a small power winch and soon swung the bell-shaped cage to the gunwale, retrieved four crabs, baited the pot, then heaved it over the side.

'By Jaysus, we'll make a fisherman of you yet, bye. Now give her some throttle and make for that one over there. I figured this morning I'd leave three for lunch.'

When they had the third pot cleared, Dan Archie left Frank at the wheel, and told him to turn to starboard.

'You see that red cliff there, make for that ... a bit more juice ... there yez are.'

Dan Archie busied himself with the kids who were squealing over the crabs.

Just beyond the red cliff was a small beach, inaccessible except by boat or, as Jonathan suggested, the Westmount Fire Department with rappelling tackle. Dan Archie anchored in twenty feet of water, retrieved the dinghy, and rowed them in to the beach in shifts.

'You little ones can have a dip while we get your lunch ready. And don't be going too deep. Brittany and Jonathan, go over to those big rocks there and fill this bucket with mussels. Make sure they don't have too much seaweed onto 'em, and be careful because the rocks is as slick as oiled ice.'

Frank had brought sandwiches, wieners, buns, apples, carrots, celery, and cukes. Dan Archie produced a loaf of homemade style bread, some plastic containers, a pitted enamel pot, several tin pie plates, and a piece of plywood. He started a fire of drift wood, poured into the pot a few inches of water from a plastic jug, quartered an onion with his jackknife, then threw it in with some pepper. 'Can I steal a few sticks of carrots and celery?' These he chopped roughly and added.

When the foragers returned with the mussels, Dan Archie used the jackknife to clean the beards. When the water was boiling, he dropped in the crabs, then tipped the mussels around them.

'You've got a bruise on your leg, Jonathan – does it hurt? How did it happen?'

'On the rocks over there. It only hurts a little.'

'Good boy yourself,' said Dan Archie. 'It won't hurt you at all, at all.'

'It'll be a lot uglier than it feels.'

Simon had scraped his elbow getting into the dinghy, but with the example of his brother before him, it only hurt a little too.

'How will we know when the mussels and the crabs will be cooked?' Jonathan asked.

'Och, dey're helpful creatures – dey'll sing when they're done.'

Jonathan looked doubtfully at Frank.

'I expect we'll find out.'

Dan Archie covered the pot with the plywood and they laid out the food. The little.ones didn't need to be called.

They busied themselves with munchies and bread, opening and spilling drinks, and squealing, squabbling, and laughing. Every few minutes, Dan Archie gave the pot a few circular shakes. After ten minutes, he removed the plywood, tipped the pot on an angle, plucked out the mussels, and put them on a tin pie plate.

'Dere yez are, byes, you won't get mussels that fresh in Montreal. You let dem cool a minute, and yez'll have a feast yez can't buy anywheres.'

Frank finally realized that Dan Archie was heavily overplaying his Tobermory burr when he spoke to the children. Brittany and Sean each took a mussel shell in their fingertips, broke off one shell, and bit off the meat.

'Will I like mussels, Dada?'

'You'll love them.'

Soon all were eating.

When Dan Archie had the crabs on another pie plate, he broke off a piece of bread and dipped it into the juice.

'Now dere's a soup yez can't buy either. Yez can sop it up like dis, or yez can take a cup of it to drink, but don't stir up the sand from the bottom.'

The soup was also a success.

Dan Archie went at the crabs with his hands and jackknife, breaking the legs into segments and squeezing the meat out the end, and in a few minutes had a pile of cleaned crab meat on a pie plate. He flipped the top from an old margarine container.

'Dat's your Aunt Mary C's homemade mayonnaise. Watch ... do it like dis ...'

He dipped some meat into the mayonnaise, set it on a piece of bread, and popped it in his mouth.

'By Jaysus,' he said with eyes closed, 'don't talk to me about your economically depressed areas. Eh, Frank?'

Frank put some bread and crab in his mouth.

'It's ... I don't have the words for it ...'

While they packed up the picnic gear and the garbage, the children swam. Frank had suggested they go in as well, but Dan Archie demurred, saying he had things to do, though the chores seemed done. Then Frank remembered that Tobermory fishermen usually did not learn to swim. The reason, as he recalled, was superstition – as long as they could not swim, they would not be made to swim, their boats would never founder. He and Dan Archie strolled the beach.

'So you made her down in one day from Montreal, I hear. About seventeen hours, was it?'

Frank described the problems between Fredericton and Sussex.

'Tell you what, Frank, you get your map of New Brunswick and look for a road straight north from Moncton to a place called Renous, then straight west through the woods to Plaster Rock and Grand Falls. It's a good hundred K shorter and no traffic, saves almost two hours.'

'Thanks. I'll check the map and maybe give it a try.'

'I'll be going that way myself when the fishing is over, going to see my brother in Sarnia.'

'And how is the crab this season?' Frank asked.

'Och, I don't think I'll get my money out if it this year. Cost of the gear, the fuel, lost pots, low prices ...'

'I don't have any friends in the tax department. And I wouldn't talk if I did.'

Dan Archie patted him on the shoulder.

'In that case, I'm doing some good, and the tuna starts in a couple of weeks. When they slapped the quotas on the cod, we thought she was buggered good. The salmon berths is nearly gone, and they're not granting new ones, you see, and they've upped the size limit on the lobsters – well, everyone's whining about that but it makes sense – you can't be taking the chickens, the little ones, or there won't be any big ones. Och, it was crazy, the size of the ones they were taking. The crab aren't making us rich, but they mean you'll break even at least, and most are after making a profit.'

'Will it last?'

'Och, I don't know. Things'll change, I expect, but for better or worse – I don't know. At the worst, we can sell fresh locally, but frozen fish is what the big shippers wants, and the factory ships can pull the nets up into the stern, and the catch is cut, sized, packed, and frozen an hour later. We'll just have to wait and see what comes.'

'And if it ends, what'll you do?'

They stopped over a broken lobster pot half buried in the sand.

'Och, there's work around if you want it. I do carpentry, plumbing, some welding. I don't touch wiring, though, I'm not fussy about shocks. Haul pulp, haul gravel, get some road work if they'd get rid of this damn government, and you can usually find some pogey for month or two. A man can make a life of it if he's after being handy and doesn't ask for a golden gearshift.'

The children had dragged a great log into the water and were paddling it about. The men began to walk back.

'You can manage a life here, Dan Archie – I couldn't.'

'Not meaning anything, you know, I think you're right.'

'Specialized labour has to go to the specialized job.'

'Yes, and, you know, the cost of living is higher here. Not a house, mind, or land, but everything else. Back in the sixties, a lot of hippies tried to settle around here, but most had to give it up. You can build your own, but nails and tools and wiring and plumbing is all more dear than in Montreal or Toronto. Taxes is higher. You can grow your own food and freeze it, but power is way more expensive in Nova Scotia. And you can't get around without a car or a truck, and they're dear, and parts is dear, and gas is dear. You got to have cash coming in to keep her all going.'

'I'm surprised anyone manages.'

'Oh, there's ways and ways. And Tobermory's not what it was when you used to come here summers.'

'No, I can remember when they paved the road up from Hawkesbury. It was a big year when you'd see a new house going up. Now there are lots of new houses along the road, and lots around here.'

'Yes, and there's even some as are paid for.'

Dan Archie joined the children and gradually convinced them that piloting their log about was not nearly as much fun as getting back to the boat. His arrangements for the ferrying order were done with a diplomacy Willis would have envied.

As he waited alone for his turn, Frank scanned up the cliff to where an eagle perched on a wind-twisted spruce, watched a silver dot lay a contrail across the sky, a jumbo from Europe on its flight path to Boston or New York perhaps, shaded his eyes down past the sun to the sea, the whale road indeed today, crab kitchen, mussel ... mathum, maðum? ... sea gulls, sea mæws wheeling ...

The children would be early to bed this night.

When, on the second last evening, they pulled into Aunt Sal's driveway, the porch light and the kitchen light were on, but Aunt Sal was not in the garden, and though she would have heard the car did not come to the door. Frank told the boys to check on the humming-birds, and knocked on the kitchen door.

'Aunt Sal?' he asked through the screen.

He heard an answering voice, too light to make out the words. Inside he called her name again and traced the reply to the front room. She was lying on the couch under a blanket, a book, page down, on her lap.

'Frank? Yes, I thought it might be you. Turn on that light, would you.'

'Sorry, Aunt Sal, I just dropped in to say goodbye.'

'Did you bring the boys?'

'They're watching the hummingbirds.'

'Well …' She put her arm over the back of the couch, struggled with the other to push herself up.

'Don't bother; I'll call them in.'

'No, no … If I can just …'

'Here, let me help you.'

'Yes, perhaps you should.'

She sat up, a shrunken little woman, changed from last week, from years ago. Of course.

'Well,' she said, 'I expect you want me to hustle up a meal for fifteen hay-makers in ten minutes.'

'Don't bother with anything. They had supper just before we left.'

'I can manage some cookies. Give me a minute to catch my breath.'

'The boys don't need cookies, Aunt Sal. Let me just bring them in and then we'll go.'

She coughed several times, and held a hankie to her mouth.

'Old age, Frank. I'm not the woman I used to be.' She smiled rue-fully and touched her left breast. 'I'm not even the woman you see. They had this one off eighteen years ago.'

'I didn't know.'

'Eighteen years after a cancer operation is good. But it's back. I don't suppose it ever goes away. In the spring, Dr Ramesh said he was optimistic, but he was probably lying. The other day I asked him if I should get an early start on my Christmas cards, and he admitted I probably needn't bother this year.'

'Aunt Sal!'

'Oh, don't get all dramatic and weepy, Frank, you're too realistic for that. Old enough to know better. Come, I'll put the kettle on and you can watch the boys don't drown themselves.'

She had recovered her perkiness, and in ten minutes Frank called the boys.

After she was done her second cup of tea, Aunt Sal went to the front room. She returned with her hands behind her back.

'Now, Simon, pick a hand.'

'That one ... no, yes, that one.'

Frank saw that picking either hand would win the same gift.

She produced a copy of Robert Louis Stevenson's *A Child's Garden of Verses*. Simon, who had been hoping for a video game, was visibly disappointed, but Aunt Sal was not distressed.

'That book was my son John's. He got it for Christmas one year, and he was disappointed. He wanted a BB gun. But he liked it afterwards. You look at the pictures now, and when you get back home tonight, your Daddy will read some of the poems to you.'

When she returned from the front room and Jonathan chose, she produced *The Birds of Nova Scotia* by Robie W. Tufts.

'I used to know him way back when,' she said, 'so it's a book by a friend. See, he's signed the title page to me. That's always special, isn't it? You could use this book in Montreal, but I expect you'd best leave it in Tobermory for your next visit.'

Jonathan relieved his father by saying a warm 'Thank you, Aunt Sal,' and opening the book to look at the pictures.

'And you take these, Frank,' setting a pair of opera glasses in his hand. They were of bronze or brass with mother-of-pearl barrels. 'These belonged to my mother when she was teaching in New York back around the turn of the century.' She returned them to their leather case. 'Then she came home to look after her brother when his wife died, and my father married her, and they haven't been used from that day to this. There's precious little grand opera around Tobermory ... though there's plenty of the soap variety.'

'You've made that joke before.'

'Don't be saucy to your elders, Frank.'

'Thank you, Aunt Sal, you really shouldn't.'

'Why shouldn't I? My three will never use them, and if they're lying around when ... well, little things like this have a habit of disappearing ...'

When the gift-giving was over, the boys asked if they could go and look for the muskrat.

'Just for five minutes or so,' said Frank. 'And don't fall in the brook.'

'And be quiet as a mousie.'

'We will.'

Aunt Sal allowed Frank to help her with the dishes.

'So you're going back on Saturday – and you'll not be happy to get there, I'm guessing.'

'Well, a funny thing happens when I get close to the Quebec border – a kind of tightening of the muscles, stomach seizing up – and I'm not the only one to have noticed it – others tell me they feel it too.'

'Yes, I can imagine. But I can also guess there's something else. Emma's ghost haunting your house? Not literally, but you know what I mean?'

'I know what you mean. No, I'm getting used to that.'

'Then it's your in-laws.'

How ...

'Of course I never met them, but your mother did.'

'I thought Mum liked the Hatchers. She only ever met them at the wedding. And for a few hours the Christmas they came to Montreal. What did she say?'

'Well, Kate was a lady, and she knew how to handle them. And what to say to you and Emma. I said the other evening Kate was a ditz – I didn't say she was a fool. To make a long story short, she said Emma's parents were racist snobs and bigots, the worst sort of jumped-up petty bourgeois she'd ever seen. Those are her very words: "the worst sort of jumped-up petty bourgeois I've ever seen". She said Emma's father was a humourless stuffed shirt, and he bullied his wife terribly. The wife she described as a borderline hysteric, a fidgety, stupid, narrow-minded prig. Now is that about right?'

'I hate to say it, but she was dead on. Oh, they're decent enough in their own way, but ...'

And they weren't petty bourgeoisie: they were Westmount, and there'd been some money in both their families for several generations.

'You needn't make excuses to me for them, they're nothing to me. And I seem to recall there's a sister who shares the worst qualities of her parents – a nasty, insincere, whiny little bitch, excuse my language, but I'm only quoting your mother.'

'Yes, I'm afraid that's also true.'

Aunt Sal folded the tea towel and hung it on its rack.

'She said something else, but ... Well, I suppose you have the right to hear it because it's from your mother. She said, "They're terrible people, Sal, terribly selfish and cruel. God help poor Frank if he ever runs foul of them, if there's a divorce or something." Just what she said. And she said something else: "But he's safe as long as he has Emma to protect him." She said that sitting on the swing in our old garden. I can remember it as well as ... Well, it's getting dark; you'd best gather up your boys and get them home to bed.'

When the boys were safely buckled into their seats, Frank came round to the driver's side and hugged Aunt Sal long and gently.

'Drive safely,' she said.

'I will, Aunt Sal. And I'll call you.'

'I'll be glad to hear from you. My own are pretty good to call, but sometimes a month goes by ...'

He decided to call at least one Sunday a month.

'And Frank, if you've got trouble with those ... people we mentioned, tell me about it. I can't help, but I can listen.'

'Thanks, Aunt Sal.'

'There is trouble, isn't there?'

'There was. A bit. I expect it's blown over.'

'What was it?'

'Well ... they wanted to take ...' He reached over the car roof and pointed down.

Aunt Sal shook her head.

'What kind of a world is this we're living in?' She shook her head, laid a hand on his arm. 'Can they do it?'

'I don't think so, but I don't know the law.'

'Perhaps you'd better look into it.'

'I guess I should. In the meantime…'

They hugged again, and he backed out into the road. The trees, the road were blurred by the tears.

Return

The New Brunswick shortcut did save them two hours, for which Frank was grateful. From Moncton north, the road ran parallel to the CN track, and although it passed through a few towns, it was fairly straight and level and they made good time. The westbound stretch was hillier, but they met little traffic and had numerous passing stretches.

'I still wish I could have gone to Sean's house to play Nintendo64.'

'Maybe next summer, Simon.'

'Dad, is New Brunswick all trees?' Jonathan asked.

'They do have a lot of them, don't they?'

'We haven't seen a house since about when we got gas, have we?'

'Well, I'm just guessing, but I think this stretch from Renous to Grand Falls used to be just a logging road. You noticed the side roads into the woods, and the places where the trees have been cut. So sometime in the last few years they paved it so we can use it, while most people take the Trans-Canada, as we did when we went to Cape Breton.'

'It doesn't look like anyone lives here either.'

'No, and only that one gas station we passed a while ago. I expect that was the halfway point.'

'So what would happen if we ran out of gas or had an accident, like?'

Frank crossed his fingers.

'I guess we'd just wait for help.'

He explained about siphoning gas, and how siphons work.

Jonathan made jokes about New Brunswick, and trees, and boredom.

The morning after they got home, Frank was stowing the suitcases in the basement when he noticed an oil smell. A quick check with a flashlight revealed a small pool of oil under the tank beneath the stairs. A few calls to neighbours for names, a few more calls, and the next day a short man named M. Maltais came and checked the junctions around the feed line and the filter.

'Well, your joints are clean. A leaky joint I could tighten in five minutes, but what you've got here is you've got a pin-point leak.'

His explanation of condensation, rust, and inevitable leaks in time accorded with what Frank had been able to learn.

'If I can find it, I can put a temporary patch on it, do you a week or two, but I can tell from looking at it that this tank is going to go. See, it's from the early fifties ... look here, no handle. Every tank since '56 has a handle, so ...'

'So I need a new one.'

'Yes, and you're lucky this one lasted as long as it did. They're good for twenty, twenty-five years. You've had this one nearly forty years.'

'And if I hadn't spotted it in time, I could have written off the basement?'

'By God, yes. The smell ... well, it gets into the whole house, takes a year ... I just did this place up on Grosvenor ... oh, you wouldn't believe ... the wife crying, probably has to throw out all the winter clothes she had stored down there ...'

It would cost six hundred, and if Frank paid cash there'd be no sales tax. So much for any savings from his summer pay; there would be no elasticity in the budget this fall. Of course, the tank could have burst, or the roof could have gone, or the car. M. Maltais agreed to install the new tank on Friday.

Shortly after M. Maltais finished his diagnosis, the Hatchers called to demand the boys for the weekend at their country place because, as Mrs Hatcher said, 'They'll have almost forgotten what we look like, and we missed them so much when you took them away from us. I don't understand why you had to go all the way to Nova Scotia when the Townships are hardly an hour away and ...'

The boys deeply resented the intrusion, having expected to spend the weekend playing computer games with their friends.

'And we were going to make the pesto, weren't we, Dad?'

The basil the boys had planted in the back yard was ready for harvesting, and for three years now they had reserved a day just before school started for the making and freezing of pesto. Even Simon remembered last year's event.

'Well, guys, I expect the basil will last another week; there's no danger of frost.' Except from up the hill. 'Anyway, you'll enjoy the cottage, I'm sure, and Grandma and Grandpa really missed you.'

They were not convinced, but they agreed.

Frank was preparing supper when the phone rang.

'Is that Associate Professor Wilson?'

Ellery Culp.

'I knew you said you were going away for a while, but I forgot when you were returning. I've been calling all week.'

Reflexively, Frank apologized for his absence.

'At any rate, I'm calling to offer you my congratulations.'

'Ahh.'

'And to be the first to welcome its newest member to the Department of English of the University of Eastern Ontario.'

It was all so unlikely.

'You were a shoo-in. A consummation devoutly to be wished, as someone once said.'

'I believe it was the actress to the bishop.'

'The … Oh yes! The actress to the bishop, of course! That's a good one.'

'I just hope it's not that sort of consummation that's meant.'

'That sort of … But of course not. I must say, Frank, you seem to taking this very lightly after I …'

'I expect it's the unexpectedness of it, Professor Culp. I still don't quite understand why your university wants me.'

'Ours not to reason why, Frank – it's settled, the committee was unanimous, and you have the job. On Tuesday the fifth of January you'll be walking into your first class up in the AHC.'

'Well, I guess so. It's tenured? There's no question of being laid off?'

'The first year is probationary, but unless you commit unspeakable acts with the president's wife, it's a formality.'

'And the dean and the budget committee approved the appointment?'

'Everything tickety-boo, ship-shape, and Bristol fashion.'

'There'll be paperwork to do about the pension transfer and all that.'

Not to mention selling the house, buying a house, getting the kids into a new school, finding a moving company, packing, teaching the term here ...

'Oh, there's lots of time for the paperwork. If your administrators are anything like ours, three months ought to be enough for the job.'

'Yes, well ...'

'So I can report to them that you have accepted?'

A long pause.

Doubt.

'I ...'

Temptation.

'Now don't let us down, Frank, don't go back on your promises.'

Promises?

'Frank?'

The newspaper lay beside the telephone; its headline:

PQ HAS CLEAR LEAD: POLL

'All right, I accept.'

Resolution.

What would the boys say?

The Hatchers?

With the boys in sports camp, Frank went to his college's registration day. He took the galleys of a scholarly article; he did not really expect to have time to do the proofing, but he could find nothing he wanted to read. In any case, he found Eleanor was also on duty so sat next to her.

'How was your summer, old fellow?'

'Quiet. Yours?'

'I spent it all on the wretched book.'

'Did you get away at all?'

'Yes, I was in England for two weeks in July trying to get a fix on Waugh's relations with Lady Diana Cooper. I had a terrible time.'

'Couldn't track down any documents?'

'Oh, I found lots of documents, but not the ones that count. The families are being very tight about the business....'

She began explaining the problems, the dates, the places, the people who knew and wouldn't talk, the people who didn't know and would, the people who were long since dead and the other biographers who had a lock on various batches of papers.

'I always knew I was better off with Jane Austen – no secrets.'

The first rush of students arrived looking for course openings.

When they were spelled off for lunch, Frank and Eleanor found a shady table on the west lawn of the campus.

'But how was your summer really?' she asked. 'How was Cape Breton?'

'Marvellous. So marvellous it was unreal. I couldn't decide whether I was in the middle of *Whisky Galore* or *Goin' Down the Road*. Mostly the former.'

He sketched their sunlit days.

'So you're keeping the house there?'

'I might as well, I guess.'

'And you'll retire there?'

'Could be. I'll see. I have at least twelve years to go; fifteen, probably. That's plenty of time.'

'Fifteen more years of this place – we'll be lucky if we can walk upright by then.'

The time had come.

'Well ... it looks as if I may not be taking my retirement from here.'

Eleanor was suitably surprised. When had this happened, how long had he known, when was he to start, what about the boys, the house, the courses he was to teach, his hours, his salary?

'But it's wonderful, you old bugger. I can't think of anyone I'd rather see getting it. And you've been really unhappy here since ...'

'Not just since Emma. For twenty years. I'm tired of the place. I just want out. I think it was being in Cape Breton again that ... They have hard lives there, but at least they don't have this fog of politics drifting constantly through their lives ... Something like that. I expect their lives are a lot harder than I can imagine, and I expect I'm just a whiner – others manage – but ... I can't really explain it.'

'Have you told Arty?'

'No. I suppose I should, eh?'

'Well, there are deadlines for this sort of thing. You'd best get moving on it. See him this afternoon.'

'Yeah.'

'Warn me so I can watch. I can't wait to see the expression on his face – the sleaze-bag will be furious that you're escaping from his clutches.'

But Eleanor was wrong. Perhaps because of their chat at the shop, Arty seemed genuinely pleased for Frank.

'You may not have low-enrolment courses like here,' he said, 'but nine hours a week – hell, you'll have all the time you need to get onto something like the Vin Maison. Hey, listen, if you'd like a franchising deal, maybe we can ...'

'Thanks but no thanks, Arty.'

'You're a sucker, Frank. You'll live and die a wage slave. You've got to take your destiny into your own hands.'

'This is real life, not a movie.'

'Okay, but perhaps in a year or so ... keep me in mind. I'll make you an offer you can't refuse.'

On Friday morning, Frank saw M. Maltais settled into the job, dropped the boys off at Westmount sports camp, then drove to the college. In the personnel department, Chantal began the paperwork necessary for his departure. She had him fill out the application for a one-year professional leave of absence and explained that he would only be able to transfer his pension equity if he resigned.

'If you take a leave, instead of resigning,' she advised, 'you'll still have your old job if you find you're dying to come back to the distinct society.'

'I expect I'll be pining for it.'

'Sure. But why take chances?'

'You've got a point. Thanks, Chantal.'

'You're welcome. We're going to miss you, Frank. Bring the boys in some day before you leave.'

In the afternoon, after M. Maltais took his stack of hundreds and departed, Frank decided his bank account wouldn't be substantially worse if he treated himself to an evening out. He confirmed with Sholem Birnbaum that some of the old gang were still getting together on Friday evenings.

Simon had played soccer at sports camp and had a bandage on his thigh when Frank picked him up.

'Does it hurt?'

'A little bit, Dada. But just after I tripped, I scored a goal.'

At home Frank took off the bandage. He found a slight scrape in the middle of a large bruise. After swabbing the scrape with peroxide, he applied a fresh bandage and had the boys ready to go when Mr Hatcher arrived.

'It should be all right by tomorrow morning,' he explained. 'If this bandage lasts the night, I don't think he'll need another in the morning. And I expect he'll be in the water all day, so …'

'Don't worry about it, Frank – rest assured, he'll get the best care possible.'

Darkness had come by the time Frank stepped out the door. But even now, in late August, the evening air was soft as he made his way along de Maisonneuve and into Westmount Park. To his right the last of the shrieks sounded from the swimming pool, and under the lights the tennis courts were busy. Frustrating game, tennis. Keep that wrist straight, oops, missed the sweet spot again. Culp had a game the day I was there, so there are tennis courts in Port Simcoe, Jonathan should be learning the game, maybe even Simon. Along the pathways, through the trees, he saw people strolling with their books fresh from the library, couples strolling in the pools of lamplight, in the clouds of nicotiana scent, stopping to embrace. Away to the left, the traffic of Sherbrooke Street, and beyond it the mountain with the glimmering of its houses rising to the dark trees of Summit Park. Jonathan nine, Simon five, and he had never taken them for a walk in Summit Park. The pool, the playground off beyond the watercourse, the soccer field, Family Day here also, but never to Summit Park, only once to Mount Royal Park on the main mountain – what a narrow life he was giving them. Perhaps in Port

Simcoe. Surely it wasn't really happening. His terror of change was precariously balanced by his exhilaration at the idea of leaving. But how peaceful this evening. Only when you knew where to look could you see on the trees the damage from the ice storm. What stranger, strolling here like this now, could guess at the devastation of January? What stranger, strolling here like this now, could guess at the continual dull turmoil of life here? And what turmoil, really? Dull was the word. It's not Omagh, not Kosovo. As a few years ago they used to say it's not Belfast, Beirut, Sarajevo, Rwanda. And most unlikely it ever would be like any of those places with their bombs and machetes – we had the Supreme Court decision. Everyone said it – the PQ would likely win the election again and lose the referendum again. And then it would go on in the same old way again. He had lived with it these twenty-five years and more – why go now? Why indeed? Mordecai Richler was staying – why shouldn't he?

Because of Emma, perhaps? His life in Montreal bound up with Emma, so that now ... Just go. Was that it?

But he had already committed himself, hadn't he? Yes. The real estate agent coming next week to assess the house. Once it was sold there would be no coming back. Not unless the worst ... but what worst?

Emma, help me, dearest love.

Emma was decisive: think it through, weigh it, decide, act.

But Emma, half my life here is you, was you ...

In the silence, the squeak of his running shoes on the sidewalk, beneath the trees of de Maisonneuve again now he was past the park, and here the houses larger, the lawns deeper, the garden more elaborate, not like those on the highest levels of the mountain, but as large as on the Hatchers' block ... Sarajevo, Beirut, indeed. Such nonsense, over-dramatization by whining anglos feeling sorry for themselves, failing to adapt as Arty said they must, could, with such a little effort. And if the effort is too much, don't worry, the kids will manage it. A man and wife of Frank's age on bicycles, five hundred dollars each, the couple side by side, chuckling; three boys in baggy pants at the street corner flipping their skateboards, teasing, bragging; two teenaged girls on rollerblades, helmeted, knee and elbow protectors, gauntlets, shrieking with laughter – happy people enjoying a dulcet Friday evening, as he was enjoying it. What could go wrong with this, why shouldn't it just go on and on?

On the outdoor terrace of the café at the corner of Greene Avenue, tables full of diners twisting up a late pasta, raising cool glasses of white wine, spooning up the foam from a cappuccino, smiling, discussing, laughing, flirting beneath the stars ... Well, perhaps the stars are not particularly visible, although there's one, another, a third ... a quibble, merest quibble ... quibble like all my complaints, whining, despairing, passive, a mediocre life, an anglo in Montreal, a nuisance to Quebec, a nuisance to Canada, irrelevant ...

Along Sherbrooke east of Guy, half a dozen blocks of fashionable shops, couturiers, specialty gift shops, art galleries, antique dealers: nine shops closed, 'À Louer.'

Sholem and Bubba Charles were already at the round table by the window when Frank arrived.

'My God, it's the ghost of Christmas past.'

'Memories are made of this.'

'Love letters in the sand.'

'Albatross!'

Sholem and Bubba, regulars these twenty, twenty-five years. The tradition developed from the hit-and-miss drinking nights of their early post-grad years. With marriages, children, jobs, few of the gang could manage two or three nights a week, and they gradually settled on Fridays in a grubby but storied old bar. When it closed they moved on, trying a place for a few months, moving on again because of rock bands, rock videos, fights, high prices, crowds, other closings, changes of management. For the past three of four years they had been here in L'Amiral Nelson. The prices were high, expense-account prices, but the service was good and the music soft jazz.

'I'm trying to explain to Sholem some of the ins and outs of the Canadian debt-sharing in case Quebec separates.'

'I'll just be getting along home then,' said Frank.

'Sit down and learn something.'

Frank got a beer and settled in to learn. Although Bubba taught political science he had taken a minor in economics, and had kept up his interest through grad school and beyond. Frank stayed out; Sholem, a philosophy prof, was something of a polymath, and was fully engaged.

one of the flaws of Keynesian economics
ceteris paribus, sure, but

Others drifted in: Neville Arsenault, math at Concordia; Luc Vaillancourt, a politico in from Ottawa; Danny Hersh in computers; Mel Stroud and Jack Greene, history; Reuben Meyer, also computers and author of a book on separation entitled *Reparation*... others new to Frank.

playing six games over five hundred, and now
Bouchard and Landry and Beaudoin don't
the year we discovered the Peruvian restaurant

Bubba's analysis of the national debt soon petered out.

but which Wyndham Lewis do you
nel mezzo del camin del
Christy and Miriam are both trying to
whole bunch with fascist leanings
moved to Toronto and goes into

Out of the general ruck, the historians moved into high gear with a discussion of the Battle of the White Mountain and its implications. Frank was delighted.

from the time of Henry the Fowler
meshugga
Indonesian wasn't it that year
nothing like Trier, but
thought it was spelled l-o-c-h h-a-y-m-e and it was Gaelic
for viande fumée and the guy behind the counter
in last weekend's Sunday Telegraph *that*
in St Elizabeth's Hospital, but

It was like his dinner at Eleanor's without the sexual tension. Of course – there were no women here tonight.

'Reuben, when Emma and I came here, there used to be women at the table. What happened to the women?'

'They still come sometimes. Some of them objected to the smoke, some want to save on babysitting, some are just bored. I think. You've not gone all politically correct, have you, Frank?'

'Naw, he's looking for a replacement,' Neville murmured. It would have been cruel anywhere else.

'I can't imagine a replacement for Emma,' replied Reuben, and all three fell silent.

the Great Elector marches on
a reactionary rag like the Sunday Telegraph, *it's no wonder that*
formule de base which is
McGuire on the front page, but not Sosa
just in front of Rouen cathedral
a dish called Indonesian meltdown perhaps
this putz who
Elsass-Lothringen becomes Alsace-Lorraine and
decent smoked meat? In Toronto?

Frank wondered if he might announce his new job. Several times he caught his breath to begin, but it seemed an interruption, gratuitous. This was the Montreal he was leaving, deserting – a continuous course in Western civ.

But what was he adding to it? These were Montrealers; what was he?

An imposter perhaps.

Emma was at home at this table, could hold her own. And Eleanor.

the price of beer in Sweden? Would you believe
what the Germans call Schadenfreude – leave it to the Germans to
think up
talking to Terry at Nick's memorial service
pronounces Décarie 'Decorry' – a real Montrealer
Ruby Foo's
real NDGer you mean
Johnny Jelly-Bean
the Riding Academy
An imposter certainly.

On the sidewalk, as the others were wrapping up their topics, deciding whether to go on to another bar, Luc Vaillancourt offered Frank a lift home. As they paused at a light, Frank told him about the Port Simcoe job.

'And you're taking it? For sure?'

'Yes ... so it seems.'

'Do you mind if I ask why? You seem so settled here, although I know you haven't been happy about things ...'

Frank shrugged.

'Well, you know as well as I do that I don't really have anything to complain of. It's just that ... I don't feel ... well, whatever happens in Quebec in the next few years ... I don't feel ... I don't feel I'll be welcome.'

Luc chuckled.

'You don't feel welcome? Imagine how welcome I feel – a federalist French Quebecer.'

'And you wouldn't feel welcome anywhere else, that's obvious enough.'

'No. But I'll get along. And you'll miss some things, probably.'

'Yeah. These Friday nights. But most of the time I can't afford the babysitting.'

'Well, we'll miss you. I'll miss you. But I understand. And you'll come back to visit sometimes.'

'Somehow I doubt it.'

Thanksgiving

Frank swept into the classroom and hefted his briefcase onto the table. The babble abated somewhat.

'Well, I'm here at last.'

He had had to take Simon to school for his first day of kindergarten, and Eleanor had put a sign on the door telling the students he would be late.

He scanned the front row and smiled at a shy-looking girl by the window.

'Registration was fun, eh?'

'Well, sir ...'

'What?' with hammy shock, 'you mean you didn't get your first choice English course?'

'No, sir.'

'I'm amazed, shocked! Your fifth choice?'

'No, sir.'

'Your forty-fifth?'

'You're getting closer.'

From a boy several rows back: 'Try no choice, sir.'

'Right. Well, I understand. Frankly, I'd rather be lounging around Westmount pool with my little boys, but the Quebec government directed the Ministry of Education to direct the administration to direct the English Department to direct me to be here. I have the letter from Premier Bouchard sitting in my office. Well, a photocopy. But it's addressed to me, personally: Mon chèr professeur fill-in-name-as-appropriate, it begins. And it goes on to promise me thirty-five keen students. Which is you. Which means we have until December to get you writing with the polish and aplomb of Dr Samuel Johnson. Dr Johnson was a good writer, although he did his writing a while ago. Now this course is called "Writing about Literature" and in it, we ...'

An hour earlier, at Grosvenor School, Jonathan's grade three group had gone in with the other returning students. The two kindergarten

RAY SMITH

teachers stayed outside to greet the new children and their mothers
and in a few cases both parents. Frank seemed to be the only single
father. Simon, as he recognized and greeted his friends, had been
enthusiastic.

'You don't have to stay, Dada. I'll be all right. Jonathan explained
it all to me.'

'Well, perhaps I'd better just go to your classroom with you. I'd at
least like to see where you'll be sitting.'

'All right, Dada, if you want to, but I'll be all right, really. I know
all about it.'

Mrs Hatcher and Betsy came around the corner of the gym. Mrs
Hatcher threw up her hands and rushed to embrace Simon. Betsy
wore an ankle-length flowered skirt, white blouse, and sparse
makeup; walking without her usual sashay, she looked like a mother
in a low-cholesterol margarine ad, more motherly than any of the
several dozen mothers there.

'Hello, Frank,' she said. 'I expect you're glad to see us – now you
can leave for your eight o'clock classes.'

'Some things are more important.'

Four mornings a week for the rest of the term, Frank would be
driving the boys to the Hatchers' house at 7:15 or so; there they could
wait for half an hour until it was time to walk the three blocks to
school. Mrs Hatcher had insisted this was the ideal solution, and
could not understand why Frank and Emma had so rarely asked her
to babysit. Frank could not reveal that Emma had always resisted
leaving the boys in 'that house of repression and lunacy where I was
nearly destroyed and Betsy was destroyed, however willingly.'
Emma also pointed out that for every minute she served, 'Mother
would demand top wages in guilt – wages we could never afford.'

Frank had agreed with her, still did, but in the circumstances had
little choice. Linda had her own children to get to school, and in any
case it was not worth her while, or anyone else's, to mind the boys
for such a short time. Frank tried some mothers on his street, and
although he arranged car pool for the ride home some days, the
inconvenience of early delivery in the morning was insuperable.

This morning, however, he had determined to bring the boys
himself, and hadn't expected Mrs Hatcher and Betsy.

'Well,' chirped Betsy, turning to Simon, flourishing her camcorder, 'how is my little darling this morning? I bet you're just a little bit frightened, aren't you, Simon?'

'No.'

'Of course he's not frightened, are you, darling?' said Mrs Hatcher. 'He's a brave little boy who's just coping marvellously with all the troubles in his little life.'

Troubles?

Emma?

Me.

A buzzer sounded, and the two smiling teachers opened the door. The parents took their children's hands and began moving forward.

'The first room to the left for Miss Bates's English language students, second to the left for Mlle Tremblay's French immersion.'

Simon pulled away from Mrs Hatcher and ran to greet a friend. Frank smiled to the mother and they followed the crowd toward the door.

'Excuse me,' said one of the teachers to Frank, 'what child are you with?'

'Simon Wilson. Simon, come hold Dada's hand.'

'Good morning, Simon,' she said. 'You're Jonathan's brother, aren't you?'

'Yes, but it's not my fault.'

She repressed a laugh.

'Well, I think you're in Miss Tremblay's class.'

'Yes, that's right.'

The teacher turned to the Mrs Hatcher and Betsy.

'And you're with?...'

'I'm Simon's grandmother and this is his aunt.'

The teacher bit her lip. 'I'm afraid it's parents only. The room is only big enough ...'

'But I'm his grandmother! How can ...'

'I'm sorry, but the crowding ... we have to think of the children first ... making them feel comfortable ... first day ...'

'I've never in my life ... my own grandchild!'

'Yes ... I'm afraid ... there are so many parents this morning ...'

Betsy played her trump card.

'You don't understand, miss. Obviously you weren't told that Simon's mother, my sister, passed away last year, so that I'm the only real mother he has …'

'And his only grandmother, family …'

'The reassurance and support that only a woman can …'

The teacher looked to Frank in appeal.

'I understand about the rules, but perhaps if you could …'

'Well, I can let you in, or let them in, but not all three. The space is really …'

Simon cried out, 'Dada, Dada, I want you to come with me, please, please, please, Dada …'

'Well,' said the teacher, 'Simon seems to have settled things. I'm afraid …'

By now, they were the only ones left outside. Mlle Tremblay gestured Frank and Simon through the door.

'I'm sorry, Mrs Hatcher, I'm afraid we're holding things up.'

As he followed Mlle Tremblay, Frank could hear Mrs Hatcher and Betsy together renewing their attack on Miss Bates.

the child's only family

the most special event in

can't understand why there can't be an exemption in view of the tragic

most certainly take this up with the principal

mother and his aunt here went to this very school so

Frank glanced back and saw that they were now through the door as Miss Bates retreated to her own classroom. Triumphantly, the two women rushed to catch up. Mrs Hatcher was fizzing with indignation:

'I must say, Frank, I am shocked that you offered us no support whatsoever. But I suppose I should have expected that from you …'

Betsy managed a cooler reaction, pulling her sunglasses down her nose and fixing him with her eyes.

'You don't know me very well, do you, Frank? Of course, I'm very different from my sister. But we do have one thing in common: don't get mad, get even.'

'It doesn't sound like Emma.'

'Perhaps you didn't know her very well.'

Mlle Tremblay was calling the names of the children and leading them to seats around half a dozen large round tables. The parents followed and knelt by their children. Simon solemnly took Frank's hand as he followed Mlle Tremblay.

'And the table is red, your favourite colour.'

Simon was busy examining the plastic box on the table in front of him.

'Jonathan says I put all my things in here, Dada. This is my box for my drawings and books and markers and stuff.'

'Sometimes it's a big advantage to have an older brother, eh?'

'Yeah. Okay, Dada, now you can go.'

'I think I'm supposed to wait until Mlle Tremblay tells the parents to go.'

In French, because the children weren't to know she spoke English, Mlle Tremblay told them that there would be a welcoming evening for parents the following Tuesday, and that if those parents who were here thought their children were settled, they could go now, though they were welcome to stay longer if they wished.

Frank kissed Simon and moved toward the door. Mrs Hatcher quickly took his place, remarking, 'I thought this was supposed to be so important to you, but I must say you can't wait to rush off.'

Back in his office after class, Frank knew he should do a quick grading of the students' ex tempore writing. But the tension of meeting Mrs Hatcher and Betsy, along with the obligatory bonhomie of the first class, had drained him. Four hours until the next class. No time to waste; do something.

He rested his head in his hands.

Emma?

On a rainy day in Edinburgh, Jonathan with a neighbour, Frank's grocery shopping done, and Emma returning early from the university, they met in Clark's Bar, their local, near the bottom of Dundas Street, on the downhill fringe of New Town.

'This weather,' she remarked, 'is all one needs to explain the Scottish character, and why the Scots were the real empire builders. And I'm getting toughened by it. My 23 bus was packed with Edimbourgeois, not one of whom had had a bath or shower since the Old Pretender, I got jostled all the way here, but I still feel fine – fetch me a dram of straight malt.'

'Get a job and we'll stay.'

'If they were hiring at EU, I'd take it, I really would.'

She ran a finger over the back of his hand.

'I mean, I'm glad to be here, glad to be alive, glad to be with you and Jonathan.'

She kissed him lightly.

'Glad I can keep on keeping on, despite the weather and the unwashed Edimbourgeois.'

Emma at her most winsome.

Keep on.

Keep on keeping on.

He had to get the mail, collect some handouts from photocopy, put some books on library reserve, pick up some supplies from the bookstore.

Do it now.

Go.

He went.

Half an hour later, his chores done, he pulled the stack of student writing from the envelope, noted a comma splice, a spelling mistake, another spelling mistake ...

The grading done, he got his sandwich from the fridge in the staff lounge. Eleanor's door was closed, and her fall schedule not yet tacked to her bulletin board. He knocked, waited, returned to his office. He set the sandwich bag on the August page of the desk calendar, poured coffee from his thermos.

Breakfast was at ... seven, wasn't it? Twelve-thirty, five and a half hours later and still not hungry.

The calendar page, unmarked. He picked up his pen, held the point over the day's box. Slowly, deliberately he touched pen to paper, wrote in block letters as he did on every fresh calendar sheet: NEMO.

At ten to one, Sid slouched in with an overflowing briefcase in one hand and a basketball under his arm, complaining of a hangover.

'Mouth like the bottom of a birdcage.'

'I've never tasted the bottom of a birdcage. Describe it to me.'

'Piss off, Frank.'

Sid dumped the briefcase on the desk and lobbed the basketball into the wastebasket.

'What's the number of the order desk at the bookstore, bastards didn't get *The Sound and the Fury* and ...'

At five after one, Sid grabbed up a chaos of papers and headed for the door and his class.

'The Eagle is about to land,' he smirked.

In his afternoon class, Frank timed the sample writing so he could leave the room at quarter to three and phone home from his office. Jonathan answered.

'How was your day?'

'Fine.'

'Do you like your new teacher?'

'Yes.'

'Can you get your long legs under your new desk?'

'Yes. Dada, do you know who's in the class? William and Anthony and Dylan and Tara and ...'

Once started, the boy poured out his delight. After a bit, Frank could hear Simon in the background wheedling for the phone.

'I'm glad to hear that. Look, I've got a class just now, so I can't stay on long. Let me talk to Simon and you can tell me all the rest at supper.'

Apart from the fact that he hadn't been allowed to sit in the front seat on the way home, a colossal miscarriage of justice, Simon had had a good day too. He listed his friends, explained the toilet arrangements, and sang 'Bonne fête' which they had learned to honour the birthday of a boy named Julian.

'And do you know what else, Dada?'

'What else, love?'

'Gamma and Auntie Betsy stayed until recess. They were the last grown-ups to go.'

'And did they help sing "Bonne fête" to Julian?'

'Oh yes, and Auntie Betsy got on a chair and waved her arms and the chair broke.'

'I hope she didn't hurt herself.'

'Not much. But she said the s-word.'

'I wish I had been there. To help.'

'Yes, Dada, and do you know what?'

'What?'

'I love kindergarten, and we got to play on the jungle gym in the playground, and ...'

Presently Frank was able to hang up. Loping along the corridor, he smiled at the picture of Betsy flailing her arms as the chair collapsed beneath her. Perhaps this was the support he had been expected to offer. Then he wondered how she would pin the blame on him.

Despite the nuisance of the awkward schedule, Frank soon fell into the routine of car pooling, classes, hasty runs home, hasty suppers, tight weekends. He rose at six-thirty and usually managed to get to bed before twelve. Despite the need to keep the house immaculate for prospective buyers, he fell behind in most chores. He had managed to wash the windows before term began, kept on top of vacuuming and dead light bulbs, put new washers in all the faucets, and neatened the garden for winter. But he pulled clothes hot from the dryer and laid them flat to avoid ironing, put off sewing indefinitely, delayed haircuts for himself and the boys.

When the house insurance came due in mid-September, he was able to reduce the policy from a year to six months, thus saving nearly a thousand dollars, but there was little left for the inevitable expenses of the coming move. Then his agent called and suggested that with a fall election looking more and more likely Frank might shave twenty thousand from his asking price.

'Do I have any choice?'

'Sure, rent the place and pray the entire PQ is attacked by flesh-eating bacteria.'

He had Ellery Culp send the classified ads of houses for sale in Port Simcoe. The difference between likely values would give him perhaps fifty thousand in profit to take with him. But that wouldn't be in hand for some months.

In the meantime, he tried to cut twenty dollars a week from the budget. When Eleanor invited him to dinner, he reluctantly refused without telling her he couldn't really afford it.

But in mid-September he conceived the idea of pre-empting the Hatchers by inviting them for Thanksgiving dinner. Not on the Monday, but on the Sunday, so that the boys would be able to stay up a bit late, and he would not have to teach the following morning. Doing it right would cost between one and two hundred, but it should prove he was not only on top of things, in control, but reaching out, mending fences, building bridges, family oriented – enough clichés to satisfy even Mrs Hatcher.

Well, no, that was asking too much.

Proper delivery of the invitation was crucial. He thought of telephoning just before supper when Mrs Hatcher would likely be cooking and Mr Hatcher would answer the telephone – 'Now, don't argue, George, it's settled, you're coming here, the boys are looking forward to it' – but with Betsy and Willis in residence, anyone might answer.

Written invitations!

The sanctity of documents, the validation of formality!

Separate cards for all four!

Signed by the boys!

Better still: cards made by the boys!

And delivered by the boys!

They made up the cards on Sunday and the boys delivered them the next morning. Frank expected a call Tuesday or Wednesday, giving him nearly a two-week lead on the day.

The call came Friday, suggesting there had been lengthy debates up the hill. Mr Hatcher got the job.

'Frank, thank you for the invitation for Thanksgiving dinner. However, I'm not sure ...'

At least there was doubt – they would come.

'The invitations were from the boys, George, not from me.'

'Yes, but, of course, Babs was planning ...'

'The boys have been planning too. And this is for Sunday, not Thanksgiving Day itself. If she wishes, Mrs Hatcher could give a dinner on Monday.'

'I'm not sure she would want to ...'

'Well, reasonably enough – Mrs Hatcher has had to slave over a hot stove for all the other festivals this past year, and this time it's my turn.'

'Yes, well, I was going to say that I think we can make it. It is a sacrifice for Babs, and, well, you know your financial situation better than we do, but ...'

'Now, Mr Hatcher, we use the term "financial situation" when talking about houses or pensions, not a family dinner. So it's settled. We won't take no for an answer.'

Mr Hatcher conceded, with just audible complaints from Mrs Hatcher in the background.

At five o'clock on Sunday afternoon they entered a house that was vacuumed, neatened, and well-lit, to find the boys dressed up in their best, Frank in his best, the meal under control, the kitchen counters cleared of the preparation bowls, the table set, the silver and glassware gleaming, the candles ready, the bar well stocked, almonds on the coffee table, and a tray of mixed hors d'oeuvres on the warmer.

After Frank took her coat, Mrs Hatcher ran her finger along the top of a picture frame and was clearly disappointed to find no dust. Betsy inspected the lower level of the coffee table and was chagrined to find the latest *New Yorker*. Willis, sneering at the boxed paperback set of Churchill's *The Second World War* was taken aback to find beside it A.J.P. Taylor's *The Struggle for the Mastery of Europe 1848–1914*.

'You've read this one?' he asked.

'Years ago. I expect I've forgotten everything but the famous footnote "except the Italians" on page three or whatever.'

Mr Hatcher, popping almonds into his mouth, stared indecisively at bottles of Famous Grouse, Macallan, and Lagavulin.

'You must spend a fortune on booze, Frank – three Scotches and two of them single malts. Not even I can keep a bar like this.'

'Surely you remember that the bar is left over from the old days when we used to entertain. I never drink anything but this,' holding up his beer. 'They've been there so long, I expect most of the alcohol has evaporated. But help yourself.'

'Well,' with a glance at his wife, 'as long as they're low alcohol.'

Mrs Hatcher had a weak G&T to which Frank triumphantly added a wedge of lime, while Betsy had a dry Noilly Prat on the rocks. Another wedge of lime.

'The footnote is in the introduction,' said Willis. 'Page xxiii.'

'As I said, it has been years.'

Willis poured himself three fingers of Macallan and drank off two of them. He smacked his lips delicately, diplomatically.

'What's a footnote, Dada?' asked Jonathan.

'Uncle Willis will show you. I've got to get the hors d'oeuvres on the table.'

At dinner, Mrs Hatcher insisted Simon sit by her; Betsy led a reluctant Jonathan to her side of the table.

Avocado and real crab.

Frank's special Mediterranean fish soup flavoured with anise and saffron.

Three roast ducklings, stuffed with sausage, apple, and the first chestnuts of the season; scalloped potatoes; braised Belgian endive; carrots with capers.

Light green salad with Frank's own vinaigrette.

Crêpes filled with vanilla ice cream and topped with strawberries marinated in balsamic vinegar.

'Well, Frank,' Mr Hatcher admitted, 'You've certainly done us proud. I can't remember a feast like this since ... oh, the Beaver Club with ... who was it, Babs?'

'Yes, I remember,' said Mrs Hatcher. 'It's far too much, far more than anyone needs. I always say ...'

'Well, I can give you this testimonial, Frank: you could hold down a position as a chef in any embassy I've ever served in.'

'Thanks, Willis, but I think not.'

'Well, if you ever need a job ... Did I see some cognac in the bar?'

The time had come to tell them. As Willis returned with cognac and Scotch with glasses, Frank said:

'Ladies and gentlemen, I have an announcement to make.'

'You're getting married,' said Willis.

'Willis!' cried Mrs Hatcher. 'Such bad taste, if nothing else ...'

'Sorry.'

'You're pregnant.'

'Betsy, don't be coarse. And in front of ...'

'No, it has to do with work. Now, I'm making an adjustment to my career which, I think, will solve several problems both for me and for you.'

'You've been appointed to the Canadian Senate.'

'No, Willis, I'm neither dishonest nor decrepit enough to earn that. No, I have known for some years that the family would be happier if I were a professor in a university instead of a simple college teacher. And I know Mr and Mrs Hatcher are planning to move to southern Ontario; this has a number of advantages for you, but the disadvantage that you would be five or six hours' drive from your grandchildren. I might add that I could use more pay, and that I'm not entirely happy here in Quebec.'

'What English person could be?'

'Speak for yourself, mother.'

'You and Willis are here on what is virtually a foreign posting, dear, it's not the same.'

'No, it isn't, Mom, it's my home, and ...'

Frank tapped his glass.

'Therefore, I have accepted a position as an associate professor at the University of Eastern Ontario in Port Simcoe. I begin in January. Depending on where you choose to live, we'll only be an hour or two away from you.'

Silence.

Mrs Hatcher fussed with her napkin and glanced at her husband for her cue, but Mr Hatcher was regarding Frank with a curiously amused smile. Willis scratched his jaw, while Betsy cocked her head quizzically.

Despite his claim that the move would solve all their problems, Frank knew he was tossing a large spanner into the works.

Mrs Hatcher recovered first, throwing her arm around Jonathan. 'But the boys,' she cried. 'What about Betsy ... our plan ... I thought it was settled ... how can you ...'

'Never mind, Babs,' said Mr Hatcher. 'I think Frank has pre-empted us. Is it certain, Frank? Signed, sealed, and delivered?'

'As near as I can tell.'

Mr Hatcher smiled over his glass. 'Well done, Frank. Very neatly done.'

Mrs Hatcher was not appeased.

'But what ... what if we don't move to Ontario, what if...? It's not certain yet ...'

'Then you'll still only be three and a half hours away.'

She cast about desperately.

'But the house ... Betsy ... Emma's ... where she rests ... and the place at the lake ... so cruel ... to spring it on us like this ...'

'Well, you perhaps want to digest the news with your digestifs. I'd like to clear away a few dishes – no, please, it's easier if I do it myself – and in ten minutes ... what do you say, guys? Bedtime, eh.'

Mrs Hatcher was torn between her reflex to help with the dishes and her desire to ingratiate herself with Simon and Jonathan; she stayed in her seat.

Betsy got up from her chair. 'It's a good thing I don't have to eat your cooking,' she cooed, 'I'd never keep my figure.' She had obviously been caught off guard not just by the announcement but by the number of wines. 'I think I'd best repair my war paint.'

She was five minutes in the powder room and paused, leaning on the door jamb, when she returned. With a stack of dessert plates, Frank had to turn sideways to get by her. She leered blearily, her makeup heavy now.

'So is this the sort of meal you cooked for my sister?'

'Every day.'

'She was a lucky girl.'

Frank put the stack of plates on the kitchen counter. Betsy followed him.

'Course Emma was lucky in everything.' She spoke quietly enough that she could not be heard by the others. 'She got the big front bedroom and I got the little one on the side, she got the new skates and I got the hand-me-downs, same with clothes. She got the scholarships, and I got passing grades, she had the hunks sniffing around the house and marking the front steps, and I had to go out and find my own nerds and dinks and creeps.'

'You seem to have done well enough.'

'Hah.'

Frank went to the dining room for a handful of glasses. When he returned, Betsy was sitting at the kitchen table.

'Everyone agrees Willis is a better catch than I am.'

'By "everyone" you mean them,' pointing toward the dining room.

'Anyone who knows the family.'

He was about to set the glasses on the table when she put her hand on his crotch.

'You really stuck it to me tonight, Frank. Bravo. I like a man who can stick it to me. Why do you think my great catch liked Frisco so much?'

'Betsy, don't.'

She squeezed gently.

'If you move, I'll scream and say you groped me.'

'Betsy, please.'

'Do you know why he loved living in Frisco? Because of the boys. Him. Wilma, I call him. Wilma just loved Frisco for the slim boys, sailor boys, leather boys, bath house boys, iron pumping boys, heavy metal boys, black boys, Chinese boys, all boys together. He hasn't touched me in ten years. Not that I'd let him, no doubt he's HIV positive. I told you not to move.'

She squeezed tighter.

'Look, I have to get the kids off to bed, and someone is going to want to go to the toilet, and I have these glasses. Perhaps we can have this conversation some other time.'

'No, we can't. Not unless I can get pissed with you again. It's the booze talking.'

'Betsy, please, I'm the wrong guy. I have no money, no time, no energy, no interest, no ... nothing. And I'm moving away. I'm sure there are lots of men around who are willing to ...'

'To accommodate me?' She laughed. 'Sure, good old Betsy can just drop round the squash club and take on all comers.'

But she released him, the tears tracing the mascara down her cheek.

Frank put down the glasses, laid a hand on her shoulder.

'Betsy, I'd do what I could, if I thought there was anything I could do.'

'Funny, isn't it? I dress like a slut, I look like a slut, I act like a slut, and I suppose I am a slut. A few little affairs, a few quickies. But do you know what I want, all I've ever wanted? Not sluttish dirty week-ends in the No-Tell Motel, not groping behind the azaleas at the bar-becue, not tumbles in the rough off the seventh fairway, in the week-ender sloop anchored in some secluded bay, quickies in the can at the cocktail party, membership in the mile-high club …'

'Betsy, you shouldn't tell me this, it's none of my business.'

'Children. That's all this slut has ever wanted. And who got them? Emma, the divine Emma. Emma, with no makeup, wearing sloppy jeans, nose stuck in a book, Emma who was as far from a slut as you could get. Emma, who never even wanted children – don't you kid yourself, you may have been married to her, but I grew up with her, and I know, I know what she was like.'

'People change, Betsy. Emma loved the boys, she was a great mother.'

'Oh, after, sure. Sure, sure, she was. She was a great learner, top grades, top of the class every time. And I got second class marks, and second-hand clothes, second-hand men, second-hand Wilma, I'm second-hand Rose from Second Avenue.'

She sang the phrase.

'I really have to go, Betsy, the boys are exhausted.'

'And that's why I want them, why I deserve the boys. I always got Emma's cast-offs, so why shouldn't I get the boys? Why should you take them away to bloody … what's it called, this place you're going?'

'Port Simcoe.'

'Port Bloody Simcoe. No little boys for poor Betsy.'

'For heaven's sake, Betsy, they're human beings, not second-hand sweaters or skates. And I am their father.'

'So I'll take you too. They need a mother, you need a wife. To hell with Wilma in there, I'll ditch him, come and live here. You'd be amazed at how civilized I can be when I'm sober.'

'Well, the boys are becoming uncivilized. I've got to go.'

She mumbled more, but released him.

Having diverted Mrs Hatcher from clearing away, Frank was the more obliged to accept her help putting the boys to bed. Taking turns, they read to each of them, saw to the brushing of teeth, the toilet calls. The lights were out by quarter to ten.

Mr Hatcher and Willis appeared happy to kill the rest of the scotch, but Betsy, seated at the head of the table, was clearly near her limit.

'Back so soon?' she slurred. 'I'm just telling Dad a story, I mean, Willis has heard it, he was there, a very funny story ...'

'Perhaps later, dear,' said Mrs Hatcher. 'I think perhaps we should go, George. Certainly the evening has been ... a ... a disaster, a tragedy for me.'

'No, no, Mother, you have to hear this story.'

'When we get home, dear.'

'It's a really hilarious story about this consular party we went to in San Francisco last year. So let me just set it up again. As I was telling Dad, it was in this apartment where ...'

Mrs Hatcher grasped Betsy's shoulder.

'No, dear, we're all going home. George ...'

Betsy shook her shoulder and slapped at the hand.

'Willis, perhaps you can ...'

'Certainly, Mrs Hatcher. Come along, dear ...'

'Get your goddamned hands off me, Willis, I'm a grown woman, and I'm not in the service. I come and go as I please.'

'Now, Betsy ...' began Mr Hatcher.

'And you too, Dad, leave me alone, the whole damn bunch of you, I'll go when I want to go ... in fact, maybe I won't go, maybe I'll just stay the night. You got a bed for Betsy, Frank?'

'Afraid not, Betsy.'

'Ah, but I know you have. Course, even if you didn't have a spare bed ... well, I'm sure we can come to an understanding ...'

Betsy's naughty hints, complaints, threats went on, but Willis soon had her in her coat and out to the car.

'Well, Frank,' said Mr Hatcher, 'it was a magnificent meal, just magnificent, leaving aside, of course ...'

'Even if I overlook the cruelty of your sudden ... just springing it on us like that ...'

'For heaven's sake, Babs, how was he supposed to do it gradually?'

'Yes, George, take his part, take anyone's part but mine, no one has ever taken my needs into account, just tell Babs to be quiet and take the affronts and the slurs and the insults.'

'Babs, are you sure you aren't under the same influences as Betsy?'

'The pot calling the kettle black.' She squared her shoulders and turned to Frank.

'And quite aside from your … announcement, as you call it, I'm shocked, Frank, that in the presence of the children you would force that much alcohol on people. Betsy is a sweet girl, but she needs firm guidance, and certainly does not need to be tempted as she was so grievously tonight. I just wish people thought it was possible to give thanks for all our blessings without becoming animals, as the rest of you have. I am most disappointed.'

I am most seriously displeased – Lady Catherine de Bourgh.

'Well, I am very sorry to hear you say that, Mrs Hatcher. I had hoped to repay some of the fine meals you have served to me. However, if you …'

'The food was wonderful, as you very well know, and I am grateful. But there was far too much of it, and far too much to drink. I wonder you can afford it, but of course, you know more about your financial situation than I do. As for the other thing … well, I'll say no more on the subject for now.'

'Very wise of you, Babs. Come along now, old girl.'

'And I'm not an old girl, I'd appreciate it if you could, just for once …'

Frank closed the door and waved from behind the glass.

Willis, gay?

Possible, or course, but doubtful, even improbable.

Betsy, deranged?

Certainly.

Arguing with the Hatchers was like arguing with …

No, don't think about that.

Hallowe'en

The Hallowe'en mischief began about noon. Frank was sitting in his office eating his sandwich and picking through the mail, while Sid was on the phone to an auto repair shop:

'Whadya mean, 350 bills?... Yeah, I realize that, but the whole ... No ... Yeah, but ... Aw, shit ... Yeah, awright, go ahead ... So when ... Tomorrow! But how am I supposed to?... Yeah, yeah, okay.'

He hung up.

'Shit.'

'One of those days, Sid?'

'And not only that, the wife is on the warpath about ...'

The litany of woe went on.

'And where the hell is my copy of *Light in August*? How am I supposed to teach a ... you got a *Light in August*? Shit.'

'Sorry, Sid, if Jane Austen didn't write it, I haven't got it.'

Sid rummaged through the midden on his desk.

'Bloody anglophile. Colonial lackey, bootlicker.'

'For a Canadian, Faulkner studies would be just as imperial.'

'Well, I'm an American. And I'm not trying to con anyone into believing I'm a critic. But if you're going to be a critic, you got to back a fast horse, get into a growth industry. Canlit, for example, not that Britshit you shovel.'

'Actually, everyone's bullish on Jane Austen these days. How about all those recent Jane Austen movies – Emma Thompson's *Sense and Sensibility*, the BBC's new *Pride and Prejudice*, *Persuasion*...'

Sid glowered into a file drawer.

'*Two* versions of *Emma*...'

'Those aren't movies of Jane Austen stories, they're movies about English country houses, same as all that Brit stuff on PBS; it's all a by-product of the tourist industry, cheap charters on 747s.'

Frank held up a brochure.

'Norton offers a critical edition of *Light in August*, though I don't suppose you can get it before class today.'

'I think Marcia has one.'

Sid hurried off.

The last of the mail was a form letter from the dean. Matters of high policy, no doubt, interpretations of ministerial directives, of bureaucratic initiatives, of …

Grade Change Summary?

Re: 603-102-04-32-W98 JANE AUSTEN
After a careful and concerted review, for administrative purposes, it has been determined that the grade(s) assigned the following student(s) (has/have) be(en) amended as noted:

9608-2386　　Farman, Tiffany　　　80

Frank recognized the name but couldn't put a face to it. He found last term's file, and scanned down the Jane Austen list: the classroom took life in his memory … Gino with his big grin, left front … Mary and Carmella whispering … Orville in his red Bulls jacket … Jane with red hair … other names with faces in their usual seats … Farman, Tiffany, however, remained formless. He ran his finger across the details of her performance: nothing on tests, weak pass on prewriting, one failed essay, sporadic attendance for five weeks, then nothing to the end of term; final grade, eighteen.

A memory loomed: largish, dark-haired girl in jean jacket, quiet, sitting by the window about halfway down, staring out the window, alone usually, perhaps alone always. Yes. Left early several times, once complained about being marked absent when she arrived twenty minutes late.

But eighteen changed to eighty?

He telephoned student records and learned that Farman, Tiffany had graduated at the end of the spring term.

He strolled to the next office, dropped the sheet beside the essay Eleanor was correcting.

'The grade I gave her was eighteen.'

'And she wangled an eighty, I see.'

'And on this sheet … here's the line which lists her accomplishments and enthusiasms; I see nothing which might be converted to stardom. Perhaps you can explain it – you have at times enquired deeply into the skulduggery of the administration.'

'Well, old fellow …'

'What "administrative purposes?" What *are* "administrative purposes" – beyond the feathering of nests, building of empires, covering of asses, and passing of bucks? And did the administrative purposes compel the grade review or did they compel the grade change? I mean, this is some of the most opaque prose I've seen in …'

'Is this Tiffany a Black? Muslim? Jewish? Native?'

'White Christian as far as I know.'

'Let me put this as delicately as I can: has she been performing White House intern services for you?'

'Have I been soiling her blue dress? Considering her attendance record, I'd have been hard put to shake her hand.'

'Yes, Frank, I know that, and you know that, but Lucille doesn't know that.'

Lucille was the dean of arts.

'But how do "administrative purposes" get translated into "suspected inappropriate D N A"?'

'Adminspeak. See, she obviously requested a grade review, not for academic reasons because that would have gone through the department, but for personal reasons, so she probably started with the ombudsman or counselling. The usual complaints are racial or religious prejudice or sexual harassment. Since race and religion don't appear to be …'

'But I hardly knew her, I barely remember her. And, hey, these days I can't be bothered taking a glance up a skirt even if it's offered – I get to the other side of the room so I won't be distracted. I'm not Sid. Besides, as best I recall she always wore jeans, and was about as sexually provocative as … the business section of the *Gazette* … uhh … Hooker's *Laws of Ecclesiastical Polity*.'

Eleanor shrugged.

'Well, my guess is she complained, the complaint worked its way up to Lucille, Lucille believed her – or pretends to believe her – so she gets a pass. It's outrageous, of course, but what do you care? You'll be out of here in two months.'

'I don't care about her, or care for my own sake, but … I guess I care for the other kids. This guy here, Gino Muzzo, also got an eighty, but he worked like hell for it. Two years ago, Gino looked like having a terminal case of back-row-ism, but he straightened himself up ... Ahh, you know what I mean, you've had lots of guys like Gino. But this "administrative purposes" scam makes Gino and all the other hard-working kids look like fools. It's so ... fraudulent ... so unseemly.'

'If you hadn't said that, I'd never have spoken to you again. But you want to know whether you fight it or eat it, right?'

'I ... yes, I guess so. I'm not ... sure.'

'Okay. When's your next class?'

'Four.'

'I have a two. Shall I find out if Lucille can see us?'

'Us? You mean ...'

'Of course I'll help you, old dear. Go back to your office – I'll call Lucille.'

'What can I say? Thanks.'

'Go. If you can, write a brief description of whatever your relations were with the student, and photocopy that grade record for Lucille.'

Two minutes later, Eleanor came in.

'She'll see us at one-thirty. Make that account brief and diplomatic – no Jane Austenish flourishes, no Tolstoyan sarcasm.'

As Frank wrote, he found his hand was barely controllable; his stomach felt queasy and his temples throbbed. What had he ever done to...?

He was proofing the account when Ellery Culp rang.

'Looking forward to your move, Frank?' he asked breezily.

Frank gazed at the paper before him, but resisted the impulse.

'I've never much liked moving, but I guess it's set. Or are you calling about a glitch?'

'No, no, good heavens, we're all looking forward to having you here. And the good news is that the senior members of the faculty are as averse to moving as you are – I think I can sweeten the deal in a most gratifying fashion.'

'An extra ten thousand a year and no students at all.'

'Ho-ho. No, but in a way it's better than that: an office with a lake view!'

Dear God.

'Fine, wonderful. I'm looking forward to it.'

And looking forward to finding out the reason for this call.

'Great. Now, as you requested, I have a real estate agent keeping her ear to the ground, and I think she's found exactly what you're looking for. The price is a bit more than the top of the range you mentioned, but...'

The house was a newish three-bedroom split-level with all mod cons, fireplace in the rec-room, double garage, paved drive, in a development near schools, playground, arena, and municipal pool; situated a short drive from the college – 'and the mall, of course!' – and the owners would be happy to make the sale effective January first.

'And conditional on the sale of the house here?'

'I am assured that is normal practice. But you'll want to get in touch directly with her for the details.'

'Right, I'll do that. Now, if that's all, there's a bit of a crisis going on here, so ...'

'Oh, goodness gracious, thank you for reminding me – there is just one other small detail of paperwork, just a formality, really. The thing is we had a few new staff last year who, for various reasons, accepted the appointments, then changed their minds. Two were in science – one got a research fellowship at Stanford and the other returned to his job at St F.X. – if you can imagine that. The third was an economist who was more cheerful than those dismal fellows commonly are – the dismal science, you know? – when an Ottawa ministry took him on as an adviser. Anyway, the upshot of all this is that the dean in his wisdom has decreed, as deans in their wisdom will do from time to time, that all incoming faculty must demonstrate the sincerity of their intentions with proof that they have resigned from their last jobs and must declare that they will stay with U.E.O. for at least three years. As I say, it's just a formality, but if you could fax me your letter of resignation, your dean's acceptance, and a brief declaration of intention, everything will be on track. Let me just give you the fax number ...'

Frank recorded it in large numerals.

'Look, you're asking me to take a tremendous chance here. I have to give up a solid position with tenure and seniority for ...'

'A mere formality. You have the job here, you have nothing to lose and much to gain ... I guarantee it, it's written in stone.'

Eleanor put her head round the door: 'Almost ready?'

Frank nodded, and mimed a request that she do the photocopying. He said to Culp, 'Okay, you'll have it this afternoon.'

On a sheet of internal memo letterhead, he wrote a brief note to Lucille resigning at the end of the fall term, and put it in his pocket. He joined Eleanor at the photocopy shop.

'Now, you know what Lucille is like, so don't speak unless spoken to. Understood?'

Like a cowed schoolboy, he nodded agreement. As they made their way toward the elevators, Eleanor scanned his account.

'Okay, this will do. I don't know what it will do, but it's calm and non-aggressive; with Lucille that's the best way. For you. But you haven't told me what you want. Do you just want Lucille to explain the basis for the change, do you want to protest the change, or do you want the grade changed back to a failure?'

'No, records says she has graduated, so I guess I'll settle for the protest. I'd like to know why the grade was changed.'

'Good. Because, knowing Lucille, I think that's the best you can expect, graduating student or not.'

In the walnut luxury of Lucille's eighth-floor office, Eleanor's adroit hypocrisy was a pleasure to watch. By shifting the concern from the offence to Frank to the unfairness to the other students, she got Lucille to admit, despite obvious reluctance, that the protest had referred to sexism.

Eleanor delivered a well-judged explosion of outrage: the student had barely come to class, had never been in Frank's office, Frank had never attracted a hint of complaint in all his years of teaching ... and, putting the knife in, his wife had not been dead a year at the time of the alleged ... 'Alleged what, Lucille? What is he supposed to have done? What is the nature of the incident of harassment?'

'There is no allegation of an incident.' Lucille pretended to consult her file. 'The student states, however, that the teacher's frequently foul language was offensive, and that his attempts at humour invariably contained words and material characterized by sexual and sexist innuendo. In one case, for example, he referred to a character in a Jane Austen novel as a "bimbo."'

During the first five weeks of term that would have to have been Isabella Thorpe in *Northanger Abbey*, an accurate enough term for the character, though certainly anachronistic and colloquial. Could he find it in *Time*? In *The New Yorker*? In *PMLA*?

'I hardly think such a term is appropriate in the context of a college literature class. I would certainly be surprised to hear that Jane Austen used it.'

True, although in *Mansfield Park* she uses 'slattern' and doesn't she use 'slut' somewhere? No, that's *Wuthering Heights*, Heathcliff on either Isabella Linton or young Cathy.

'And I do not think that any female student in the college should be expected to endure a term such as "bimbo" which, I'm sure you'll agree, is heavily loaded with the most foul sexist implication, and is certainly demeaning and insulting to all women.'

Hardly 'most foul'.

Eleanor ignored the implied question and returned to the attack.

'You're being disingenuous, Lucille. You and I have both heard the most innocent-looking female students using far more inflammatory language ...'

Frank saw the obvious rejoinder but Eleanor was ahead of him.

'... and while student cafeteria usage does not validate terms for classroom use, you know perfectly well Frank was simply using a bit of modern slang to enliven his lecture, to make it more relevant to students in a compulsory class who are frequently indifferent and easily bored despite the best efforts of the most experienced and capable teachers in the profession. And the student is almost certainly being disingenuous as well in making the charge.'

'You have no justification for ...'

Frank's attention wandered.

Would UEO be less politically correct? More, in all likelihood. Would Culp use 'bimbo' in his lectures? No, he would stick to recent and intriguingly provocative criticism, solidly respectable academic lectures on deconstruction before mute and uncomprehending kids ... No, he was more likely jolly and teasing, with a hint of condescension ... no ... nonsense ...

Frank shook his head and tried to pay attention.

Lucille obviously considered him guilty until proven innocent, but her desire to pillory a male teacher was nicely balanced against the slim evidence and the danger of a union grievance, a course Frank had not even considered. But Eleanor played the union theme skilfully enough that Frank even caught the moment Lucille made her decision – head bent over the papers, then a turn to the window.

'Lucille,' Eleanor pursued. 'The student's complaint is based on slim evidence and the questionable assertion that she was offended by slang which is regularly used in the *Gazette*. In fact, she was a lazy student who did not read the assigned texts, who did not do sufficient written work, and who effectively dropped the course after five weeks. To grant her a pass, never mind a first-class grade, is a grotesque injustice to the other students, and her complaint against this teacher is tantamount to slander.'

Lucille tapped the papers with her pen and looked at Frank.

'You will not be lodging a counter-complaint against the student or a complaint against the administration?'

Frank shrugged.

'It seems pointless to me.'

'You're not asking that the grade you gave her be reinstated?'

He decided to submit the letter of resignation.

'In fairness to the other students, that's what I want, but I gather I'll not get it. I believe the student has graduated and has gone on to university, so failing her now seems ... unnecessarily cruel.'

Eleanor saved him further agony.

'He simply wants you to acknowledge that any suggestion that he behaved improperly is without foundation and is quashed.'

With an ill-natured nod Lucille assented.

As Eleanor started for the door, Frank said, 'Could I have a word with you, Lucille?'

Eleanor looked suspiciously at him.

'On a different matter altogether.'

'I have a meeting in five minutes,' said Lucille.

'It won't take that long.'

Eleanor closed the door as she left.

Frank slipped the letter of resignation onto the desk in front of Lucille.

'I just need a note confirming that you have received and accepted this.'

Lucille read the few lines then glanced up.

'This is a non-reversible declaration.'

'I know that.'

'You're serious?'

A deep breath.

'Yes.'

'You know you're probably making a mistake. You're going to the University of Eastern Ontario, I hear.'

'Yes.'

'Good luck.'

She made it sound less a blessing than a curse.

'Do you need it printed?'

'I gather a handwritten acknowledgement on my letter will do. It's to be faxed.'

She added a few lines and signed.

'Have Josée make a photocopy for our files as you go out,' she said as she handed it over. 'You'd better see Chantal in Personnel; you'll want to transfer your pension equity, and there'll be a few other details. I hope you know what you're doing.'

'So do I.'

But it was real – what other explanation could there be?

The Hatchers wanted the boys to do their trick-or-treating up the hill, but Jonathan and Simon begged to visit their friends' houses, so Betsy and Mrs Hatcher agreed to come to the house at six and take the boys about while Frank manned the door. Supper was by tradition quick hot dogs and salad.

By five-thirty Frank had the table cleared, the camera and the giveaways at the front door, the jack-o'-lanterns ready to be lit, and had the boys calmed down enough to begin dressing them. Both had obligingly asked for last year's costumes, Simon's Batman and Jonathan's pirate. Making up was a solemn rite: the boys stood silent and still while Frank reddened lips, blackened Jonathan's eyebrows, fitted the eyepatch. By the time the women arrived, Frank was lighting the jack-o'-lanterns.

'Three jack-o'-lanterns!' cried Mrs Hatcher. 'Such luxury! Your Dada has certainly gone all out this evening. And who are these little monsters?'

When Frank mentioned that he was to stay in the house while they went with their aunt and grandmother, both boys objected.

'Come with us, Dada, you always come with us!'

'Yes, Dad, you made us up.'

Frank shrugged to the women. 'It's supposed to rain in a while. You won't want to get your hairdos wet.'

'But Grandma and Auntie Betsy came all the way down the hill just to go with the little goblins.'

'I'm not a goblin, I'm Batman.'

With obvious irritation Mrs Hatcher accepted the arrangement. With the camcorder Betsy taped the departure. Other children climbed the steps with bags open and parents smiling from the sidewalk below.

The practice in the neighbourhood was that houses offering trick-or-treat put jack-o'-lanterns on the front porch; other houses were skipped.

Simon took Frank's hand.

'Do you know my favourite day of the year, Dada?'

'Your birthday?'

'No.'

'Christmas?'

'No. Do you give up?'

'I give up.'

'Hallowe'en. Because you get presents *and* you get to dress up. Is that smart?'

'Very smart.'

'I think it's my favourite day, too,' said Jonathan.

'Here's a house.'

For once the boys were pleasant to one another, Jonathan helping Simon up and down the steps, Simon objecting politely if his brother received less. They still did not notice that their costumes were not as elaborate or expensive as the full-suited knights, Ninja

Turtles, or tiny princesses with their lace and ruffled skirts. They were as grateful for peanuts in the shell as for chocolate bars. They discussed and agreed on the preferred route.

After forty-five minutes, however, they were passing the end of their block and Frank thought it best to give Mrs Hatcher her chance.

'Hey, guys, how about we drop the stuff you've collected at the house.'

'Yeah, good idea, Dad.'

'Yeah, then we'll have room for lots more.'

'And maybe some people when they see our bags are empty will think we haven't had anything at all yet and they'll give us more.'

'Yeah, right, Jonathan, you're really smart.'

'And perhaps Grandma and Auntie Betsy can take you for a while.'

'All right, Dad,' said Simon. 'Because perhaps you're getting tired.'

'Well, a little bit.'

What had Scrooge said of the boy who bought him the goose on Christmas morning? Intelligent boy? Remarkable boy? Delightful boy?

When they arrived, Mrs Hatcher was fretting at the door. She turned and called to Betsy.

'We weren't expecting you back so soon,' she cried. 'Betsy is ... she's using the washroom I believe ...'

Frank was helping the boys pour their loot into other bags when after a minute Betsy sauntered down the stairs with the camcorder bag.

The upstairs toilet?

'A camcorder in the toilet?' he asked her while her mother fussed on the front steps.

'I'll send you a copy.'

I thank you for my share of the favour, said Elizabeth ...

'The boys are waiting and the rain will be coming soon.'

Three children were coming up the steps, so Frank went to the door with the treat bag.

The next day Frank called the real estate agent in Port Simcoe. She gave him more details about the prospective house, and made it seem he was buying a mansion worth far more than the owners were asking or the even lower price she was confident they would accept. She arranged to send the documents he would need to make the offer. In the meantime she would confirm with the owners about the mid-December signing and New Year transfer dates, but assured him she could anticipate no problems.

He shivered as he considered the change rushing down on him.

Ringette

The ringette players, mixed boys and girls, crowded about the gate to the ice surface as the Zamboni made its last circuit. Dressed in full hockey gear including helmets and face masks, they would have appeared bizarrely threatening save for their wavering ankles, their piping happy voices. As the Zamboni rolled off, the referee skated out from the timekeeper's box and threw half a dozen rings onto the ice. She waved and the children stepped gingerly onto the ice then skated for the rings with bright cries. The referee threw more rings toward the visiting team entering at the other gate.

Frank watched gangly Jonathan, tallest of the players, unsteady as tall skaters are, take a loose ring, wobble toward the goal, and shoot. The protective cage hid his face, hid the smile Frank knew would be there.

Happy boy.

'Do we have to wait long, Dada?' Simon whined.

Unhappy boy.

'The game hasn't even started, Simon. It'll be an hour, then we can go home for supper. It won't be long. I brought your puzzle book and the Sega games.'

'Can I have a hot chocolate, Dada?'

The hot chocolate from the machine would be scalding and watery; Simon would not be able to drink it for half an hour and then would not like it. Frank fished a fruit drink from his bag.

'How about some juice instead?'

Of course, it wasn't thirst, but a natural enough need for a favour, attention directed away from his brother. After negotiations, Simon agreed to the juice now, while Frank bought a hot chocolate and set it to cool against the wall beneath his bench. Simon wandered off in search of a friend, of some likely stranger, of any amusement.

Frank took out Jane Austen's *Persuasion*, slipped his finger along the bookmark, but withdrew it, returned the book to the bag. Later.

Simon was at the drinks machines talking with two girls. Jonathan had just missed a pass, but the opposition also missed it, as did two of Jonathan's teammates.

'Not quite ready for prime time, are they?'

Monica Something, mother of Lara, one of the more adroit forwards on Jonathan's team.

'I think televised professional sports plant the expectation of cleanly executed plays, but at this level muddle, mêlée and milling about are the norm.'

'As long as they're enjoying themselves.'

Monica-Almost-Lewinsky.

'Yes, Jonathan always comes off the ice with a grin on his face, and I think he only scored one goal all last season.'

'Lara too. Last week she ...'

Monica Lowenstein ... yes.

They settled into comfortable chat, glancing at the game, at their younger ones.

'My brother's kids are in one of the West Island leagues and the atmosphere is completely different ...'

'I've heard that. So it's true?'

'Oh, yes, they're really nasty, everything is win, win, win, the coaches yell at the kids, the parents are all screaming, "Get him, kill him, murder her!" I mean, these are eight-and nine-year-olds we're talking about!'

'I think the Westmount Recreation Department people have a lot to do with it, don't you? They set the tone, keeping things friendly.'

'Exactly. I remember when Lara was playing soccer last spring, and ...'

Monica was a pleasant, genial woman, happily married as Frank understood, and obviously a wonderful mother. Her abundant affection, however, habitually spilled onto acquaintances as touches on the shoulder, the hand, the knee, and this unnerved Frank enough that he found himself shifting sideways, turning his shoulder, crossing his legs away from her. This evening she was in animated good cheer and more than usually hands-on. Frank considered chasing after Simon, but decided to wait for an opportunity. None came for five minutes, when Lara scored a goal and Monica went to the glass to cheer. There she began talking with another mother, and Frank looked about for Simon.

The boy was not in sight, so Frank picked up the hot chocolate and strolled toward the drinks machines. Simon was not in any of the locker rooms, nor at the drinks machines. The girls he'd been talking to were also gone. Frank scanned around the hockey rink, but even with his hat on Simon would hardly be visible. He was not in sight.

Frank became moderately concerned. Simon would not likely have gone outside, but it was possible. More quickly now, Frank walked across the north end of the small rink and down the west side, past the visitors' bench and past the bleachers where some of the parents sat. At the home team bench, he asked Jonathan if he had seen his brother, but he had been following the game and hadn't seen him. At the south end were several utility rooms with power tools, barrels of chemicals, and other potentially dangerous supplies. No Simon. The lone maintenance man shook his head.

Seriously worried now, Frank walked more quickly round the corner to the east side and scanned the full length to the north end; from what he could see past the obstructions, Simon was not there.

The Zamboni bay.

Perched in triumph in the driver's seat, Simon was holding the wheel and making 'brumm-brumm' noises.

Relief flooded his nerves; but was quickly transmuted to irritation, then anger. What if he had fallen, what if he had damaged it, what if the key was in and he had started it?

'Simon!'

The little boy jumped and turned, his face reading shock and fear.

'I'm sorry, Dada, I wasn't ...'

'Here, come down ...'

Frank reached to grasp the boy who was scrambling to climb down, his feet groping for the foot rests.

'What were thinking of, don't ever do that again, how many times have I told you ...'

The boy safely on the ground, Frank slapped his bottom padded inside the snowpants and, grabbing his arm, pulled him out of the garage bay and along the walkway, the boy crying, Frank spluttering his protests, the time-hallowed accusations, he dimly realized, of parents whose own negligence has endangered a child:

'… and what if it had started, what if it had gone crashing through the boards and onto the ice, the cost of a new computer for sure, and what if you had been hurt, off to the hospital …'

The boy, scrambled to keep up with Frank's strides, sobbing convulsively, crying his defence:

'I won't … I won't do it again … I didn't mean … Don't hurt me, Dada …'

As his glance roved in agitation, Frank saw something which froze him: a figure in the bleachers on the far side with a camcorder to his face … Willis? Frank looked away at once, resumed walking but more slowly; stopped talking; bent and lifted the sobbing child to his shoulder. The boy buried his face in Frank's neck, the unhappiness shaking his little body.

'Well, you're all right, Simon, that's the main thing, Dada was worried, and …'

Shamed and humiliated by his anger, his loss of control, his hypocrisy, Frank slipped behind the wall of the timer's booth, hugged the boy and wept with him.

Between periods, Willis came round from the bleachers, ankle-length black coat billowing out, a wide-brimmed black hat tipped back jauntily, the camcorder at the ready.

'Don't look up, guys, just keep reading your book,' he said. 'Biggest mistake in film is looking at the camera. Okay, roll 'em!'

Frank obediently read: 'So Snuggie said to the Chief Monster, "But I don't like being a mean monster, I want to be a friendly monster." "Monsters aren't friendly," cried Zogbu, "it ain't their nature."'

'If I was a monster, I'd be a friendly monster, wouldn't I, Dada?' said Simon.

'You sure would, little fellow, very friendly.'

He hugged the boy.

'Cut!' said Willis. 'It's a wrap.'

When he had both boys in bed and their lights out, Frank slumped on the couch. He had not even enough energy to open the TV supplement. As so often lately, increasingly often it seemed, he felt limp, despondent.

Whose fault was it? The Hatchers'? Willis and Betsy's? The Ministry's? Lucien Bouchard's?

His fault.

How many people with fewer advantages managed to cope – Linda, for example, Linda with her rented slum, her disastrous taste in men, her two kids, her lack of education, lack of skills, lack of job; Linda in danger of being hunted down at any moment by well-fed civil servants who suspected her of under-the-table payments. Yet Linda managed to be in good cheer most of the time, managed to raise her children reasonably well, managed, it seemed, a social life.

His fault and no excuses.

When Emma died, the strength went out of his life. But also, perhaps, the joy? Their marriage had seemed reasonably happy, the children seemed as cheerful and contented as most other children they knew, they were more or less in control of the money. But now? Were the Hatchers right? Was he perhaps not up to the job alone?

Eleanor always told him he was doing a marvellous job, but when did she ever see him with the children? She never saw him losing his patience over a lagging breakfast, a splashy bath, dirty clothes left in the middle of the floor, homework left waiting while Jonathan snuck half an hour for his favourite television show.

Losing his patience over the Zamboni.

No joy, no excuses.

Keep on.

He pulled himself to his feet, microwaved a coffee, flopped down with the remote.

Surely there must be more to life than keeping on?

Keep on drinking coffee, keep on wasting time before the box.

He muted the sound, began at the bottom, and flipped slowly through the channels: commercials, guns and crashing cars, talking heads, announcements, sitcoms, sports ... a British mystery from one of the PBS channels – *Prime Suspect*? Yes, there was Helen Mirren. He had almost certainly seen it ... Emma had probably seen it with him, one show they always watched together ... Yes, he had seen it twice, *and* had it on cassette. Another sitcom ... When had it become acceptable practice for actors on a set to deliver a punchline and look at the camera? Was verisimilitude old hat? ... Polar bears ...

He switched it off, managed to get to bed, slept fitfully.

The Hatchers decided to make Betsy's birthday party in early December a combined family occasion and social event, with cocktail party and buffet dinner.

'A goodbye to fall weather,' George explained, 'and a consolation for what's coming. Of course you'll bring the boys.'

'Are other children invited?'

'Yes, some of Betsy's friends are bringing their children. They'll have the rec room. There's the computer and there'll be videos and games and snack food, the usual thing.'

They wanted the children at the party, but out of the way, not making nuisances of themselves; they wanted the idea of children.

'And, Frank,' sotto voce, 'you needn't think in terms of an expensive gift – we understand your financial situation. Babs suggested perhaps a place setting of the Rosenthal – we'll be leaving that one with Betsy and taking the … what's it called?… you know, the flowery dishes.'

At a guess, a place setting of Rosenthal would cost a week's grocery and spending money, five to ten times what he and Emma had spent on one another in the last half dozen years.

'Or … let me see, Babs wrote it down for me but … an "open veg"… You're a great chef, does that make sense to you?'

'Yes.'

'Good, well, we'll expect you about four-thirty on Friday.…'

Simon had been agitating for a large bedroom like Jonathan's. Frank saw no need to keep the big back bedroom for himself, and decided to begin by doing something about Emma's clothes.

Emma had a matched pair of bureaus in their room, but hung her clothes in the closet of the spare bedroom. Frank scanned the rank of hangers briefly, then plucked them in manageable bunches and laid them on the bed: blouses, sweaters, slacks hung by the cuffs, jeans folded on hangers. From the shelf above he took folded sweaters and sweats. Could the Sally Ann want second-hand shoes? Could anyone? Despite her hint, Betsy could not reasonably wear any of her sister's clothes. While Emma was generously built, Betsy was thin, borderline anorexic even. But perhaps Linda … Linda couldn't wear anything closely fitted or fitted for height, but would she like some of the loose sweaters or blouses?

Frank cleared a space on the bed and sat to ponder his dilemma. Linda must have thought about Emma's clothes, but had not mentioned them. Nevertheless she might well be grateful for some of the things, and those that didn't fit her might fit her mother. And hadn't she spoken of a sister? And if things didn't quite fit, couldn't they be taken in?

Yes. Put them all back, even the shoes.

The bureau drawers held handbags and jewellery, lingerie and hosiery, sweat socks, and more folded sweaters. From the jewellery box he took Emma's charm bracelet with mementoes of their stays in Edinburgh, London, the continent; a jade (actually plastic, he suspected) pendant and earring set he had bought her for their tenth wedding anniversary; a Chagall-inspired brooch he got her one Christmas from the museum shop; and an allegedly Celtic or Pictish pendant from Scotland. Betsy could have the rest.

Would Linda take the lingerie, or would she be offended by the offer? Not the panties, of course, and the bras were probably the wrong size, so he put them all in the reject pile. Bathing suits also useless. But perhaps the slips and half-slips? He piled them on top of the bureau. He culled the athletic socks with bits of lace and saved the plain white ones for Jonathan. Surely Linda would not want the washed pantyhose? He examined the unopened packs of new pantyhose: size C, according to the table of heights and weights on the back, seemed to include Linda as well as Emma; they'd no doubt be useful, and Betsy favoured gaudy colours and designs quite beyond Emma's utilitarian beige; even the 'silky evening sheer' in 'barely midnight' might be too restrained and Linda would certainly appreciate …

The envelope was smaller than the pantyhose packs and fell free when he lifted the stack. It was addressed to Emma at her McGill office; the return address was the Department of Economics at the University of Alberta; the return addressee was 'C. Wert.' Wert? Carl, wasn't it? Yes. He had been part of the lunchtime crowd Emma knew from the McGill grad students' club several years ago; he had come to a party at the house once, and Frank had two of three times chatted with him in the grad students' bar. Rather stout, a bit of a spare tire, sandy-haired, clean-shaven; actually wore cowboy boots. Good sense of humour, rich laughter.

The note was on buff U of A letterhead paper and dated ten days before Emma's death: computer down, so using snail mail, chatty bit about U of A politics, teasing bit about Quebec politics, dismissive bit about Reform Party politics – surely he was a Reform supporter? – then:

> I've booked us a room at the Tumbleweed; it's a bit out of town, so it's not one of the conference hostelries, but I'll have the car, and there's a great view into the coulee of the Oldman – reminds me of my favourite view – gulch in the foreground, flat middle ground, mountains in the distance. Sorry I can't pick you up in Calgary, but the departmental meeting that morning is …

Frank folded the letter, replaced it in the envelope, put it in his pocket. He put the pantyhose packets on top of the bureau with the slips. He put the used pantyhose in the garbage bag with the other rejected lingerie, took the plain socks to Jonathan's bureau. Returning to his own room, he closed the two empty drawers. Linda could come and clear what she wanted of the rest.

He took the letter to his study and slotted it in between the printer and the computer. No, boys might see it; on the bookcase shelf beside … the postage rate brochures, they'd never notice it there.

Downstairs he microwaved a coffee and sat on the couch. Why had she not left the letter in her McGill office? More prying eyes there, probably, or more chance of accidental discovery. Why had she not destroyed it? Perhaps she figured simply throwing it out was not enough – burn it, or snip it into little pieces, or get it into a garbage bag as it was going out for collection. In any case, she could reasonably have considered it secure where he'd found it. Was the letter her last thought as the car…? No, leave her the privacy of those few moments …

And what moments had she taken for ... 'bonking' as the Brits say these days, a better word than ... the alternatives. It would have been quickies, probably, Emma too busy, too obsessed for languid afternoons in bed. In her office? Surely not. Carl perhaps living near McGill, student ghetto, was that it? What difference?

For what does it matter now? Emma is dead.

Was Carl the first, or ...

It doesn't matter, don't think about it.

He had not liked Carl, had not disliked him particularly, for Carl was cheerful, genial, amusing, polite, but had felt uneasy with him. 'No, Frank, it's my round. Got to distribute some of those oil patch profits here in the east ...' Piecing together scraps of anecdote, he gathered Carl had first taken a bus-admin degree, had gone into an oil company or a brokerage, something to do with oil; had multiplied a parental legacy; had, after ten years or so, taken his profits and gone back to school. A few references to a broken marriage.

Arm on the shoulder.

Eye contact from just a shade too close.

Confident smiles.

'It's my round ...'

Smug smiles, it seems.

The term papers could wait no longer; could not possibly be done now, could wait no longer.

He microwaved another coffee, went to his desk, bent to the job.

Birthday

Because the boys were slow making their birthday cards, Frank did not arrive until just before five. Warned that 'real guests' needed the front hall closet with spillovers in one of the front bedrooms, he put their coats in the back bedroom. The Hatchers obviously rated the party Class A: the dining-room table, supplemented with several side tables, was moved toward the far wall, the lot covered in white linen, and stacked with rented crockery and cutlery. A smocked woman from the catering service was distributing bread baskets. A huge ham decorated with pineapple rings and cherries was flanked by a pair of triple chafing dish frames, the dishes themselves yet to come from the kitchen. Three candelabras awaited the match. In the living room, all the lights were lit, and dishes of nuts sat on all the tables. Mr Hatcher was talking before the fireplace with a man his own age. '... at least the pollsters got a black eye by predicting a landslide ...' Mr Hatcher was saying. Frank's brief wave was returned with a nod. 'I'll just park the boys,' he murmured, and escaped. In the nook beneath the stairs, another covered table served for a bar; behind it a young man was slicing lemons. Frank thought of offering greetings to the kitchen, but the smocked woman came bustling toward him, so he beckoned the boys and headed for the basement.

Betsy stood beside a woman who was kneeling before two unhappy children. Betsy was in black dress which Frank took to be sedate by her standards: it covered her from her throat to the knees of her black stockinged legs. Perhaps Mrs Hatcher had made suggestions. As Betsy flounced toward them, the mother threw Frank and the boys a perfunctory glance.

'Hi, guys, come to wish me a happy birthday?'

'Happy birthday, Auntie Betsy,' Simon cried.

'Yeah, happy birthday,' said Jonathan.

'But there are lots of toys, Brendan,' the mother was saying, 'so if you don't want to share with Allison, I'm sure you can find something else to do.'

The mother gestured vaguely about the room.

'But I want *that* Turtle,' he insisted.

The pouting girl was clutching one of Simon's cast-off Ninja Turtle figures.

'Perhaps he wants to play with my boys,' said Betsy. 'This is Jonathan, and this is Simon. They can show you some computer games.'

'That's a great idea, isn't it, Brendan? Why don't you go with ...'

The woman, in a red cocktail dress, turned, exposing a stunning amount of bosom. Frank hurriedly knelt beside Simon.

'Can you show Brendan how to play Destruction Derby?'

'Demolition Derby. Okay, Dada ...'

Sociable Simon at once went to Brendan and began explaining the game in intricate detail.

'Can you find something to do, Jonathan?'

'I suppose I can watch a video.'

'I did warn you that you'd have trouble getting time on the computer.'

'I know, Dada.'

'It's only for a while, then there'll be lots of nice stuff to eat and cake and ice cream.'

'Okay, Dada.'

'Good boy.'

Two more women came down the stairs followed by three children who peered cautiously into the unfamiliar room, but who came readily enough when they spotted the computer, the television, the children already there. Simon turned to inspect the arrivals. 'It's all right now, Dada,' he called. 'There are enough kids now. You can go.'

The mothers laughed.

'Thank you, Simon.'

'Yes, Frank,' Betsy leered, 'you go play with the big boys upstairs.'

'Yes, I think the guys are all right.'

'But keep your hands off the big girls,' she murmured. 'How about a birthday kiss?' She pressed against him.

'Don't start, Betsy.'

'Can't I *raise* any interest in you at all?'

She moved her hips against him, lifted one leg between his. He pulled back.

'Betsy, don't – it's all so meaningless, beside the point. Don't demean yourself like this. It's pointless flirtation.'

Her eyes hardened.

'Everything I've ever gotten I got through flirtation. But I'm not a tease – I come across. When I get my payoff, you get your payoff, all you want of it.'

'Don't be offended, Betsy, but nothing you can offer would pay for what you want. I'm dead to … flirtation … dead to … all this sort of thing.'

She turned, hissed over her shoulder, 'But I am offended. And that should frighten you.'

As she walked toward the others, she flipped up the hem of her dress, giving Frank a private view of her legs stockinged in black stay-ups, her behind in skimpy black panties.

He turned and went up the stairs, reflecting that after three months of mornings in the house, along with other encounters, the boys at least were comfortable with Betsy.

Willis was just coming in the front door with half a dozen plastic bags of ice cubes. Frank went to help carry them to the bar. Mrs Hatcher, fluttering from the kitchen, cried, 'Finally you're here to give some help, Frank. If you had come earlier, you could have saved Willis the trouble of going out for the ice. You obviously think a party simply organizes itself.'

'I was getting the children settled in …'

'Oh yes, blame the children, it's always someone else's fault, and you never so much as … And that blue blazer again – why do you go out of your way to disgrace the family, don't you even have a suit? You'll have to do better than that if you're expecting to fit in at the University of Eastern Ontario … But I see Ellen and Ralph coming up the steps. Take this ice to the bartender, and try to keep away from the drink, try not to make a spectacle of yourself the way you usually do … We go to all this effort and what thanks … Ellen! How wonderful you look!…'

Willis winked at Frank. 'Yeah, pull up your socks, pal, you want to make a good impression.'

'I expect it's hopeless: I went to the wrong schools.'

Willis pretended to consider this statement. 'Yes,' he agreed, 'You did; and you are hopeless.' He gave his bags to the bartender. 'But do try to stay reasonably sober. J & B on the rocks,' he said to the bartender. 'On second thought, make it a double.' He patted Frank's shoulder. 'Momentous questions about the guest list, old pal. How many friends of Betsy's, how many of the Hatchers'? Foreigners from the office were okay, even blacks and Orientals, because they're diplomatic, but they also had to accept some local French. But no spiky hair, quota on local Jews, and absolutely, positively no gays – Mrs H is terrified of getting AIDS from her toilet seats. Be thankful you missed it.'

'I can use the bog in confidence?'

'Yeah, but tell me ahead of time so I can turn off the security video.'

'It wouldn't be a pretty sight.'

Frank would have preferred a beer, but decided a gin and tonic might avoid a charge of debased origins, vicious breeding, unbridled barbarism. 'And light on the gin,' he said.

The party had been well launched while Frank was in the basement. Willis immediately joined a group, clearly of Betsy's friends, an attractive blond woman with two men in suits, Willis's hand on a shoulder, a ready quip igniting laughter above the murmuring voices.

courses in economics 101 and real estate 401
Marco Island – that's just south of Naples
since Charest won the popular vote, Bouchard has to
old diplomats never die, they just go to Ottawa
about Mordecai's article in last Sunday's
first Bourque and now Bouchard – I mean, what in God's
if he thinks his National Post *will*
got into Bre-X at about two-forty

Frank lingered just inside the door searching for a familiar face. More than a dozen people were now arranged about the living room in the diffused yellow light that glowed on faces, dusted the suits and dresses with a glow, flared from the drinks, the glasses, the ice; authenticated the paintings. Laughter, baritone rumbles, soprano trills.

don't think Bouchard ever 'has to' anything
and sold off just before
just the Daily Telegraph *with the brains kicked*
fly to Tampa, although Miami is actually closer
saw Ted – you know, the Jane Austen of Westmount
the Asian meltdown, but you can't
restaurants in Ottawa, so
I mean, Reagan the Teflon president had nothing on
without planeloads of the usual Miami people … if you get my meaning
and that was on margin!
knew him when he was going to Bishop's, and even then he

Effete, barren, irrelevant, ultimately provincial: perhaps Mrs
Hatcher was right to complain. Even Emma had at times chided him
for his shyness. He did not want to be here, did not want the advantages of mingling with the select, but did the boys perhaps deserve
the chance of upper Westmount acquaintances who would be a help
later?

the main advantage of winter in Montreal
so Mordecai said
junior mining stocks, but
the launch of Nick's book and
wife of his? Christ, bazooms out to
prefer West End, Grand Bahama, although now

Was he justified in keeping them out of the private schools where
their classmates, to the tune of ten thousand per capita per annum,
were the future lawyers, bureaucrats, captains of industry and
finance? Sensitive, reserved, mathematical Jonathan being offered
friendly hands up the social ladder, the professional ladder, groomed
for cut-throat negotiations in the walnut-veneer of the thirty-fourth
floor, in smoke-filled rooms, groomed for positions Linda's children, for example, could never hope for? Or was this just more effete
moralistic hypocrisy? Give the boys every possible advantage in the
desperate struggle for jobs in a bleak world?

in Grumpy's on a stool between Nick and Dick when
cockroaches wherever you
at least put off another referendum, but
no gardening!

in Chatelaine *or something that they were real, but no one*
stadium has about as much chance as
the last page of Barney's Version *and*

Money, power, a house on the Mountain, mid-winter Caribbean
vacations: Frank had never sought them, nor had Emma; surely he
was right to continue as they had begun? Surely Emma would not
have wanted the boys in private school where, she once remarked,
intellectual debate was: 'My Dad's BMW cost more than your Dad's
Mercedes.'

Costa Rica for a change and it was
set for life
the poor Trudeau boy only last spring and never imagined
that little separatist with the teeth, you know, she
daughter plays in that rock band – it's called ... uhh
from the Ritz to the Chateau and back in three minutes flat with her
VISA *Gold*

The attractive blonde woman beside Willis tilted her head back
and laughed, her parted lips startlingly red, the lipgloss glistening.

As more and more people arrived, Frank had to move from the
doorway into the hall. People were avoiding the dining room until
the food was ready, while the inevitable cluster around the bar and
the powder room blocked the hall, and several groups were already
sitting on the stairs. Frank made his way to the study at the back of
the house. More than a dozen others, Hatcher friends by their ages
and clothes, had had the same idea. Several people glanced at Frank,
but he knew none of them, and none greeted him.

so warm lately that a white Christmas may not
the fiasco the time he was running in Pointe Claire or Beaconsfield or
in the Gazette *this morning that he won the QSPELL*
Blue Mountain coffee, I mean the real thing!
Miss Piggy!
expected a black Christmas, but now that Bouchard has
about the tongue trooper and the tattooed
headline in the newspaper: 'Fresh Constitutional Initiative'
a grey Christmas

Because he was usually in the more public rooms, Frank had not often been in the study, but he had always liked the room for the generous proportions, the two tall windows, the wide desk with its brass lamp, the two leather reading chairs, the dark-stained oak bookcases that lined three walls. Apart from several shelves of *Canadian Tax Law*, *Estate Planning* and other professional series, the collection was eclectic. The shelves had not, as Emma had once unfairly suggested, been stocked with volumes bought by the yard. And the *Encyclopædia Britannica*, the *Canadian Encyclopedia*, along with several atlases and dictionaries were respectable and obviously used. AAA tourbooks for various parts of eastern Canada and the US. Books of exploration and travel – Thor Heyerdahl, Jan Morris, Freya Stark – just above three shelves of *National Geographic*; some paperback mysteries; gardening and sewing books belonging to Mrs Hatcher. Antiques: silverware, china, furniture. The largest subject was history: Pierre Berton, of course, but mainly general or popular works on Europe – all of Barbara Tuchman, the complete John Prebble on Scotland – with five shelves of World War II. Some were the obvious Time-Life series and Churchill in book club hardback. But he also had memoirs by Montgomery, Alexander, Eisenhower, and others, along with biographies of such as MacArthur, Halsey, Rommel, and Roosevelt; a shelf of accounts of escapees and the clandestine war, including Fitzroy MacLean's *Eastern Approaches*, and R.V. Jones's *Most Secret War*; campaign and general accounts such as Samuel Eliot Morison, Liddell-Hart and Prange, half a dozen works by John Keegan, and the Copps/Vogel series on the Canadians in northern Europe. Frank would dearly have loved to sit down with a stack of them; but the chairs were occupied, and his own parents and Emma had made it clear to him that reading at parties was not done.

He decided he had best return to the hall, out of the way of temptation. Near the door, he glanced along a shelf of coffee table books – *Treasures of the Louvre*, *Canada: A Year of the Land*, *Golf Courses of the Carolinas* – and noticed the McGill yearbook for 1953. An image of Ellery Culp's diploma, framed on his office wall, appeared before Frank's mind's eye. He would not likely have another opportunity of looking up Culp without wasting several hours traipsing down to the university library.

He found Mr Hatcher readily enough among the graduates, his

economics major noted. Turning back, however, he was unable to find Culp; but Culp had graduated later, hadn't he? The undergraduate photos were small and he riffled unsuccessfully through to the team photos in the sports section. He found George Hatcher among the tennis and golf teams, but Culp, if he had played, must have stayed intramural. There remained the fraternity pages: beer bottles raised above card tables, crossed eyes, tongues lolling out, guys in their underwear, the winsome sweetheart of Sigma Chi and other beauties, the annual Ritz balls with cocky guys in tuxes and page-boyed girls in flaring taffeta. And, on the Omicron Rho Chi page, in a group above a caption reading, 'Those pledges get younger every year!' a grinning George Hatcher with his arm over the shoulders of a boy with the lopsided grin of Ellery Culp. Culp, his torso naked, wore a diaper.

When Frank checked the children, he found a dozen of them picking at plates of chips, crudités, and dip between bites of hot dog. Several mothers were trying to keep mustard off the party clothes, the carpet, the walls.

Jonathan was explaining details of a computer game manual to a boy Frank recognized from school; Simon was laughing in exaggerated hysteria with two girls. Frank stayed a while, exchanged a few words with each, but both seemed happy and paid him little attention.

Many people on the main floor were doing their best to eat and drink and talk without the convenience of chairs. In the dining room, Frank found himself in line behind the pretty woman from Eleanor's dinner. Brenda? Betty? Beth.

'My God, I think I'm wearing the same skirt and blouse I wore that night. Whatever will you think of me?'

'I'm wearing the same jacket and slacks.'

She lifted her mouth close to his ear:

'And I'm wearing the same bra ... but you're not to remember it.'

'Bra? What's a bra?'

'You're my kind of lover. Brad is here. Would you like to meet him?'

'Actually ...'

'That's all right. Eleanor said you were shy. Anyway, I was just teasing.'

'I expect she said "painfully shy."'

'Well, yes, but I didn't believe her.'

'So what are you doing here? Friend of Betsy?'

'Can we talk?'

'That bad?'

'We went to Waterloo together, and we've teamed up for squash doubles a few times at the club lately. But friends? Well ... you know Betsy ... and I hope you know me well enough.'

''Nuff said.'

'I don't actually know why she invited me. Perhaps because of Brad; he's with SAE – they do aircraft simulators and control systems, so perhaps Willis wanted to meet him. Oh, look, a ham with pineapple rings and cherries – I haven't seen one of those for ages.'

Perhaps because she was Eleanor's friend, Frank felt comfortable chattering with Beth, but knew well enough that when they had finished the precarious task of getting their meals into their mouths he should make an effort to circulate. However, when they had stacked their plates on the side table with the other returns, Beth touched his hand.

'Don't do the proper thing, don't run off. Show me your children.'

In the basement they sat on the couch amid the screams and flying teddy bears.

'I'm afraid the showing won't last long,' Frank commented. 'They're getting tired. Jonathan is the tall fellow in the blue shirt, and Simon is the little blond fellow there.'

'Aren't they handsome, though.'

'Yes, and cheerful. Nice boys. Exemplary in a way. I'm very lucky.'

There seemed little more to say. They had left their frivolity upstairs with the grown-ups; here Frank sensed Emma's absence as the unspoken subject, the subtext. Beth, smiling, watched the boys for a few minutes, then looked at Frank, though without speaking. His tears didn't really surprise him, but hers, tracking eyeliner over her cheekbones, did. He found her a tissue in his pocket, another for himself.

'I'll go now,' she said. 'I'm … imposing … that is, I … think you want to take them home soon.'

'Perhaps that would be best. I don't mean …'

She brushed her fingertips along the back of his hand.

'No more words.'

She arose and slowly disappeared up the stairs.

He knew he would not get the boys out of the house without some fuss; besides coats, boots, hats, scarves, and mitts, they would have to say their goodbyes to their grandparents. In the event, Mrs Hatcher kept them all in the kitchen five minutes until she had settled some crisis over the dishwashing machine, then another five while she complained that Frank was showing insufficient family loyalty by leaving so soon: '… and no school tomorrow – what can *you* possibly have to do that's as important as …' Mr Hatcher, now in the study and breathing a heavy fog of Courvoisier, made a point of introducing the boys to everyone as 'the heirs-presumptive'.

Betsy ambushed him as he emerged into the front hall.

'Dead to all this, like hell,' she hissed.

'What are you …'

'You and that slut Beth, don't think I didn't see you.'

'Betsy, she's just a friend, an acquaintance I met at a dinner party. I don't even know her last name.'

'But I bet you know her bra size. You'll pay for this, for rejecting me. Wait till you're in court, then you'll find out.'

'Court? Is Willis divorcing you? I don't see what …'

But Betsy's eyes, her open mouth told him that he was far off the track; that she was frightened; that she had made some sort of mistake. She closed her mouth and turned toward the bar.

'Okay, guys, we're off home.'

Coffee

In the second week of December Frank accepted an offer on the house. He got ten or fifteen percent less than he might have had for it six months earlier, but his agent assured him he was lucky to sell at all. 'Despite the election, it's still a buyer's market, Mr Wilson,' she chirped.

'I'll send a bill for the difference to Bouchard.'

'Don't hold your breath,' she replied drily. The signing was to take place on the fourteenth, and his ownership ended at the stroke of midnight on New Year's Eve. This gave him a few days to get his end-of-term grading done, about a week to pack the house, then a week to close the sale on the new house in Port Simcoe. Although he was vaguely uneasy about doing what was obviously the sensible thing, Frank agreed to send the boys to stay with the Hatchers from Friday the eleventh until they moved so he could work and pack without too much distraction. December looked like being a frantic month, and January, with unpacking and classes beginning immediately after the holidays, looked no better. He made a mental note to ask Culp for book order forms for the courses; book orders at the college had gone in several weeks ago.

On Friday, he moved a carload of the boys' clothes and other things to the Hatchers' house. As the boys would go straight there from school, he decided he might join the Friday table for a final visit. He spent the rest of the afternoon grading, made himself an omelette, telephoned the boys good night, then strolled downtown. He could do some Christmas shopping before joining the others.

Although the crowds were light and the clerks obviously anxious to help, he could not get his heart into the task. Nonetheless he managed a silk scarf for Mrs Hatcher, a designer sort-of-T-shirt for Betsy, an illustrated account of the Battle of the Atlantic for Mr Hatcher, and a biography of Palmerston for Willis. Buying for the boys should have been easier. He found a prettily illustrated *A Christmas Carol* – when would he have a chance to read it? – but after half a dozen other obvious books Frank found himself wondering what superheroes they favoured these days. Super Mario, Batman, Spider-man, and the Turtles, he had been told, all 'suck'. A team shirt? Montreal Canadiens items were easily available; Frank preferred the boutique at the Molson Centre, but it was out of the way and perhaps not even open tonight. The Chicago Bulls? Charlotte Hornets? The Mighty Ducks? No, that was going too far.

Choose something next week after getting the Santa lists.

He could easily spend five hundred on computer games, but a glance at his watch told him he could not get to a computer store before closing. He trudged toward the Friday table.

Frank's elegiac mood was not echoed in the others; the teachers in the group were giddy with end-of-term release while the rest were variously looking forward to a few days off, a mid-winter week in Florida, visits from family.

He settled back in his chair to watch, listen, catch their mood rather than infect them with his own. In any case the subject was politics, Canadian politics, Quebec politics, constitutional ooze, referendum silt, language flotsam …

'Hey, gang, Wilson's here – we're supposed to stay off politics.'

'Let him drink somewhere else if he doesn't like it.'

'Are there no brasseries? Are there no coffee shops?'

'Let him hide his head in the sand of another saloon.'

'What's wrong, Frank, don't want to know?'

'I read Richler's piece in *The New Yorker* a while back – is that enough?'

'That was six years ago!'

'Seven!'

'New and exciting developments!'

'Queen Anne is dead!'

'Anyway,' Frank replied, 'if I'm not mistaken, several of you gentlemen are, as my in-laws put it, among the Chosen. How come you haven't left yet?'

After a loaded pause, Sholem replied, plonkingly, 'It can't happen here.'

Another pause, then people five tables away raised their heads to enquire into the laughter. The genial bartender lifted an eyebrow.

'In that case, how are the Expos doing?'

'It's December, Frank.'

'A bit distracted, are you?'

'The Habs, then?'

'Another thing that can't happen here.'

This was the opportunity to tell them this was likely his last night with them, but it seemed an imposition; he let go of the conversation, let it drift again to politics, let his mind drift back to earlier nights at the table, nights a decade back, two, the night he brought Emma the first time … when she savaged someone over Claude Lévi-Strauss … Terry Everett wasn't it? … Terry long gone …

Sholem wasn't deeply engaged.

'Sholem, where's Terry Everett these days?'

'London.'

'Ontario?'

'England. Computers, I think.'

Emma had been a hit, slimmer then, her black hair down to the middle of her back, glossy, her eyes sparkling, her beauty at its peak, and she passionate with life, life of the mind, while beer, jokes, gossip were only distractions to be pushed aside impatiently, the same impatience with which she pushed her hair back from her face …

No, don't think about it.

Gradually the chat drifted from politics to history. While Frank should have been entranced by early medieval migrations, he found himself thinking of real estate: values, prices, conditions of sale, insurance coverage, notarial tasks, deed searches … He had never really wanted to own a house, but with apartment rent just money down the drain, a solid down payment available, and monthly payments manageable, the advantages of building equity were obvious enough. And now selling and buying … And the other house in Cape Breton … children … He was bourgeois, despite his half-hearted youthful dreams of bohemia, of intellectual adventure, of late-night discourse rivalling that of Dr Johnson, David Garrick, Sir Joshua Reynolds … and he not even fit, it was apparent, to play Boswell, not even fit, indeed, to fill out the list of silent guests at the table, a make-weight … as he was here … a gloomy presence … adding nothing, unneeded, unwanted …

A tug at his sleeve.

'Uh?'

'Distracted?'

'Yes … sorry, Sholem, I didn't hear you. I was thinking about … the house … painting …'

For a few minutes they talked about house painting.

The others, friends, companions of a quarter century, were losing definition, the past fogging, slipping away, his mind captured by the present alone, thought without substance now …

Presently he arose, drifted to the toilet, paid his tab at the bar, slid his arms into his coat.

'Frank?'

'It's barely eleven, you're not …'

At the door, he found Luc had followed him with the bright bags.

'Don't forget your Christmas presents, guy. A bit tired from the term, are you?'

He found himself concerned not so much to understand Luc's offers of help, of a cab, a drive home, but rather to know if Luc knew the connection of 'Guy' to 'Guy Fawkes.' Yes, he probably did.

'Yes, I expect that's … or just tired … I … I think I'm better off home in bed.'

'Well …'

'It's best this way … I'm not … I'm out of place.'

He was in the street, gone without a goodbye.

At home, he took his Boswell from the shelf, scanned his list of annotations on the inside back cover for a vaguely remembered definition of conversation. Yes, Johnson to Boswell and Mrs Thrale:

> 'There must, in the first place, be knowledge, there must be materials; – in the second place there must be a command of words; – in the third place there must be imagination, to place things in such views as they are not commonly seen in; – and in the fourth place, there must be presence of mind, and a resolution that is not to be overcome by failures; this last is an essential requisite; for want of it many people do not excel in conversation. Now *I* want it; I throw up the

game upon winning a trick.' I wondered to hear him talk thus of himself, and said, 'I don't know, Sir, how this may be; but I am sure you beat other people's cards out of their hands.' I doubt whether he heard this remark.

Perhaps it made better sense if not *I* but *Now* were italicized: Johnson was a year and a half from death and often tired from ill health. But materials, words, imagination, resolution: I seem to have lost them all.

If I ever had them.

For several days he graded, nourished by sandwiches and frozen dinners. The boys when he telephoned or visited seemed content to stay at the Hatchers' and produced daily lists, which Frank promised to mail to Santa on his way home. Each evening he drove downtown or out to a mall, buying gifts in nearly empty stores.

The night before the grades were due, he stayed at his desk until after ten, then flopped on the couch with a beer and the remote control. He fell asleep on the couch watching AA tracer over Baghdad, and was awakened by the ringing of the telephone. He stumbled along the hall, trying to get his slippers on, bent over with stiffness from sleeping curled up, clicking his mouth to encourage some moisture.

'Hello?'

A pause, then the dial tone as the other receiver was set down.

Seven forty-five. For five minutes he tried to get back to sleep, considered trying the comfort of bed, thought about coffee. The coffee won.

When he went to the front door for the paper, he found a bubble pack envelope on the floor below the mail slot. No mail delivery on Saturday … indeed, no address or stamp … wrong shape for a late essay … It was a video cassette, unlabelled.

The screen flickered to life – a street, Sherbrooke Street on a sunny day; the date and time across the bottom. The camera isolated a group, then zoomed closer to show Frank walking hand in hand with Simon and Jonathan in costume for the Family Day parade. The scene changed abruptly; shaky pan of a park, people,

Westmount Park, Family Day. Then Simon's left leg was in close-up; the bruise he got when he slipped on the fire engine was clearly visible, livid red and blue.

A new scene. Jonathan was standing in the bath, turning modestly from the camera and frowning and he pulled the towel around his thin body.

Willis's voice could be heard echoing hollowly in the tiled room.

'How did you get that awful mark on your bum, Jonathan?'

'What mark?'

'That one right there ... there, see.'

Jonathan looked at the scratch then turned nervously away.

'I scratched it when I was on the slide at school yesterday.'

'Are you sure? No one hit you? Are you sure it wasn't where your father hit you?'

The incident had occurred last June. Frank could see that Jonathan was ashamed of being taped in his nudity, could sense the boy's confused irritation and fear over the question. The playground story was the one Frank had heard as well when he noticed the mark, and it was likely true, but perhaps Jonathan had been hit by another boy and didn't want to start trouble.

'Was your Dada upset when he saw the mark?'

Jonathan paused. 'A bit.'

'Was he angry?'

'No.'

'Was he sad?'

'A bit.'

'But he wasn't happy about it? He didn't laugh?'

Jonathan thought about this.

'Dada doesn't laugh.'

There followed a succession of shots of the boys dated through the summer and fall. In every case, the sequence came to a close-up of a bruise on the body of one of the boys. The purpose was clear enough: they had assembled evidence that Frank was a negligent or abusive father. They had even spotted the nasty bruise that Jonathan suffered on his ribs when he slipped getting into Dan Archie's boat.

The sequences from the ringette game were ill-lit and the sound from the echoing rink was mere noise, but they were effective, heavy with implication. Carefully selected bits showed Monica obviously fawning over Frank; because they were seen in telephoto close-up partly hidden by the boards, the glass, the penalty box, they seemed to be hiding. Even a reasonable viewer would be justified in suspicions. The Zamboni incident showed a cowed, hysterical child being yelled at and beaten by an enraged, brutal father.

The date changed to 31 October; the ringette had been later, so Willis had clearly edited to produce a telling climax. The camera was shaking and rather out of focus as it panned around Frank's bedroom. His night table in close-up. It shook more as a hand reached to pull open the drawer, a woman's hand ... a sleeve Frank recognized as Betsy's. The open drawer revealed a *Scientific American* Frank had bought years ago for an article on the dispersion of Indo-European languages ... nail clippers ... a travel alarm. The picture wavered as the hand closed the drawer ... swept to the left ... his bureau. The hand opened the top drawer. More junk ... extra bulbs for the boys' night lights ... cufflink box ... old watch boxes he meant to throw away ... never-used handkerchiefs ... The hand lifted a batch of items aside to reveal two magazines, removed them and laid them side by side on the bed. When the picture stabilized, the titles were clear: *Anal Boys, Oral Boys*. The photographs were graphic illustrations of the titles. Frank was not just abusive, but perverted. The camera shook again as Betsy's hand opened both books: more explicit photos. The picture went briefly static, then changed to a rather grubby office with German Wehrmacht officers: Charles Gray ... Donald Pleasence ... both generals ... Nigel ... something, as a sergeant, Feldwebel, wasn't it? ... Nigel Stock ... *The Night of the Generals*, unlikely Omar Sharif amusingly workable as the detective ... interesting, curious movie ... Willis had frugally taped the evidence onto a used cassette.

This obviously had something to do with Betsy's remark about 'court'. A custody suit? Were videotapes admissible? And while Frank was made out to be having an affair with Monica, was he also supposed to be in the thrall of young men?

Surely this was nonsense: the fireman, Monica, even Dan Archie could be brought to bear witness.

But:

'Dada doesn't laugh.'

Frank realized with a shock that the boy spoke the truth.

Over a bowl of cereal, Frank wondered how he could investigate the relevant laws for Quebec at eight o'clock Saturday morning. Were video cassettes considered evidence? Would he have to subpoena the fireman who witnessed Simon's fall? Or Dan Archie for Jonathan's bruise? Surely anyone could see that the pornography was planted? Would the boys be allowed to tell their versions? Would they remember the bruises? And how much would all this cost?

Frank was washing the breakfast dishes when the phone rang again.

'I hope I didn't wake you, Frank.'

Mr Hatcher.

Eight-twenty by his watch.

'No.'

'If you can manage it, Babs and I would like you to meet us for coffee.'

There was something this morning ... the notary to close the sale of the house.

'I have an appointment at eleven, then I have to turn in my grades at the college.'

'Nine then? Nine-thirty?' He named a café on Victoria, a few blocks away.

'Yes, sure, nine.'

Did notaries know about child custody?

A shower cleared out the last of the wooziness. The Hatchers were seated at a window table when he arrived.

Mr Hatcher stood up and offered his hand.

'I hope,' said Mr Hatcher stiffly, 'that we might manage to settle all this in a civilized manner.'

Frank gave a brief shake.

'I got the video cassette – what it promises doesn't strike me as civilized. It strikes me as a threat, intimidation, coercion.'

'The cassette was not our idea.'

Mrs Hatcher burst out, 'The very idea ... that we ...'

'Now, Babs, we agreed I would handle this. Frank, I didn't approve of the cassette, but it does make the point – we are willing to go to some lengths to achieve our objectives. We would prefer to accomplish them in a civilized fashion, and hope you might be willing to go along with that. Now that you understand the position you're in, I hope perhaps you may be willing to see reason.'

'I'm willing to consider any proposition which means I keep my children.'

'Well, we'll see what might be arranged. But the business is rather complicated; it has ramifications you may not have considered. I believe I explained something of the position Babs and I are trying to arrange for ourselves when I retire. I mentioned that we're letting Betsy and Willis have the house on a balance of sale at a bit of a discount as it were. As I explained, it will be hers eventually anyway.'

'And the boys would have gotten the other half, isn't that so, George? But we're going to leave them money instead.'

'Now, Babs, let me explain – I think I can put the case in a more straightforward way. The point here, Frank, is that transferring ownership of the house to Betsy is all very well in terms of estate management and avoidance of probate and the attendant duties and such. But the result is that even with our government pensions, the company pension, and my own small income – smaller than you might guess, Frank, because of the expense of bringing up the girls, sending them to private school and all – and the damn recession in the early nineties ...'

'I think we can avoid vulgarity, dear.'

'That's the least vulgar word you can use about it, all the fault of that damn Mulroney and his separatist buddies ...'

'George!'

She flourished her handkerchief.

'And even though Bouchard says another referendum is on the back burner, it's just that – delayed; two years, three, he'll call another one. But, yes, all right. Anyway, Frank, what it amounts to is that, come March first, our income is not going to be quite enough to manage ... Well, I was going to say, "in the style to which we have become accustomed", but in fact, even with a number of projected economies, things are going to be a bit tight for us.'

Frank sat motionless, wondering where this was leading. Into a highly fictional world, it seemed. Over the years, Mr Hatcher's asides about buying Alcan or unloading bank shares invariably involved 'making a tidy sum' on the deal. From this and from all Emma said about it, the Hatchers should have been more than comfortable. But perhaps those reported sums had not been so tidy. And Emma had never been much interested in money; perhaps she had been wrong. Emma wrong? No.

'Now, let me come at this from a different direction. I didn't mention this until I got all the paperwork done, but I've put the fifty thousand from Emma's insurance into an investment fund for the boys, for Jonathan and Simon.'

'That's more than kind of you, but it is entirely unnecessary. After all, it's your money, it's simply the repayment of the money you loaned us on the house.'

'But it isn't our money,' interrupted Mrs Hatcher. 'Can't you see that? It's Emma's money ... it's all she ... it's all that's left of ...' She began to sob. '... blood money ... money bought with her ... blood ... I'm sorry, I just ...' She put her face into her handkerchief.

'Well, you see how it is, Frank. Babs and I are pretty much of one mind about this. You see, we just don't feel we can take that money. Surely you can see that it is only proper that it go to the boys?'

'But the boys will get it anyway – that money has been translated into equity in our house. When I'm gone, they'll get the house, or rather the new house in Port Simcoe, between them. Surely it's all the same?'

What did Mr Hatcher's eyes hide?

'Blood money!' cried Mrs Hatcher. 'How can you talk of equity and such like?'

'I didn't invite this conversation, Mrs Hatcher. And I can talk about it because that's the term. My salary and Emma's fellowships and TA positions saw us through the first years. Emma was only just beginning to earn good money when she died, money which would have gone to pay off the house in maybe five years. With her insurance money, the house is now secure – in fact, that is precisely the reason she had insurance, that I have insurance. In an hour I'll be selling the house and using the money to buy a new house. That new house will provide capital for my retirement, whatever retirement I get. I'll likely be gone about the time the boys graduate from university and whatever value the house has then will give them a good start in adult life. Whether she is with us or not, that's the way Emma and I both saw it.'

Mrs Hatcher was still in her handkerchief.

'You needn't lecture me on the purposes of life insurance, Frank. Babs and I both understand your point, but, and I repeat, we do not feel we can take any profit from Emma's ... Well, the fact is, we haven't. As I said, I have put it in trust for the boys. We simply cannot consider it as payment toward the mortgage.'

'We just couldn't take it,' cried Mrs Hatcher. 'The idea that we would be living in luxury in Toronto on the profits of ... on money that ...'

'Mrs Hatcher, I'm no financial wizard, but the earnings on that fifty thousand would hardly make up the difference between penury and luxury. Even as an annuity, it wouldn't likely ...'

'Details, Frank. You're missing the point – we cannot, we have not, we will not take that money.'

'It would be unthinkable!'

'But you have taken it. Emma left it to me as her beneficiary, and I paid it to you. I no longer have it, and you do. The mortgage is paid down, and the money is yours to use as you wish.'

'But I keep trying to make you understand, it isn't ours – it's set aside for the boys.'

'And I have explained to you that the boys have or will have the house which that money has, in part, bought.'

Mr Hatcher shook his head in frustration.

'You are being deliberately obtuse.'

Frank suddenly got the point.

'Are you telling me,' he asked, 'that the result of all this concern for Emma's memory, and concern for the boys is that you are claiming I have not paid down the mortgage? That as far as you're concerned, I don't owe you a mere three thousand dollars – I still owe you the entire fifty-three thousand?'

'We just couldn't take Emma's legacy.'

'But you could keep me from having it.'

I can't believe what…
shocking…
the selfishness of it…

The Hatchers were fizzing with righteous vitriol.

'And you are expecting me to pay off the balance later today when I get paid for this house, or perhaps to pay at the rate of a thousand a month or something for the next eight years?'

'When you wanted to buy the house you're in, you came to me for the money, cap in hand, and I loaned it to you.'

'Emma went to you in response to your repeated and insistent offers – I had very little to do with it.'

'How dare you?' demanded Mrs Hatcher. 'Using our own daughter against us … I can't believe that …'

'So you want fifty thousand now or a thousand a month from me, when I can barely get by now bringing up the boys, while at the same time you're giving Betsy her share of the house and selling her the boys' share at a nominal monthly payment when Willis pulls down half again what I earn?'

'They have expenses you don't have.'

'They have social obligations,' cried Mrs Hatcher. 'They move in a higher social circle than you do, entertaining diplomats, politicians, the select.'

'The select usually have money, while politicians and diplomats have expense accounts for their three-martini lunches – I get free paperclips from the school bookstore.'

Mr Hatcher clucked at this naiveté.

'Willis has lost many of his allowances because he's no longer posted abroad.'

'And I never had them.'

Mrs Hatcher sought another handkerchief from her purse.

'Explain it to him, George, for heaven's sake. He simply refuses to see reason.'

'You don't have to lose the fifty thousand.'

'I'll be fascinated to find out how I can manage to keep it when I don't have it.'

'You needn't be sarcastic, Frank. I have your best interests at heart. Yours and the boys'.'

'I'm waiting.'

'Well, Babs and I have thought this through really carefully. There is an alternative.'

'I'm not sure we should have brought this up at all, George, he just will not be reasonable. I can see what a mistake we made, trying to be generous.'

Mr Hatcher shushed her, fiddled with his coffee cup.

'You must believe, no matter what the appearances, that we are concerned about the children – their future is our paramount concern. We wish they could live in a proper neighbourhood, go to a good school, make the contacts that are necessary if they are to get ahead in life. It takes money, lots of it, to provide these advantages. As I know full well, having put two daughters through Waterloo and McGill; as you have not yet realized. Now, your current job is hardly sufficient to clothe and feed them and provide the minimum amenities. Your new job is still only in a regional university, and although I expect it will pay better, it will hardly be sufficient to do a proper job of it. They would have to go to a boarding school in Toronto, at least for their high school years, and they would have to go away to university. I have to wonder if you'll be able to save enough to provide that. And you are young, you may marry again, may want to have more children ...'

'No, I have no interest in that, I'll never marry again.'

'Don't say "never", Frank. But if that's the way you feel about it now, so be it. But the point is, that if the boys stay here in Montreal with Betsy and Willis, they will have the best. And I'll guarantee that – it will mean great sacrifices, but Babs and I are prepared to make sacrifices for family. Selwyn House, St George's, LCC – even Brébeuf or the Grand Séminaire if they seem so inclined, we're not prejudiced, and with changing lines of power the French schools may offer better opportunities, who's to say.

'Now, the point of the cassette is that we can make a case against you as a competent single parent. Of course, there would be more than the cassette. That babysitter might not make the friendly witness you expect when she has a clear picture of the view the welfare and tax people might take of her finances. Then, there are the rumours about you and a female student, sexual harassment, I understand.'

How had they got word of that business? Did they know Lucille? Someone else in admin? Had other teachers heard of it? 'Bimbo.' But it didn't matter.

'Of course, your college hushed it up, but one can draw conclusions ... such as that that case is likely not an isolated one. It is well known that only a minority of sexual harassment cases come to light, and female students are often frightened of failing if they report them.'

'Yes, and those other women, too! I have to wonder about while Emma was still ... those times you went jetting off to conferences all by yourself! It needs very little imagination to ...'

'But most damning of all, to my mind, is that Betsy has reluctantly admitted that your ... approaches to her have not been ... those one should expect of a brother-in-law.'

In the past few years, since the word had become current, Emma had frequently referred to her sister as 'Betsy the consular bimbo.'

'The poor child is so upset – you can't imagine – and to think that you would ... on Thanksgiving, and again on her birthday of all days – I was shocked!'

'Now, Babs. Of course, Frank, I expect you'll be planning to drag in a whole list of friends and colleagues to assure the judge of your fitness to care for the boys.

'Before you protest, let me assure you that I probably know Quebec's child custody laws better than you do – I have had several chats on the subject recently at the club. And I can also admit to you what you would find out soon enough – that in any action we might take, you would likely win. But court rooms are funny places, I can tell you. Yes, you might win, but then again you might not. In any case, the boys will suffer tremendously from the process, and if we pursue the matter with vigour, it will cost you as much in legal expenses as it will cost us. And we have set aside quite a tidy sum for the purpose.'

Frank saw that he was to ask.

'How much?'

Mr Hatcher's eyes twinkled.

'I have a nice round number in mind – a convenient little fund which I think might be appropriate for the cause.'

Frank sighed.

'Fifty thousand?'

'You get the point with surprising rapidity.'

'You're threatening to spend Emma's fifty thousand in a series of losing legal actions not because you expect to get the boys but to bleed me of a similar amount?'

'Not bad, but you haven't got the whole point. Rather more than fifty thousand. You're forgetting the other fifty thousand we'll collect from the lien on your house.'

With fifty thousand less for the house because of the lien and another hundred thousand to spend on legal fees, Frank would be competing with students for a cheap flat in Port Simcoe.

'Of course, if you were willing to concede custody, things could be very different.'

Exhaustion descending.

Mr Hatcher took a small sheaf of documents from his pocket; several had the customary legal folding.

'This is the promised lien on your house for fifty thousand dollars. In an hour I can present this to your notary and fifty thousand will come off the top of the sale price. That'll leave you with perhaps one hundred and eighty, tops. Of that, a hundred or so will go to finance your contestation of the custody actions, leaving you eighty to buy a house and get started on your savings for the boys' future. However ... if you sign this other paper, relinquishing custody to Betsy and Willis, I'll tear up the lien. I'll do more – in this envelope is the necessary documentation for the transfer of the boys' investment fund to you. I'll return to you that fifty thousand from Emma's insurance policy ... and I'll also consider the mortgage paid in full. Instead of eighty thousand, you'll have the full price of the house without the lien, plus the insurance money. That's two hundred and eighty thousand, a difference of two hundred thousand dollars. You'd be set for life, Frank.'

'And think of the wonderful presents you would be able to afford for the boys for Christmas, for their birthdays!' cried Mrs Hatcher.

'And of course, you would be able to see them for several weeks every year, during holidays. And think of the holidays you would be able to afford. Why, Jonathan is old enough to appreciate a trip to

Paris or London. Think of it, a new car, decent clothes and proper furniture for a change. And Betsy and Willis would be most grateful if you wanted to help out with the boys' tuition fees. A whole new world would be opening to you, and ...'

Frank stood up.

'I have to be at the notary's soon. If you're planning to present that lien, you shouldn't wait here too long. Don't bother offering me a lift – I'd rather walk. Good morning, Mrs Hatcher. Here's something for my coffee and my share of the tip.'

'I told you, George, I warned you, there's no point offering the hand of friendship to his sort, they're always ungrateful ...'

On Monday the moving company dropped off several stacks of collapsed boxes. Frank left them piled in the hall. He could pack later; he had little else to do. In the afternoon, he cleared the paperwork with the insurance company, and took to the notary the necessary confirmation that the house was insured until the transfer of ownership. He got a change-of-address package from the post office and stopped in the stationery shop for a few boxes of late Christmas cards. He was reading the instructions for a microwave pasta when the telephone rang.

'Frank, I'm so sorry, I can't say how sorry I am.'

Ellery Culp.

Frank knew at once, barely heard as Culp babbled about the provincial budget, the dean, the board of governors, restraint all around.

'But I have a contract. You said I ...'

'But that's just the point, the contact was delayed, there is no contract, the college has not signed a contract with you.'

'But you guaranteed ... it was written in stone ... you made me resign from my job here ... you said ...'

'I *said*, yes, but they cut the ground out from under me. The dean's office was supposed to issue the contract over a month ago, but ...'

Frank waited for a pause, then said, 'Well, I'm getting used to legal documents – I guess I'll just have to sue.'

'Well, if you want to take it that way, you're at liberty to do so, but the legal advisers to the board have concluded that you'll get nowhere.' He paused carefully before adding, 'You see, if you think about it, you have nothing on paper. Not a scrap.'

'Fax receipts, photocopies of my application, receipts for registered letters ...'

'From you to the college, yes. But nothing from the college to you.'

'But I came to see you, I ...'

'You came to *enquire* about a job. I advised you that a position *might* open up, but I certainly never *promised* you ...'

'Do you know a Mr George Hatcher, accountant, of Montreal, McGill 53?'

Did he pause?

'No.'

Frank replaced the receiver.

When the telephone rang a few minutes later, Frank barked an irritable hello.

'Frank? It's Angus McDonald.'

'Sorry about that, Angus. I just had an annoying call and ... oh-oh, what's happened? The cottage has burned down?'

'No, the cottage is fine. I was in to check the oil just the other day. No, it's about your Aunt Sal – we buried her this morning ...'

She had managed to conceal the progress of the disease during his half-dozen calls since the summer, but Frank was not surprised.

'I know you probably wanted to come for the funeral, but I didn't think about it and when I did I thought the family was in touch. I'm sorry about that, Frank ...'

'I probably couldn't have come anyway, Angus, so don't feel ...'

Snow

After a number of tries, he managed to get Lucille at home. She confirmed that as far as the college was concerned his resignation was final: they were already in the process of hiring. The one union official he talked to tut-tutted when he admitted he had resigned: 'I'm afraid there's nothing the union can do. The contract is quite explicit. There are MEDs and part-timers who need work, and this position is now open to them; if we agreed to let you back, one of them at least would certainly grieve it. Remember when Jake resigned then tried to get back?...'

He telephoned Eleanor at their cottage.

'Are you coming for Christmas, old fellow?'

He brought her up to date.

After a long silence then some swearing: 'They're monstrous.'

'Tell me I'm imagining all this. Tell me I still have two kids, a job, and a house.'

'What can I do to help?'

'There doesn't seem to be much, does there? After this house is sold, I'll probably have to live in my parents' cottage in Cape Breton. Lend me a bed in town when the custody hearings start.'

'Look, you can't go to Cape Breton, it'll cost a fortune in travel and long distance phone calls. You can have this place. Stay with us over Christmas if you want, and when school starts we'll be back in town. You'll be close to the kids, close to the custody case, close to friends...'

It was tempting, a reasonable solution. She continued to press him. At last he agreed to come after he had cleared the house, at least for the weekend of the New Year.

Over the next days, Frank delivered the last of the boys' things to the Hatchers' house. He managed to give away or sell half of the furniture; the rest he donated to the Salvation Army. Eleanor arranged for a neighbour to let Frank into her basement with the paintings, the stereo, the china, some dishes and kitchen things, his computer, and two dozen boxes of books. His own clothes, Emma's laptop, and the few books he might read over the next week or so he packed in a few suitcases and boxes, a small enough load to get into the trunk and the back seat of the car; these boxes he stacked near the front door. Everything else he gave to friends or threw in the garbage.

He declined the invitation from the Hatchers to spend Christmas Eve and Christmas day with them. Instead, he brought the boys home for a few hours on Christmas afternoon. The house, largely stripped of furniture, echoing with emptiness and lit only by ceiling lights, was no longer a home. The little tree was pathetic, the bright show of presents beneath it contemptible.

'This morning we had presents like this,' piped Simon, describing a curve as big as a haystack.

Frank smiled.

'That's wonderful, little guy. And Santa left you lots of great presents, I hope?'

Jonathan replied, 'Grandpa got us a membership in his squash club, so now we can play there any time we want, not just on visitors' tickets.'

This was news, but not a great surprise.

'Yeah, and William and Thomas and Stephen and Jared are members too, and we can have our own lockers, and we don't have to pay when we get a sandwich, the woman just writes it down and Grandpa pays it later.'

'That's very generous of Grandpa; I hope you gave him a big hug.'

'And do you know what else Grandpa said?'

'What did he say?'

'He said maybe if we come and live there all the time, we could go to St Crispin's School. Sean and Jared are going there next year, and Patrick started in September.'

'Well, I'm not sure if …'

'And some of Simon's friends go there, too.'

'Yes, Dada, like Anthony and Eric and …'

'Well, we'll see, guys. Try to be patient. Okay?'

'Okay, Dad.'

'Now can we load StarCraft and NHL99 on the computer, Dada?'

'I'm afraid I've packed the computer, Simon.'

'Then let's go to Grandma's and load them on that one! When are we going back there, Dada?'

'In a little while. Look, guys, I'm sorry our lives are in a bit of a mess just now, but I'm trying to arrange things. I'm not sure when we'll have a new place to live, but, tell you what, when we do, the first thing we do is set up the computer and load the games.'

'We're never going to live in this house again, are we, Dada?'

'No, Jonathan, we're not.'

'I like this house,' Simon piped, 'and I'm never going to forget it.'

I hope not.

Frank got them interested in the jigsaw puzzles, but Simon solved his Star Wars puzzle in ten minutes, while Frank and Jonathan took half an hour just to get the edge pieces of Jonathan's Eiffel Tower picture; it would have to be taken apart for later solution … or for a yard sale, more likely.

The second hour was unbearable. The fruit drinks and cookies Frank offered they picked at, then abandoned. A tour of the empty bedrooms evoked not curiosity or nostalgia, but indifference. A stroll to the park was impossible because they did not have their snow pants with them. Frank offered to read to them, but they politely declined.

'Can we go soon and load the games?'

'Yes, please, please, please?'

After he returned from taking the boys up the hill, Frank slumped on his sleeping bag, exhausted.

On Wednesday, Frank packed the car, lowered the thermostat, and locked the door. From the sidewalk, the house looked smaller than it was, and desolate in darkness. The little garden he had worked over was forlorn without the covering of snow. Tears welled in his eyes, so he started the car and drove away. He delivered the keys to the notary's receptionist.

As he drove toward the Champlain Bridge, he yet again considered taking the boys to stay with the Rowans, but it was clearly impossible. Despite Eleanor's promises of acres of outdoor playground, there was in fact almost no snow on the ground and the cold was so intense as to be dangerous. Stuck indoors, the boys would quickly become impatient and irritable without their computer games. Eleanor and Magnus had not had a child about the house for some years; the noise and activity of their arrival would charm them, but it would soon pall.

Our house is silent now, no children in it, gone from us. The living room is beige, the hall is light beige, the kitchen peach.... The watercolour of the asters hung above the television, the big blue abstract in the dining room, the beach scene in the hall.... Graham Greene was on the top left shelf, then Orwell to the right, and Wodehouse below.... But was Waugh on the third or the fourth shelf? Our house, slipping away from memory.

Jonathan has light brown hair, Simon is still blond....

A horn and a glowering face from an overtaking car reminded him that although the autoroute traffic was light and the road surface clear, he had to pay attention to his driving. He concentrated on keeping the needle on the one-hundred-kilometre mark, the dashes flashing by a uniform distance to the side, used the turn lights when passing.

Most of the history books were on the bottom right shelf, with biography above them, travel above them ...

Another blast: he had pulled out to pass a van without checking the side mirror as well as the overhead.

He turned on the radio, slowed down to ninety, began playing with calculations of time and distance.

Twilight obscured the house behind the trees, but the several lighted windows suggested warmth and comfort. Frank parked next to the Rowans' car, pulled his garment bag from the passenger seat and walked toward the door. Eleanor threw it open and reached her arms to his shoulders.

'The fire is warm and the martinis are cold,' she murmured. 'Welcome, old fellow.'

'I was just thinking about warmth and comfort. Merry Christmas,' he replied, handing her the little gifts, dropping his bag by the stairs.

'Shalimar?'

'It's a whim. If you don't want it, give it away or throw it out.'

'I'll give it a try. Talk now or talk later?'

'Later.'

'Martinis by the fire first?'

'Anything first. Anything second ... third ...'

'Come on through to the kitchen. Magnus is making his famous daube ... Like? ...'

'Like Mrs Ramsay in *To the Lighthouse*.'

'Can't fool you.'

'You seem to be about the only one who can't. Magnus, Merry Christmas. That smells like a daube, and a particularly fine one at that.'

The fire was warm and the martinis – rather too many of them – icy from two hours in the freezer. The daube was indeed fine, and the cabernet sauvignon with it, and the salad, and the Lagavulin to follow. Magnus carried the conversation to British politics, to the EC, to the new Eastern Europe. He was informed, witty, genial; he and Frank never talked personally, and Eleanor, despite a shrewd and evident eye on Frank, was a willing participant. By eleven-thirty, Frank was stimulated to a point just short of wooziness. When Magnus pushed the Lagavulin toward him, he shook his head and rose to his feet.

'Bed for me.'

'So early? My God, Frank, you're ...'

'I'm the father of two little boys who get up at seven- thirty. Time for bed ...'

He escaped before the tears reached his cheeks. Eleanor, who came along to show him to his room, had seen the tears coming ten minutes ago. She turned on the bed light, pulled a corner of the covers back, and patted his cheek.

'Sleep well, old fellow.'

After a late breakfast, .the three drove to town for groceries and a salad lunch. On their return Magnus said he had a squash match. 'I'd rather do ten K on the skis, but it's too cold.'

'And there's no snow, Magnus.'

'Well, that would be a bit of a problem. We're having a rotten winter. I'll be back by the cocktail hour.'

'Now, talk,' said Eleanor when he was gone.

'Well ...'

So they dragged their way into that wilderness, trudging the wastes of lies, hypocrisy, betrayal, enmity, threats. Frank was in tears, Eleanor comforting, reasonable, practical. Yet even she could not see any hope save through endless lawsuits, and but little there. The house was gone, and most of Frank's savings with it. She had to agree that the job was gone, with the slight hope that Frank could win it back if he could prove, though more lawsuits, no doubt, that he had been tricked into resigning.

'So you agree,' said Frank, 'that the Hatchers probably conspired with Culp?'

'Well, I admit it looks likely. The U E O wouldn't ...'

'Couldn't, you mean – couldn't possibly want to hire someone with my credentials. That's not pessimistic, it's realistic.'

'But you still have the boys – the Hatchers can threaten, they can sue, they can run up your legal bills, but even they admit they probably won't get custody.'

'But perhaps they should. What if I can't care for the boys properly? What if the boys are better off up the hill? I have nothing – almost nothing, because the money I do have will be gone in a year or two. And even if I could qualify for unemployment, welfare, whatever – and I can't – it would be too little, and it would run out soon enough. In two years, my babysitter Linda will be better off than I am.'

'But you may find work. It's not hopeless.'

'Perhaps. But money is not the point, is it?... What can I offer them, really?'

'Love!'

'That's just what I doubt most ... Love needs presence, strength ... When a ... weak person, weakling, loves, that love is ... perhaps it is sentimental, unhealthy, big on hugs and tears ... perhaps clinging, cloying ... it strives to capture the loved one, to bind him, her, it is selfish, grasping, hothouse, narcissistic, it ... seeks to hold, to tie down, it finally demands love while pretending it is giving it. But good love, healthy ... valid love, is generous, it values the loved one for her own or his own valid self ...'

'But yours is good love, that's clear.'

'Perhaps, but … It has always seemed to me that a parent's love for a child is best when it comes from strength, when it loves the freedom, the integrity of the child's soul. The greatest – one of the greatest – sicknesses in a parent is the desire to make the child into a replica of the self. "Be like me, this is your proper future." The finest love is love of difference, not of sameness. I feel like a … a broken thing, entirely self-absorbed. I don't know if I have the moral strength … the strength of character, to bring them through to … to adulthood … to the futures which are theirs, rather than just my dreams. As we weaken – or see ourselves as weakening, which comes to the same thing in practice – we cling tighter to what we have, we seek more and more the reassurance of stasis, sameness … we fear change, movement. The boys have been up the hill for nearly three weeks now, and they seem happy enough. And they have grown away from me, I'm becoming a bit of a stranger to them now. They survived the death of their mother, why not the departure of their father? What if moving really is better for them? Granted, my coming poverty is the result of a conspiracy, but it will be poverty nonetheless. And it's not so much the financial, but the spiritual poverty: "Dada doesn't laugh." My future is … questionable … my present is … well, look at me, just look … am I fit to care for those two marvellous boys? As for the past, I have accomplished little: an overweight, balding, middle-aged and mediocre teacher, a footnote of a scholar, a friend of no great merit, with little wit or geniality …'

Eleanor sighed, poured more coffee.

'I find it difficult to read them, to figure out the details. Is Willis gay?'

'It's possible, of course, but I doubt it.'

'So why did Betsy have those magazines?'

'For her own amusement? Who knows? Who knows what she's up to? I doubt if she does. Half the time she's threatening me with murder, mayhem, maiming – and the other half she's flashing the flesh and breathing heavily. She's as crazy as her mother, just more out of control. No, the really dangerous ones are Willis and Mr Hatcher – they plan carefully and they carry out their plans. Like the separatists, they're religious zealots and they pursue their mission with single-minded, self-obsessed conviction, against all evidence, against all logic.'

'Perhaps it would be easier to hate them if they actually were French.'

'It wouldn't make any difference. They're us, the French are us ...'

'That was sloppy of me – I shouldn't have said "French" – I should have said "nationalists" or "separatists". It's the booze talking.'

Frank shook his head.

'I understood what you meant. But when I say they're us, I don't just mean the French are decent people like us, I mean ... nationalism ... romanticism ... the will to a national state, which implies that minorities –' and slipped into tears, incoherence '– the Holocaust ... as I grow older ... it seems to me the Jews are us and the Germans are us, too –' grasping at lines of argument '– there are always others ... others to blame ... as the Hatchers blame me, as the separatists blame us –' babbling bits of his reading, of remembered Friday nights '– the Prague Pan-Slav Congress of 1848, my nationalism but not your nationalism –' flapping his hands in frustration '– and when we argue with them, we use their terms, and we become them ... measuring signs ... probing ancestry ... blood –' giving in ... 'lunacy ... monomania ... fascism –' giving up '– this Quebec ... the times ... nothing ... I know nothing ...'

Slumping in exhaustion.

'Nemo.'

After some minutes, when he had recovered some, when his convulsive tears had stopped, Eleanor murmured, 'You're missing Emma. I mean, you need her strength, her absence is undermining you, isn't it? You were different when she was with you.'

'Yes, well, I've been meaning to tell you ...'

Eleanor was surprised by the news of Emma's affair, but not shocked.

'You must have been devastated,' she concluded.

Frank shrugged.

'No. Hurt, I guess, but not ... I mean, it was a casual thing. She loved the boys far too much to let it come to any crisis – she obviously wasn't planning to leave me, to leave the boys. Emma was too strong, too self-confident to need someone like Carl. So future and present may be crumbling, but the past is solid. But the past ... is gone. Finally, though, it was trivial for her, and she loved me. I'm sure of that, I believe that, I know it, I know she loved me.'

He arose and went to the window.

A touch of snow under the spruces in twilight.

'Perhaps we should get some food ready for Magnus – he's going to be hungry.'

'He's going to be thirsty – we'll mix some martinis first.'

Despite another evening of alcohol and chatter, Frank was up by eight-thirty the next morning. He tiptoed downstairs and soon was sending the aroma of coffee though the house, but the others remained in bed.

He must not think; he must divert his thoughts, himself.

On the bookshelves on either side of the living-room fireplace he found a miscellaneous collection of outdated academic works, unwanted coffee table books, the *National Geographic* 1964–66, and light holiday reading. His hand paused over an Eric Ambler, but he would not have time to finish it. *Treasures of the Uffizi*? He decided on *Their Finest Hour*, from Churchill's *The Second World War* and was soon immersed in the Battle of Britain and the Blitz.

But after an hour of the delights of 'The Wizard War', of Mr Jones's tale, of the countering of Knickebein and the X-Apparatus and the Y-Apparatus, he was relieved to see Eleanor in her robe coming down the stairs.

'Coffee!' she rasped.

Frank pointed to the kitchen and lofted his cup as proof. When she returned, they chided one another for their overindulgence, promised to avoid a repeat for at least eight hours.

'Other than that, old dear, how are you getting on?'

He held up the Churchill.

'About tonight. We're invited to the Ibbotsons' New Year's Eve party just down the road, and of course you're invited as well. They'll all be very pleasant and easy, but I know what trouble you have with strangers, so you can come with us or you can stay here.'

'I'll stay.'

'Now look, I mean this just as I say it and I don't mean to imply anything by it: if you'd rather not be alone, if you'd just like someone to sit with you and chat, I'll be perfectly happy to stay here with you. No, really, it will be an enjoyable party, but I don't mind missing it. Magnus is happy enough to go alone. We can watch TV, watch a video, play cards, talk, read, whatever you want.'

'It's not necessary. Really. I've had more booze in two nights than I usually have in two months, and you needn't worry about me here alone.'

'Okay. If you change your mind through the day, just tell me.'

'No, I think a quiet day is the thing for me. And a quiet evening. I may even try to do a little work – something on the recent Jane Austen movies – *Pride and Prejudice*, *Sense and Sensibility*, *Persuasion*, and two versions of *Emma*.'

'That many? I knew about ...'

'And *Clueless* – Emma Woodhouse as a Valley girl.'

'How many novels did Jane Austen write? Five? Six?'

'Six.'

'So that's two-thirds of her work. You'll be a vedette, old fellow!'

'Jetting off to expense-paid conferences in Lugano and Buenos Aires and Auckland.'

'Offers of jobs in a temperate climate, pay increase with tenure and tax-free booze.'

'Private office with no Sid and a lake view, students who have all read the oeuvre three times – complete with the juvenilia – before the course begins.'

'Compliant coeds with pneumatic chests and legs up to here.'

'You're mistaking me for Sid.'

'Sorry, old fellow. Still, that's the spirit. You go do some work, and I'll turn on the fax so the offers can roll in.'

Eleanor did not need to tell him he might make free of the telephone, so in the languid afternoon, he thought to call the boys. But the one phone was in the living room and he was too shy to ask for privacy. He would wait until he was alone.

He had no energy for writing, but he did have an article which needed editing, so he went to his bedroom and opened Emma's laptop. He had never used it, but the instructions for start-up were in the carrying case, along with the AC adaptor, the battery charger, and a collection of cables. In time he managed to get it running, entered the word processing program, and inserted his own diskette.

The article was an examination of the taciturnity of Jane Austen's leading men. For several hours he worked to fine-tune his perceptions of Darcy, Knightley, Captain Wentworth, and the others. He gradually realized he was going to need a section on the contrasting villains with their easy charm. The only Jane Austen Eleanor had in the house was *Pride and Prejudice*, so he lay on the bed and began reading of Elizabeth's early encounters with the plausible Wickham. In ten minutes he was asleep, to be roused by Eleanor in darkness. When she turned on the light he saw she was dressed for the party.

'It's seven-thirty, old dear.'

'Umm, sorry.'

'Don't apologize, you obviously needed the rest.'

'Haven't had a real nap for years. You're wearing the Shalimar.'

'Yes, I thought this was the right occasion for it. How do you like it?'

'Marvellous. Very ... evocative.'

'I won't ask what it evokes.'

The Shalimar didn't really suit her.

'Now then, Magnus and I are going in a few minutes; they're serving a buffet at eight-thirty. If you change your mind later, turn left at the bottom of the driveway and it's the white house on the right just before the bridge. But if you're determined to stay here, there's some of Magnus's daube in the fridge, or you can scrounge whatever you find.'

'I'll be fine. The daube, I think.'

'I can still stay with you.'

'Did you know Jane Austen wrote a Canadian scene?'

'No, she didn't.'

'It's in *Emma*: a big snowstorm, Mr Elton gets drunk and makes unwelcome advances to Emma. Could you get more Canadian than that?'

'All right, I guess I can trust you. I've left their number on the table by the phone. If you need me, I can be back in five minutes.'

'I'll be okay. Go and enjoy yourself.'

'I expect I will. The Ibbotsons never invite amateur drunks like Mr Elton, and amateur drunks are the curse of New Year's Eve parties.'

He microwaved a helping of daube, then picked at it with the Churchill propped before him. After he washed the dishes, he decided he should call the boys. But remembering that Emma's computer was still running, he went up to the bedroom to turn it off. Hitting the unfamiliar keys in the familiar steps he would have used on his own machine, he found himself not saving to diskette and exiting, but looking at a list of directories on Emma's hard drive. He was about to change the display when he noticed a directory called EMAIL.

For a long moment he stared at it, motionless. Carl had mentioned 'snail mail' so perhaps he usually sent e-mail. Frank reached forward and moved the highlight bar down, paused, tapped the enter key. The alphabetical list of EMAIL files got as far as F; Frank moved to display to the end of the alphabet. There were about a dozen files named WERT25JA.TXT, or other dates. Frank sat back on the bed.

Letters in Jane Austen, he reflected, are ... After Elizabeth Bennet reads Darcy's long letter: 'Till this moment I never knew myself' ... Emma Woodhouse nearly learns the great secret because of Jane Fairfax's trips to the post office, while Captain Wentworth leaves his letter to Anne Elliot, looks at her 'with eyes of glowing entreaty' or ...

But these letters were from Emma to Wert, not to himself. Indeed, did he want to know? What else could he lose? The children were still his, the memory of Emma's love, despite the affair, was still his. That passage from *Othello* was apt:

> I had been happy if the general camp,
> Pioners and all, had tasted her sweet body,
> So I had known nothing.

Surely Othello was right? Better not to know, certainly better now that Emma ... What could he want to discover? How often they...? Smutty details. How much she had cared for Wert? Whether she had seriously considered ending the marriage? But she wouldn't have left the boys, and she wouldn't have expected Frank to let them go with her? Would she?

> O, now for ever
> Farewell the tranquil mind! Farewell content!
> Farewell the plumed troop, the big wars
> That make ambition virtue!

What a grotesque joke, farce! What wars, what ambition? What royal banner, and all quality, pride, pomp and circumstance of glorious war? What tranquil mind, come to that? Complacent mind, more like.

> Make me to see't; or at the least so prove it
> That the probation bear no ... something-something
> To hang a doubt upon

For if he did not look, if he erased the files, he would always suspect, thinking the worst when the truth was perhaps as trivial as he had assumed it to be.

He moved to the desk chair, reached forward and tapped the Enter key.

The truth came directly:

> Darling,
> Neither loyalty to 'dear old McGill' nor fear of Edmonton winters restrains me from applying, though I have to wonder about job security there in the face of Klein's obviously determined and continuing budget cuts. No, the crumbly rock upon which this and all my projects threaten to founder is the Old Shoe himself. He's perhaps competent to teach junior college there, but even if there was a job on offer he is too timid to apply, and would bungle the interview if he did. In any case, taking him with me is hardly the object of the game, is it? Talking him into letting me take the boys would be a delicate business, but he is so

compliant, so agreeable, so submissive, so decent, so anglo! so Canadian! that it will be as easy as kicking off a pair of flip-flops.

No, the problem is that he is incapable of standing on his own. If I leave him – and it's not quite yet 'when' I leave him – he'll simply fall apart. It's not so much loyalty I feel for him, or even the memory of long-ago fondness, but pity, that sad ghost of fondness. He really is the comfortable Old Shoe, and while I'm eager to wear new high heels, I shall feel a touch of melancholy, of affection for the old pair as I throw them into a box in the basement, to be worn, perhaps, when gardening or painting the spare bedroom.

But if the job is there, I rather think I shall take it. Get your ear to the ground, scout. First, continual monitoring of the budget situation; second, immediate identification of the hiring committee when it is constituted; third, personality profiles of the powers and politics of the department – before I approach the front door, I want to be sure I know all the back door gossip.

Love, E.

It was Emma's style, certainly: bright, chipper, confident, edged with sarcasm.

Numbered campaign plan, as confident and demanding as a Churchill memo to General Ismay.

The sentences rather more convoluted than in her published work, and the metaphors trite, but these flaws were doubtless excusable on the ground that she was probably writing quickly.

Frank found himself descending the stairs.

High heels?

Coffee?

Perhaps there was a cup left in the pot.

Emma hated high heels.

Spare bedroom was good; succinct in its contempt.

But it entirely failed to redeem *Old Shoe*.

Hackneyed, that.

But perhaps she had avoided high heels because she'd been nearly as tall as him.

After he tapped the numbers the telephone rang several times, no doubt so someone could get to an extension. Simon answered.

'Happy New Year, Simon.'

'Is that you, Dad?'

Sylvia Plath: *Daddy*.

'None other. How's it going?'

'All right.'

'Going to bed soon?'

'I guess so.'

Daddy Dearest?

'That's good. Having a good time?'

'Yeah. Sort of. Jonathan gets to play the computer more than I do. See, he got up first this morning and so he played for an hour to start, then we went to the squash club, so ...'

Frank quickly lost track of the tale, was too tired to try picking it up again.

Black Shoe: that should do the job, apt substitute for *Old Shoe*; but, no, Plath's 'Daddy' was also *Panzer-man*, Nazi brute, not wimp.

'Perhaps you could get up first tomorrow. That way you could get a head start.'

'Maybe.'

'Anyway, Happy New Year.'

'Happy New Year.'

'And perhaps I can talk to Jonathan now.'

'Okay.'

Scuffling sounds.

'Hi, Dad.'

'Hi, Jonathan. Happy New Year.'

'I guess so.'

'You don't sound convinced.'

'Are we going to live in an apartment or are we going to stay here?'

'For a while at least, you'll be staying there. I'm not sure how ...'

'So, like, since we're staying here can we, like Grandpa said, can we go to St Crispin's School? I was talking to Sean yesterday, and he said he's starting at St Crispin's next week, like, instead of next fall, so I was wondering if ...'

'Well, I'm not quite sure just now. There are new ... developments I have to think about. You'll hear, one way or the other.'

'Okay. I've got to go before Simon exits from my game.'

'Sure thing. You go. Goodbye.'

But the boy had already hung up.

They were gone from him.

I love you, my boys.

Tranquil mind.

He threw his things in his bag, turned off some of the lights, checked the kitchen stove, and scribbled a brief note of thanks and apology to Eleanor.

Cold outside, frozen, like him, like his mind, like his soul.

Frozen tranquillity.

After starting the car he checked the map for the way north to the autoroute. With a quarter of a tank he could easily get to an open station; there should be some all-nighters at the Drummondville entrance to eastbound Autoroute 20. He drove away.

In little more than two hours he passed Quebec City, and made good time as far as La Pocatière, but then light snow began. In the hills between Rivière-du-Loup and Edmundston driving would be difficult, he guessed, and hoped that the road would not be closed. At least there would be little traffic, and he likely wouldn't meet anything at all on that empty hundred kilometres or so of shortcut across New Brunswick. Toward midnight, just past Rivière du Loup he gassed up again at a station shining brightly into the deepening snowfall. Frank started the engine, pulled onto the highway and drove on, craning forward over the steering wheel, peering into the white wind.

Half a life ago, he reflected, I drove into Quebec in a second-hand car with a trunk full of clothes and books. And now ...

Jonathan has light brown hair, Simon is still blond ...

The living room is beige ...

Or is it?

He could not laugh, managed but a smile, as he stared into the winter night, at the snowflakes whirling, filling the night, chill in the swirling dark all about, multitudinous, lost.

BURT COVIT

Ray Smith is from Mabou, Cape Breton, and grew up largely in Halifax. Since 1968, he has lived in Montreal where he teaches at Dawson College. He is the father of two children, the exemplary and remarkable Nicholas and Alexander.